What people are sa

Flight of the Eternal Emperor

James Rogers is a superb writer, a jack-of-all-trades. Over the years I've always enjoyed reading his short stories, never knowing if the next one will be horror or supernatural, humour or crime. His science fantasy novel, *Flight of the Eternal Emperor*, is an entirely gripping read, filled with fascinating characters and sharp, timely, unexpected twists. You'll be thinking about this wonderful debut novel long after you've finished reading it.
Colum McCann, National Book Award winner and author of *Transatlantic* and *Apeirogon*

James Rogers is a tremendous writer. And now he's turned his hand to science fantasy. You're in for an unsettling but gratifying read. *Flight of the Eternal Emperor* is the real deal.
Larry Kirwan, author of *Liverpool Fantasy* and *Rockaway Blue*

Flight of the Eternal Emperor

A Novel

Flight of the Eternal Emperor

A Novel

James Rogers

COSMIC EGG
BOOKS

Winchester, UK
Washington, USA

JOHN HUNT PUBLISHING

First published by Cosmic Egg Books, 2023
Cosmic Egg Books is an imprint of John Hunt Publishing Ltd., 3 East St., Alresford,
Hampshire SO24 9EE, UK
office@jhpbooks.net
www.johnhuntpublishing.com
www.cosmicegg-books.com

For distributor details and how to order please visit the 'Ordering' section on our website.

Text copyright: James Rogers 2022

ISBN: 978 1 80341 319 8
978 1 80341 320 4 (ebook)
Library of Congress Control Number: 2022914775

A CIP catalogue record for this book is available from the British Library.

Design: Lapiz Digital Services

UK: Printed and bound by CPI Group (UK) Ltd, Croydon, CR0 4YY
US: Printed and bound by Thomson-Shore, 7300 West Joy Road, Dexter, MI 48130

We operate a distinctive and ethical publishing philosophy in
all areas of our business, from our global network of authors to
production and worldwide distribution.

For Siu, Liam, Áine and Cian

She stepped from the elevator, holding her baby girl on her hip as she took her keys from her pocket. "Don't run," she called to her son as he took off down the corridor. She shook her head and sighed as she watched him trail his hand along the filthy wall.

As she tried to get hold of the apartment key, the bunch slipped from her fingers to clatter on the tiles. "Damn." She went on her hunkers to retrieve them. The baby wriggled, eyes flickering open. She thought she saw a smile. She smiled back. Standing up, she saw her son had stopped halfway down the corridor, his back to the wall as he watched an older boy approach from the other end. She recognised the teenager, a bully from two floors up. She started towards her son, anger bubbling. Why should he have to live in fear of a brat like this?

She stopped when she realised her son appeared confused rather than scared. She looked at the bully. He had stopped in the middle of the corridor with his eyes wide and his mouth slowly stretching open. His hands groped blindly as he staggered, then fell back against the wall. Plaster dust showered from the ceiling.

Her heart leaped into a higher gear as she recognised the symptoms. A pitiful croak escaped the boy as, sliding down the wall, he grappled with unseen fingers at his throat. Goosebumps rose along her arms.

"Quick!" she called to her son. "Come!" They ran back the way they had come, away from the damned.

She pressed for the elevator. The motor whirred, then stopped. She pressed the button again. The baby squirmed, cried a little, as if her anxiety were being transmitted to her daughter. Her son pressed up against her. He peered out from behind her leg at the teenager. She tried to ignore the sounds, the gagging, the dull thump of a leg slapping against the floor. "Don't look at him." She could hear clunking from the elevator below, but no motor. She grabbed her boy and made for the stairs.

The boy was too slow. He could only take one step at a time. She grabbed him under his arms and lifted. Down they went, with her almost falling twice. To the corridor below, to her friend's apartment. It was locked. She pounded on the door. "Please!"

The baby cried. The boy's lip trembled. She went to her knees, pulled the boy towards her and pushed the baby against his chest. Confused, the boy pushed back.

"Mammy," he cried.

"Stop it! Move your hands!" She squeezed her children together, making them one.

"What's the matter?" an unfamiliar voice spoke. She looked up at a man in the sky-blue robes of the Order of Lurg, the God of Light. "Is the child sick?"

"Take the boy," she pleaded, pushing her son towards him. "Please. Take him away."

The priest frowned. "Why? I don't understand. What's the matter?" he reiterated.

"Take him!" she yelled. The baby started to choke. "No!" she screamed. "Please, no!" In horror she looked down at the little face, the eyes screwed up, the tiny mouth opened, tongue protruding as the little one struggled for breath. She could actually see the neck tightening. "Please," she whimpered. "Don't. Please."

A terrible croak emanated from the delicate creature before the little head lolled to one side. She cradled her daughter's head in the crook of her neck and stroked her hair, rocking back and forth and crying till her throat cracked. The boy took a step back, whimpering. The priest didn't move.

***

After a quick smoke, I re-entered the pub to find Johnny looking into my laptop. He straightened up. "Oh," he said guiltily. "Sorry. I was just looking."

"That's all right," I replied as I sat down by the fire and took a sip from the fresh pint Johnny had delivered in my absence. "What do you think?" I asked. Johnny looked sheepish. "Go on. I don't mind."

"Well, I only had a quick read. It's good. Not a comedy, though."

"No. It's not."

"What was it killed the baby? Some sort of ghost?"

"He wasn't a ghost then, but maybe you're right. Maybe he is now."

Johnny gave me a funny look as he went back behind the bar. Above him on the television the American President defended his country's destruction of a Chinese space station. They'd fired a missile at it from a warship in the Pacific. The Chinese said it wasn't theirs. Two men at the bar argued with Johnny. They believed it was Russian.

I didn't bother informing them that they were all wrong. I would have had to tell them how I knew, and that would've involved explaining what I am. And even though Johnny doesn't believe in ghosts, he'd be quicker to accept them than the notion of sentient beings without physical form darting about the universe (ostensibly to observe and learn, but more often, at least in my case, to be entertained). Earth's scientists were only then beginning to approach the truth. After all, what is matter? Right down at the infinitesimal, there's nothing there at all. So Johnny and I were not all that different. He only seemed to be made of something. It's all an illusion.

***

Nevertheless, I quite often take physical form. Not because I need to, but because I want to. Like right now, click-clacking these words onto an electric screen, the pungent smell of burning peat in my nostrils. I pause for another sip of this marvellous beverage. I like the feel of the creamy head against my upper lip. A slight tilt of the glass and the smooth, dark liquid beneath pushes through. Across the tongue it hints of burnt coffee, then slides to the back of the throat. A wonderful sensation.

That's the reason my fellows and I, the Grid Riders (a grandiose title I've just now decided to apply to the incorporeal immortals), enjoy returning to the physical realm; we long to enjoy the organic senses again. I especially like taste.

Which is part of the reason why, on a world very like Earth but on the far side of the universe, I sat by an open fire, drinking ale. My companion was Arnelius. This is his story.

Prologue

The river laughed and tumbled over the rocks as it made its way down the hill towards the valley. On reaching level ground, it spread out into a wide calm lake, as if it wished to rest. A horse galloped along the stony shore in the direction of a small, thatched hut. Collapsing at the near end, it had one square window, a rotting timber door and a hole in the thatched roof from which a twisting column of smoke rose into the darkening sky.

The rider in black halted his mount in front of the shack and nimbly jumped to the ground. As he turned to the door he was met by a tormented scream, which shattered the silence of the slumbering scene. The horse jumped with fright, then galloped away. Arnelius ignored him. With fearless determination, he entered the smoky room. Almost subconsciously, he increased the pace at which his pupils dilated so that his eyes quickly became accustomed to the dark. In one corner a young girl sat on the clay floor, her arms wrapped about her knees, pulling them towards her chest. She stared uncomprehendingly at the woman lying in the far corner, at the long tangled hair turned snowy white. Out of a face frozen in horror, the mother's eyes stared back at her daughter. But they were lifeless eyes. She had departed with her scream.

Between the mother and daughter stood Destlar. His prominent and pointy nose sat above a small mouth with thin lips almost as pale as his skin. Two tiny black eyes, as black as the hair on his head, looked out at the newcomer. There was fear in those eyes. They seemed to shrink further as Arnelius took a step closer.

Arnelius relished the task of destroying Destlar. To have the unfathomable arts bestowed upon oneself, and to such a degree, was an honour. The Gods chose few. To then use those gifts in such a despicable and unholy manner was simply unforgivable.

1

***

Destlar staggered, ecstasy abruptly dispelled by the arrival of the dreaded moment. During the act of torture, and for a short time afterwards, his normal senses were attenuated and his whole body was suffused with a heat that somehow made him shiver. But the feeling didn't last and the depression that followed left him cold and weary and angry. He would argue with himself, plead with himself to be more discreet, to be more careful, for he knew the day would come when another of his order would confront him.

Now, it was worse even than he'd feared. The invincible Arnelius stood before him and Destlar was terrified.

With a slight movement of his head, a gesture rather than a necessity, Arnelius threw Destlar out the door and into the fading light. Destlar cried out as he landed heavily on the hard ground. Arnelius advanced, his face animated with rage and repugnance.

The fallen magician writhed in the soil as his destroyer, through nothing more tangible than the will to do so, attacked every limb, every organ. Destlar's throat tightened and his lungs burned. His eyes watered, blood ran from his nose and ears. Fire raged in his gut, intensifying with each passing moment as Arnelius squeezed the life from him. As the heat spread through his body, panic swept through his mind. He was dying. The dark empty chasm awaited.

Arms flailing as if he were indeed falling, the fire reached his fingertips, then shot forth. Suddenly it was over. No pain, no sensation, no light. Just thought. Would this be it, for eternity? Had the Gods chosen this particular punishment for him, correctly divining its appropriateness? Panic began to build once more, until he noticed the soft light through his eyelids.

He wasn't dead. And yet the attack had ceased. Had Arnelius given in to pity? No, more likely he was just playing with his victim, dragging him back up and out of the abyss, just so he could enjoy driving him over the edge once more. Destlar lay still, eyes screwed tight, awaiting the renewed assault. It didn't come.

He opened his eyes and stared into a darkening sky as he sucked air through a raw throat. His muscles ached and his stomach and lungs burned. He rubbed his hand under his nose, then looked at the blood on his fingers, dark in the low light. He licked his fingers and swallowed slowly, relishing the salty, metallic taste. Wheezing with the pain, yet enjoying it, he raised himself onto his right elbow. Arnelius lay on the ground a few yards away.

With grunts and sharp, painful intakes of breath, Destlar got to his knees, then slowly crawled over to Arnelius. The man was unrecognisable. His face and head were covered in angry burns and most of his hair was gone, the remaining clumps singed a sooty black. Yet he lived. Destlar so badly wanted to finish him off, but he didn't have the energy. He collapsed onto his back and passed out.

***

Destlar awoke. The sky above was alive with stars. After a moment of confusion, he remembered, then smiled. Had all his fears been unfounded? If he could destroy Arnelius, then who would stand in his way? He looked at the familiar constellations, the names of which he could never remember. These stars looked down upon the entire expansive Empire. Why was he hiding in this barren and rocky land? He had underestimated himself. He had no one and nothing to fear.

He stood up, invigorated and renewed. At his feet, Arnelius groaned as he regained consciousness. Again, Destlar smiled, then closed his eyes and reached for Arnelius's mind. Without understanding the mechanism, he began to play with his subject's personal clock; for Arnelius, time slowed. With anticipated delight, Destlar reduced the flow even further. He took pleasure in observing his prey's descent into madness. To the outside world, only minutes would pass, but for the victim in his cocoon where all external sensations were blocked, millions of years of emptiness reduced the hapless creature to insanity. Once released from the spell, death was welcomed adoringly.

That's what usually happened. But not this time. Destlar held the wizard inside the decelerated time bubble for longer than usual, desperately trying to see inside the mind, to witness the horror. Somehow, he couldn't get in. He'd never before practised the spell upon a fellow magician, and he attributed the disappointing opaqueness to the peculiarity of the sorcerer's brain. When he finally dropped the spell, almost 12 million years had passed in one timeframe, while the moon had risen in the other. Frustrated, Destlar kicked the corpse.

Then he remembered the girl. He turned, walked into the hovel and stepped to one side to allow moonlight to stream in through the open door. The girl was still there, asleep with her arm draped across her mother's shoulders. Destlar kicked her awake. She whimpered. He was about to administer time dilation once again, then stopped, wondering. Could he repeat that trick with the fire? He closed his eyes. For a moment, nothing happened. Then, as naturally as drawing breath, a spark in his belly grew into a flame and advanced through his chest and along his arms. He jerked his head to one side and gritted his teeth as the pain increased. Bright light erupted from his outstretched hands to strike the girl on the dirt floor. The whimpering ceased.

Chapter 1

Jeseque Debrone rinsed her long black hair. Rivers of white foam streamed down her flat belly, along her thighs and shins and swirled through the plughole. For some reason, she always found the sight pleasing. She stood under the spray of warm water and watched the last of the bubbles disappear.

In the bedroom, her computer beeped. Jeseque's head snapped up. She turned off the water, grabbed a towel and stepped from the shower onto the cold tiles. Wrapping the towel about herself, she entered the bedroom and sat before the computer. With a few taps on the keypad, she had the message open. As her eyes ran across the phrase "SpaceExpress Maintenance Centre", she threw her hands in the air and let out a little shout of satisfaction and relief. She'd been assigned to the space orbital maintenance crew, the very post she had hoped for.

It was unusual for a woman to make it through military school, and despite arriving in the top ten percent in her chosen speciality, avionics, she had expected to be assigned to some boring job, spending all her time compiling requisitions or scheduling meetings. Perhaps she had been a little unfair on her superiors. Perhaps they really were trying to accept women on merit. This was a genuine engineering position, and she would gain valuable experience. If she did well, she might even be rewarded with a transfer to the orbital itself, travelling to and from the space station. In the meantime, and more importantly of course, she would gain access to a lot of important and sensitive information.

Jeseque got into a pair of dark blue jeans and a plain blue short-sleeve top. She slipped into white canvas shoes, grabbed a jacket and left the apartment in the Academy's accommodation block, smiling. She couldn't remember feeling so good. As she walked along the busy street in Wesmork, capital city in Destlar's empire, she pulled on the jacket against the slight chill. In centuries past the region would have been quite warm at that time of year. Not any more, with the ice inexorably encroaching from the poles.

She entered a public network station. It was a narrow space, poorly lit. Along the left-hand wall there were five terminal booths. Only one was occupied, its frosted screen pulled closed for privacy. Jeseque approached the counter where a young man sat reading a book. She handed over a few coins, enough for five minutes of network access. It would be more than adequate.

Hardly lifting his head out of the book, the attendant took the money, then pointed at the nearest booth. Jeseque entered, pulling the screen across behind her. The terminal came to life. She entered a code, which she knew by heart, then typed a short message, informing the Northern Allied Liberation Organisation, NALO, of her new position at orbital maintenance. It was a message she dared not send from her computer back in her apartment.

**

Jeseque shivered, wrapping her arms about herself. Even the large coat did little to keep out the cold. The old train carriage wasn't generating much heat itself, and she couldn't afford a ticket in the luxurious carriage up front.

She sat with her back to the direction of travel. Looking out the window, she could at least admire the scenery that slowly rolled past. The low hills were covered in snow, peaceful and untouched. It was beautiful, but making a living off such land was tough. The snow and ice would melt for a while in the summer and enough grass would grow to feed a few sheep, and to save a little hay for the long winter months. A farmer could work long hard hours and still not have enough to get by.

Farming had to be combined with work in the coal mines in the mountains that Jeseque could see beyond the hills.

With the intensifying roar of the engine and the slowing of the train, Jeseque knew they were about to climb Cairn Hill. She had always been a little anxious during this part of the journey, wondering if the train would make it across. Somehow, it always had. This time she found herself hoping it would fail. It was years since she'd visited her mother and she wondered why she was bothering to make the long journey now. Was it something to do with the new job? Was she hoping to start afresh? Jeseque shook her head as she considered getting off the train at the next stop.

Annoyed by this sense of uncertainty, by her own indecision, she closed her eyes and cleared her mind. The hypnotic clack of wheels on rails helped her relax.

A moment later she jumped, shocked by the incoherent shouts of a young boy across the aisle. The boy's mother quickly shushed the child. Jeseque judged him to be about eight years old, and it was apparent he suffered from some kind of mental condition. She reckoned his mother must have been desperate to risk bringing him out in public.

The train crested the hill and picked up speed as it rolled down the far side, the engine sighing its relief. Minutes later it began braking and the countryside suddenly disappeared as a stone building popped into view alongside, barely three feet from the window. The featureless concrete ran alongside for a few seconds, before the buildings shot back to make space for a platform.

Jeseque's heart leaped at the sight of two policemen. She couldn't believe the mother's luck. She pressed her head against the glass in order to keep the policemen in sight as the train continued along the platform. With a jolt, the train stopped. Jeseque looked across at the woman and her child. Sitting on the other side of the carriage, the woman hadn't noticed the police. Jeseque considered warning her, telling her to hide the boy. But there was nowhere to hide.

She had seen this many times before. The dreaded blue uniforms, with the round metal helmets adorned with the Emperor's insignia—in a ring of fire, a dark figure on a white throne—lazily making their way from one carriage to another, picking on people whose appearance somehow offended them, demanding identification and taking pleasure in the delay they were needlessly causing.

Jeseque saw terror form in the mother's eyes as the flunkeys slid the door to one side and entered the carriage. They stopped at the first row of seats. "ID," grunted one to a young man with long hair and a beard. The policeman took a quick look at the proffered plastic, threw it back and moved on.

Jeseque decided to act. She jumped from her seat and walked up to the policemen. "Why are you delaying us all with this nonsense?"

They looked at her with wide eyes. They were unused to having their authority challenged, especially by a woman. "ID," demanded the one with the moustache. "Now!"

Jeseque's heart hammered. "You have no authority over me," she replied, trying to keep her voice steady.

They grabbed her, painfully squeezing her biceps, and dragged her towards the end of the carriage. "We'll teach you some manners, you cheeky bitch." Jeseque resisted, half-heartedly. She wanted them quickly off the train. Once on the platform she would show them her military ID. That might be enough for them to let her go, as the flunkeys were fearful of the military.

But it didn't work. They were almost through the door when the boy started babbling again, his mother pleading with him to be quiet. The flunkeys turned around, instantly losing interest in Jeseque. Realisation dawned as they pushed her into a seat and strode back down the carriage.

"Identification!" the moustache yelled. The frightened woman handed over her card. "And him."

"Please," she cried. That's all she could say.

"You never registered him. You managed to keep the little freak hidden. You should be ashamed of yourself. What a fucking waste of resources." Together they reached across the woman and dragged the screaming boy from his seat by the collar of his shirt. "Shut up, you crazy shit!" The woman was now screaming too, pounding and grabbing and scrabbling at the uniforms with her tiny fists.

The moustache carried the flailing child to the door and threw him onto the platform while the other took the gun from his holster and hit the woman hard on the temple with the butt. She staggered. He hit her again and she dropped to the floor. Jeseque, looking on helplessly, wondered if he had killed her. Everyone else on the train and on the platform did their best to remain invisible.

The unconscious woman was dragged along the aisle and thrown into the snow beside her son. The boy crawled towards her, sobbing. As he tried to put his arms about her neck, he was dragged away. A gun was aimed at the back of the child's head and fired. The shot rang out and then there was silence.

The Emperor's instruments of peace and harmony kicked the inert woman in the ribs. "Bitch! She should be thanking us for putting that thing out of its misery."

"Get this train moving! Holding up the whole line."

With the child's blood soaking into the snow like spilled wine on a tablecloth, the noise from the idling engine slowly grew in volume. The train jerked forward and then gradually made its way from the station. Jeseque slowly returned to her seat. Her quiet sobs seeped into the emptiness.

***

It was twilight and she'd been on the train for almost seven hours when she finally reached her destination. The journey had taken her approximately 400 miles north, to the small town where her mother lived. The temperature had dropped the whole way and it was bitterly cold when she stepped from the carriage, her bag on her back. A new layer of snow crunched beneath her boots. Jeseque tried to concentrate on the familiar surroundings, on the shop fronts that hadn't changed since she was a child, on the locals who went about their business in these icy, windy conditions with a casualness born of experience. She tried to remove from her head the screaming, the blood, the brutality.

She stopped in a coffee shop, desperate for any kind of interaction, something to focus on. "Coffee, please," she said to the teenage girl behind the counter. There was only one other customer, a middle-aged man sitting at a table down the back, newspaper spread before him.

The girl handed her the steaming mug. Of course it didn't contain real coffee, just some kind of synthetic product. It was dark and strong and bitter and full of caffeine. Jeseque had often heard people remarking on how it tasted nothing like the real thing. She wondered how they came to this conclusion as she was sure they, like herself, had never tasted real coffee; only the wealthy could afford the bean that was becoming ever more scarce. She felt it was just one of those things people liked to say, or to be heard saying.

Jeseque shivered. "That's good. So cold out there."

"That's nothing. You should have been here last week."

"Really? That bad?"

"You're not from here," the girl stated.

"Actually, I am," Jeseque replied, dropping a few coins on the counter. "I grew up in this town. But I haven't been back in a while and I'd forgotten how bad the weather gets."

"And things are cheaper than you remember," the girl said as she pushed one of the coins back.

Jeseque smiled as she pocketed the coin and lifted the mug. "Thanks." She sat down at the nearest of the small round tables.

While in military school, Jeseque had learned about the planet's gradual descent into another ice age. She was aware of the scientific studies into climate change, and the little progress that had been made; so far, no one knew why the global temperatures were dropping.

But to the people of the North, the reasons behind the long hard winters weren't so important. They were concerned with getting by, day to day. Fruitless research didn't interest them. It didn't feed them or keep them warm.

Jeseque's eyes wandered down the street to the old shopping centre. Sipping her coffee, she watched an endless stream of people going in and out of the big double doors. As grey and dirty as the place appeared from the outside, it was obviously as popular as ever. She guessed a lack of choice had a lot to do with it. Still, it was a place she'd enjoyed as a child, even if it was only because it got her out of the cold.

She found herself almost smiling at the memories.

***

The security guard held the door open for the skinny girl, as he quietly admonished the parents for letting a child so young out and about on her own. "Thank you," the girl mumbled.

A wicked wind was swirling between the buildings, so Jeseque was glad to get inside. She was supposed to be doing the grocery shopping for her mother, but her feet were freezing inside her light shoes. She walked to the back of the large shop and down a flight of stairs to the shoe department. She didn't waste any time, but quickly decided upon a pair of sturdy brown leather boots. Now to find her size. She hunted amongst the rows of boxes. "Why can't they put some kind of order on this?" she whispered to herself. Eventually she found them. Quickly she sat down and slipped the empty backpack from her shoulders. She always brought the backpack; it was easier than lugging bags of groceries all the way home, the plastic handles cutting into her fingers. Her back supported the weight so much better.

She tried on the boots. Perfect. She walked over to a mirror, then back. So comfortable. And she had enough money in her pocket, but it was to be spent on food and soap and things like that. Necessities, her mother called them. Jeseque thought her toes were necessities.

She sat down again, staring at the plastic ribbon hooked through the left boot's top lace hole. No way to take it off. No way to get out unnoticed with it in place. She pictured herself running down the street with the security guard after her.

Could she pretend to her mother they were on sale, and that she'd bought them with the change from the shopping, only to have the shopping stolen? No way. Her mother wouldn't fall for that. And even if she did, she'd go nuts about the shopping and would hold her daughter solely responsible.

With a sigh, Jeseque removed the right boot. No ribbon on it. She laughed at the idea of stealing just one, saving one foot, letting the other freeze.

A thought occurred to her. She jumped up and looked inside another box, then another and another, but her heart sank further each time she saw the ribbon was always on the left boot, never the right. No chance of making up a ribbonless pair. "Pity they're that much organised," she mumbled, sitting down again and reluctantly removing the left boot. She put on her own ineffectual pair and got up to go. But as she put the boots back on the shelf another idea popped into her head. She was stunned by its simplicity.

She hunted about until she found a second pair of the same boots in her size. Grabbing the box, she peeped inside to make sure they were the right ones, then slipped them under the shelf, where no one else would find them. Then she took the original pair and paid for them at the counter. The cashier removed the ribbon and was about to put the boots back in the box when Jeseque stopped her. "Actually, I don't need the box." The cashier slowly slid the boots into a plastic bag. Jeseque felt like shouting at her to hurry up. She was giddy with excitement. Finally, the woman handed over the bag. Jeseque took it and spun around.

"Your receipt," the woman called.

"Oh, yes," Jeseque said, turning back. "Thank you." She pocketed the receipt, silently cursing herself. Without that little piece of paper, the plan wouldn't work.

She made her way back to the shelves, pulled the boots from the bag and slipped them inside her backpack. Then she wandered about a while, trying to appear casual. A few minutes' stroll took her back to where the secreted pair of boots lay beneath the shelf. She stooped, slid out the box and popped it into the plastic bag. Then she headed back upstairs to the exit.

As she went through the doors, the alarm went off. "Excuse me, miss," called the security guard. Jeseque turned to him, frowning. She held open the bag. "May I see your receipt?" She handed it to him. He nodded, then peered inside the box. "They forgot to take it off," he sighed. "Just a moment." Jeseque stood at the exit, heart pounding, giddiness replaced with anxiety. The security guard went over to the nearest cashier. Jeseque watched her remove the ribbon from the left boot, just as her colleague had done with the twin that was now nestled in her backpack. The guard strolled back. "Sorry about that," he said with a smile as he handed Jeseque the bag.

She went out, around the corner, then came back in via another entrance. With the hard part over, she was excited again. It was hard to believe there could be such a gaping hole in their security procedures. And yet she couldn't see how she could be caught now.

She headed straight for the customer service desk, popped the plastic bag on the counter and told the lady she'd changed her mind. With no fuss, she got her money back.

Now the only tricky bit would be explaining the new footwear to her mother.

***

About 15 minutes after leaving the coffee shop Jeseque reached the old familiar apartment block, drab grey concrete with dull aluminium-framed windows, each one somehow conspiring to reflect the sunlight at slightly different angles and intensity, giving the entire edifice a random and haphazard appearance. Jeseque felt it was well in keeping with the state of the building in general. She wasn't surprised to find the elevator sitting lifelessly on the ground floor. For her mother, it didn't really matter as she lived on the second floor, unlike the poor souls who had to traipse up five or six flights of stairs with heavy shopping.

Jeseque climbed the stairs and walked down the corridor to her mother's apartment. Just as she reached the door, two little girls came running around the corner. They stopped in front of her. "Hello," the black-haired girl said with a big smile. The red-haired girl stood back, timidly looking out from under her eyebrows.

"Hello," Jeseque replied, returning the smile. "Having fun?"

"Yeah," the black-haired girl yelped. She took off down the corridor, the shy one at her heels.

Jeseque chuckled as she walked through the front door that opened directly into a small living room. A feeble lamp did its best to light the space in the growing darkness, but only managed to illuminate one corner. The middle-aged woman sitting in the armchair beneath it was of similar potency. "Who were you talking to?"

"Two little girls. Adorable."

Her mother grunted. "The twins," she said with a sneer.

"Are they?"

"Of course not. They don't even look alike."

"Not all twins are identical."

"Are you hungry?"

"Yeah," Jeseque said, glad to have the conversation steer away from the dangerous path along which further talk of the twins might have taken it.

"There's a pot of stew on the stove. Heat it up."

"OK." Jeseque dropped her bag by the circular table and went into the tiny kitchen. Turning on the burner under the stainless-steel pot, she looked about the familiar space, grimy but tidy. Nothing had changed, except perhaps the dark patches about the cupboard door handles were a little darker and the brown water stain in the sink seemed to have etched its way deeper into the white ceramic. How many times had she stubbornly fought that stain, determined to remove it? The stain won, every time. It stayed around longer than she did.

Jeseque looked out the window to the little park below. With the traffic on the other side of the building, the window was reasonably clean. Through the skeletal trees she saw children in the snow, wrapped up in coats and hats, climbing through a concrete tunnel and jumping over a stone tortoise. How small the tortoise seemed now, the green paint completely worn away to leave pitted grey stone. She pictured her little self, standing at the window, watching in envy the kids at play, sickened by their screams and laughter, knowing that if she went to join them, they'd leave. She'd hated them because they feared her.

It seemed to take an age for the heat to work its way through the steel and into the stew, but eventually Jeseque heard a few pops and bubbles. She went to the drawer beneath the sink's draining board. It screeched as she pulled it open, as it always had. Wood on wood. She took out the largest spoon and returned to the pot. As she lifted the lid, her mother called out. "Stir it!"

Jeseque rolled her eyes. "Yes, mother." She swept the spoon through the thick brew. Carrots, parsnips, potatoes, peas and big chunks of chicken. She breathed deeply through her nose, relishing the smell. Her mother always had been a good cook. Though young Jeseque's feet might have been cold a lot of the time, her belly was never empty. And yet the aroma brought with it mixed memories. Wolfing down a delicious meal after school, fighting the guilt. She couldn't be blamed for her mother's actions. Should she push the food away? Go on hunger strike? Who would that help? And anyway, her mother wouldn't have allowed her. She would have complained about the ungrateful brat who didn't appreciate all her mother did for her. And would she be wrong? Hadn't the woman done her best, in the only way she knew? Hadn't she learned it from her own father? And after her husband walked out, what else could she have done?

Jeseque filled two bowls with the steaming stew and took them and a couple of spoons to the living room. Her mother pulled a lightweight folding table closer to her knees as Jeseque placed one bowl on it and handed over a spoon. Jeseque sat at the larger table.

"Use the mat," her mother said.

"Of course." Where else would she have put the bowl but on the placemat? That's what it was there for. It and its fellows about the table had always been there. She wouldn't have been surprised to find they were fused to the wood beneath. Their plastic tops had originally been red but were worn away to almost white by the heat of ages.

"This is very good," Jeseque said after taking a mouthful.

"It's all right."

"It's more than all right. I haven't had something this good in ages."

"You should come more often if it's a decent meal you're after."

Jeseque returned her head to the bowl. Why had she come? To tell her mother about the new job? She didn't care. She'd never shown any interest in her daughter's studies or her career choice, except to say it wasn't for women. Women should stay at home, look after the house and child.

And maybe do a little work on the side. A little freelancing goes a long way, buys you plenty of chicken.

Jeseque finished the stew, sat back.

"Are you pregnant?" her mother asked.

"What? No, of course not."

"Good. I see these women and their bellies and I ask why. Isn't the world full enough? And one's not enough for them. You think they'd keep their legs tight, but they don't, despite the law. Or to spite it."

"Mother, please."

"Resources dwindling and these selfish cows aren't happy with one. Oh but it's their right. They think they should be allowed to have as many sprogs as they want."

"We don't have to talk about this."

"Look at those twins," her mother said in that mocking voice Jeseque hated so much. "They're not twins and everyone knows it. But nobody says a word. Except me."

"You didn't."

"Of course I did. Any responsible citizen should. Not that it made any difference. They're still running about the place, free as birds."

Jeseque's anger and dismay were building together. "Why shouldn't they be free?"

"So there's no consequences for breaking the law?"

"Children don't break laws."

"Their parents did? And yet they're all still living together. They didn't even take the father away."

"Stop it! Stop talking like that."

"The law is the law, girl."

"Bullshit! You don't care about the law, just or otherwise." Jeseque suddenly felt nauseous. An all-too-familiar musty smell invaded her nostrils, more noticeable now that the stew was gone. She could feel it in the back of her throat and all the way down, into her gut. Her eyes fell upon a rack of faded clothes drying next to an expensive-looking electric heater. "You betray your neighbours, just for a bit of comfort." The building's feeble central heating system barely did enough to ensure the residents didn't freeze to death, while her mother sat in her toasty living room. Jeseque was certain she didn't have to pay the exorbitant electricity bills. "It's disgusting."

"You come all this way just to talk to me like that? You didn't complain when it was your comfort too."

"I had no choice. What was I supposed to do?"

"I've never reported anyone without good reason."

"Rubbish! Rumour and suspicion, that's all you need."

"No, I listen. I gather information. You provided me with very accurate information on one occasion. You must remember."

Jeseque winced. The heartless comment flicked a switch inside her head; painful memories strobed her mind. Kicking and screaming and crying. And the eyes. The eyes that had, in another world and another time, been filled with kindness and laughter, they blazed across the years with such fierce hatred that Jeseque screwed her own eyes shut in a futile effort to block out what was already within. Would those unforgiving eyes torment her for eternity?

"I should not have come back," Jeseque whispered.

"Who asked you to?"

Jeseque dropped her head. She stood up slowly, took her bag from the floor and walked out of the apartment. When she got to the top of the stairs, she stamped her foot. "Damn it! I'm not going to cry, not twice in one day." She wiped the dampness from her eyes and walked down the stairs.

Chapter 2

As Lord Oulezandur Luckran opened the heavy white door to the Emperor's private quarters he almost bumped into a teenage girl hurrying from the room, her hastily gathered clothing bundled in a ball and clutched to her breast. Because he was small in stature, they were momentarily face to face, and Luckran could see shame and humiliation in those brown eyes. Relief was also evident. They both knew there were many such girls who never emerged from the Imperial bedchamber alive.

Luckran, the Emperor's First Advisor, stepped aside to let the girl scamper away. He then entered the large living room, soundlessly closing the door behind him. To his left, double doors to His Majesty's bedroom were slightly ajar and Luckran could hear movement within. He waited patiently.

The huge living room was bright with the early morning sun that shone through the large floor-to-ceiling windows, their heavy white curtains held open by hooks of solid gold. Gold-threaded white wallpaper reached to within two feet of the ceiling, the intervening space filled with a deep plaster moulding of elaborate design. From the moulding's circular counterpart at the ceiling's centre, a large crystal chandelier hung. When the palace was first occupied, a century and a half earlier, each evening a servant spent half an hour lighting the many candles. Since then, the fixture had been modified, first for gas, then for electricity.

Luckran, a slightly bent figure dressed in pale green robes, wandered about the room, his soft shoes sinking into the deep blue carpet. He could recall the original carpet being laid in this room, as he had supervised the construction of the magnificent palace when the Emperor had finally but reluctantly agreed to relocate to more hospitable climes. It was fashioned after the gigantic structure further north that had once been the seat of

19

Neiron, the Emperor whose throne Destlar had taken centuries earlier.

The history books describe Destlar's spectacular defeat of Arnelius the Wizard, and how he subsequently conquered the Kingdom of Rustletov with a show of titanic power, the climax being the murder of the King, Neiron's cousin. Rustletov's nobility, never content under Neiron's rule, had been quite happy to accept this forceful new leader and his plans to invade the Empire itself. Under normal circumstances, Rustletov's army would have been no match for Neiron's, but Destlar rode in the vanguard, decimating the Imperial forces with immense claps of thunder that shattered eardrums, and raging fires that neither sand nor water could extinguish. Neiron sent his best magicians into the field, but they too found themselves enveloped in flames and had to use all their might to put out the fires and escape. Witnessing this, Neiron decided Destlar would not be stopped; the old Emperor ran, making space for the new.

Through a simple and logical policy of reward for the faithful and obliteration of any who might resist, Destlar had, over the centuries, expanded the Empire to the point where the entire planet was his domain. All religions were banned, except for the one founded by a long-forgotten prophet who had preached tolerance and forgiveness and who had lived in the western region of the original Empire two hundred years before Destlar was born. Destlar declared himself head of the Church and Velkren of the Gods, one of the angelic beings, intermediaries between humanity and the divine. A move seen as arrogant and derisory at the time, it proved wise as, with the passing of the years, most of the faithful accepted without deliberation Destlar's celestial nature. His immortality was very convincing.

During his unparalleled reign, there had been a few moments when a people won autonomy. But it was always short-lived and not since the Mazeranian massacre had any real resistance flourished.

"Luckran," the Emperor called in his high nasal voice as he emerged from the bedroom in his habitual black robes. "That damn wizard!"

"Wizard, Your Majesty?"

"Don't pretend to be confused. Put on last night's news."

With Destlar standing before the large television screen attached to the wall, Luckran pressed a few buttons on the remote control. He knew exactly what the Emperor wished to show him. In a moment, an image of a snow-covered town square appeared on the screen. At the centre of the image was a man in brown robes, standing on the back of a truck and gesticulating wildly. Luckran purposely kept the sound low.

"He's threatening some grand demonstration of his power and purpose," Destlar continued. "Any idea what he's up to?"

"No, Your Majesty. I believe he's all talk."

"Yet he gathers a following."

The television images showed a group of people standing before the truck, looking up at the magician. But they didn't seem to be taking the man seriously. It looked like they were enjoying the spectacle. "Not many. He's considered a bit eccentric, mad even. He spends long periods away from his wife and son, in the cold and barren mountains. Meditating, it seems."

Destlar grunted. "I hope you're right. There's something about him I don't like. I thought by now he'd have disappeared."

Luckran knew that the Emperor, despite his extraordinary abilities, feared magicians more than anyone or anything, save death itself. For that reason, the First Advisor went out of his way to keep all magicians happy, content and harmless, providing each with a large stipend, basically for doing nothing.

Destlar crossed the room and settled himself into the large sofa between two windows, adjusting his robes and arranging the many cushions about him. "I'm surprised you haven't taken care of him."

Luckran switched off the television. "I really don't think there's any need, Your Majesty. It's better not to react at all, so that soon he'll be forgotten. I'm not even withholding his stipend. And I notice he's not refusing it."

"All right. I'll leave it to you. Now, I believe you have news."

"Yes, Your Majesty. MatScan is now fully operational. Yesterday afternoon, a human being was disintegrated, transmitted to a receiver, where he was successfully rebuilt. The subject is alive and well."

"Very good. How far away is this planet you've found?"

"Thirty light-years. But distance doesn't come into the equation with MatScan. The only tedious part is setting up the receiver; it will take a little over thirty years for our spaceship to reach the planet. Once it's there, MatScan can transmit enough materiel and troops to take control of the new world."

"Thirty years. Still some time to wait."

"But we are fortunate to have found a suitable planet so close to Earda. On a cosmic scale, thirty light-years is not far at all."

Destlar reacted to the news of MatScan as if it was a new type of train. The almost identical planet in orbit about a relatively nearby star was no more exciting or amazing than the discovery of new lands beyond the endless ocean several centuries earlier. But the First Advisor was not surprised by such muted response. He knew the Emperor's interests lay elsewhere.

"Perhaps not far enough," Destlar said. "What if they decide to attack us?"

"I assure Your Majesty, there is no chance of that. They are primitive. They haven't yet harnessed electricity. And they have no magic." Luckran liked to remind Destlar there were no magicians on the new world. "Thirty years from now," Luckran pronounced, "Your Majesty's domain will span two solar systems."

Destlar rose from the couch. He regarded Luckran with piercing black eyes, looking down either side of his long and pointy nose. Perhaps he was searching for a hint of sarcasm in his First Advisor's bearing. But he must have been happy enough with what he found, or didn't find, for he gave a quick nod and turned in the direction of the dining room. It was the attitude of a man who believed things were as they should be.

Luckran coughed quietly.

Destlar turned. "You have more to say, Luckran?"

"I am assuming Your Majesty would care to visit the new domain."

"Perhaps."

"With the worsening climate, I believe it would be wise to have such a journey planned out in advance. Shall I proceed?"

Destlar grunted his approval, then turned for the dining room again.

Luckran bowed to the retreating back. He was a satisfied man, leaving the Emperor's quarters. The most important part of the meeting had come right at the end, when he broached the subject of Destlar leaving Earda, the slowly freezing home world. He could see the Emperor wasn't too pleased with the idea, and Luckran felt it would take no small amount of persuasion to get him to leave, but at least now the seed had been planted.

For the Emperor, spaceflight was not an option. The notion of 30 years in deep space with most of that time spent in hibernation would terrify Destlar. Luckran didn't expect Destlar to find MatScan very appealing either, but he believed the time would come when the Emperor would be relieved that an escape route existed, despite the risks inherent in such a novel form of transport.

***

Luckran entered the small conference room. Sitting either side of the table were two men, one dressed in a dark suit, the other in military uniform. The civilian was dark-skinned, the soldier white, like opposing chess pieces. Together they rose from their seats. "Thank you for coming," the First Advisor said. "Please, sit down."

Luckran sat at the head of the table and introduced each man to the other. "Dr Rendal Rubyan, scientist, engineer, commissioned to develop certain technologies, the details of which are classified. General Aldon Meckreen, Commander of the Imperial Engineering Corps. Amongst other sensitive projects, this unique division has been entrusted with the construction of the Emperor's villas, the existence of which are kept secret from all save the Emperor, myself and those within the general's staff who need to know."

Luckran handed the general a brown folder. In red letters it was marked as classified. "General, I am assigning you two projects, though together they form one system. You will begin construction of a new villa in the Swutland mountains. On the surface, it will appear ordinary, but in the extensive basements Dr Rubyan's apparatus will be installed. You will begin searching for a suitable site immediately.

"At the same time, you will begin construction of a spaceship in orbit. This ship will also contain equipment provided by Dr Rubyan." He pointed to the file. "Details are within."

The general frowned. "My Lord, are you expecting us to carry out the construction of a spaceship in secret?"

"No. That would be impossible. The official story will be that a new space station is being constructed."

Meckreen nodded. "Very good, My Lord. I look forward to the challenges."

"As outlined in the documentation, Dr Rubyan will be available for consultation and two members of his team will join your division for the duration of the spaceship construction, and afterwards on the villa."

Meckreen's eyes opened wide. "With respect, First Advisor, and no offence meant to Dr Rubyan, but I cannot accept outsiders."

"I understand your concerns, and indeed appreciate them. But I personally vouch for these men. They and Dr Rubyan can be trusted implicitly. Now, I'm sure you want to get started. Good day, General."

For the briefest moment, Meckreen's face betrayed his concern. Then he snapped out of his seat, put on his cap and saluted. "My Lord!" With the file tucked under his left arm, he left the room.

Luckran looked at the other man. "How about lunch, Rendal?"

***

After lunch, Lord Luckran and Rendal Rubyan sat in two large leather armchairs beside a fire of spitting logs in the lounge of the Governors' Rooms, home to the most enviable of clubs. A seat on the Imperial Assembly guaranteed admission, but from time to time, others were granted membership. Dr Rubyan was one of those few, thanks to his association with Lord Luckran, his long-time friend.

The lounge was on the ground floor of a three-storey building, four centuries old, hunkered between two giant office blocks in the centre of high-rise Wesmork. The teak panelled walls and deep red carpet added to the room's sleepy character. It was quiet and cosy.

The two old men sipped brandy from hundred-year-old crystal goblets. They had been presented to Luckran years earlier by a viceroy who'd imagined the gift would garner favour. The disappointed man was long since dead. Luckran liked to drink from them, as they reminded him of the egocentric stupidity of man.

"Meckreen's men won't figure out what all that machinery's for?" Luckran asked.

"No. They're closed boxes, with instructions on how to wire them together. It's common practice in engineering to connect inputs and outputs according to documentation, without necessarily having any idea of what's going on inside the devices themselves. They'll be curious, but they won't consider it strange. I expect they'll be more confused about the apparent lack of propulsion for the ship, but we'll tell them it's to be fitted later."

"You've done well, Rendal."

No one other than Luckran knew that Rubyan and his team were in fact magicians. In total secrecy, they had combined magic and engineering to develop a most fantastic technology, MatScan. It was imperative that Destlar remain unaware of the fact that magic was involved. He did not trust magicians, which Rubyan found mildly insulting. Perhaps it stemmed from earlier times when the world was less stable and the Emperor was forced to fight those magicians who enviously eyed the throne.

Still, Rubyan wondered that the Emperor didn't guess the truth. With classical physics, as he referred to it, MatScan would be impossible. Only by effectively combining the electromagnetic field with the more elusive, esoteric magical field could such technology become a reality.

An essential element of the remarkable mode of transport was Deep Sleep. When a live subject was undergoing the process of disintegration/reintegration, it was first necessary to place the organism in suspended animation. Rubyan and his team had spent years developing the technology and the magic that together slowed the heart rate down to about ten beats per hour. And of course Deep Sleep had a secondary function. It would allow a ship's crew to spend most of a long and uneventful journey asleep.

While testing the system on monkeys, Rubyan was disappointed to find the simians could not survive more than three months in hibernation. Human subjects—criminals sentenced to death—lasted longer, but few beyond 20 months and only a single individual beyond two years. A perplexed

Rubyan tried to discover the reason for this limit, but time constraints forced him to move on. Though he considered it inelegant, the solution was simple: the crew would awaken at regular intervals during the voyage. After a brief spell relaxing, they would return to sleep. The hibernation periods were set at 12 months.

Rubyan took a sip of brandy, his long dark fingers encircling the glass. A tall, thin figure, he looked much younger than his 76 years, with a full head of curly black hair and a face free of wrinkles, except when he smiled, which he did now. "You know what I always say: nothing's impossible to a magician."

"If only," Luckran sighed. "Now, I've another job for you."

"Ah, no. Come on, Oulezandur, you promised me that was the last one. I'm to help General Meckreen, but other than that, I get on with my research."

"You can't complain, Rendal. You keep talking about how much you've learned, thanks to the projects I assign to you."

Rubyan reluctantly acknowledged this fact. Luckran prevented other magicians from working with scientists and engineers. He was afraid of what they might come up with. Something that, in the wrong hands, might pose a threat to the Emperor. "You're right," Rubyan admitted. "I've done really well out of our relationship. But I want to study magic. I want to find out what it really is, rather than simply use it."

"And you will. But I need you one more time. If I'm to persuade the Emperor to leave Earda, the MatScan terminal in the Swutland mountains must be completely secured."

Rubyan frowned. "You're very determined to have him leave."

Luckran thumped the armrest. "Well of course I am. I want to get off this planet before I'm sandwiched between two walls of ice."

"Ah, yes. The immortal think long term. And of course you need His Majesty to go too, as he's the one keeping you alive."

"Yes, thanks Rendal. Rub it in."

"How old are you, exactly?"

"Never mind my age."

"You must be a couple of centuries by now. I remember learning about you in school," the magician said with a widening smile. "The man upon whom the Emperor bestowed the unique gift of immortality, reward for unstinting service to the welfare of mankind."

"Few have gained so little for doing so much," Luckran said. Despite the gravity of his voice, or perhaps because of it, Rubyan laughed.

A waitress approached. "Can I get you gentlemen another drink?" She was dressed in a tight short black skirt with matching waistcoat and a white blouse. Luckran noticed Rubyan's eyes travel up the girl's legs and along her hips to linger on the ample bosom that was putting considerable strain on the waistcoat buttons.

"Yes," answered Luckran for them both. "Two more." The magician's eyes continued to follow her as she went around the corner towards the bar.

Once she was gone, Luckran put the conversation back on topic. "I need a completely secure terminal, with the Deep Sleep unit at the centre. Impervious to any kind of assault, conventional or mystic. Could you erect such a barrier?"

Rubyan looked into the fire for a moment, thinking. "Yes, it could be done, but such a spell would take years to fashion, one layer on top of another, so to speak."

"Time we have. It will be thirty years before the MatScan terminal is in place at the other end."

"All right. I'll put one of my magicians to work on it."

"No," Luckran interrupted. "I want you. I'll trust no one else."

"I don't think you were listening, Oulezandur. This spell will be decades in the making. And it will be hard work. Most days now, I take a nap after lunch. No, you'll want one from my team to take on this task."

"No, Rendal. They're good, but nowhere close to you. It has to be you."

"Sorry. I'm not able for it. Besides, I'd be dead before it was finished."

"Nonsense. You're as healthy as an ox. Anyway, you'll enjoy the challenge. Nothing pleases you more than trying something new."

The waitress arrived with the drinks. "Thank you, my dear," Rubyan said as he took one of the glasses from the proffered tray. She smiled and walked off.

"Do you want her?" Luckran asked.

Rubyan laughed sheepishly, embarrassed that he'd been caught staring at the girl.

"I'll have her placed in an apartment," Luckran stated, "and she will be yours. A gift from the Emperor, for all your hard work. Your wife need never know."

Rubyan's pulse quickened as he imagined the fun he could have with such a beautiful woman. Then he shook the images away. "You're joking. She'd want nothing to do with an old man like me."

"She'll hardly believe her luck. It will mean permanent absence from the Imperial harem."

Rubyan sat up. "You mean she's one of the Emperor's wives?"

"Of course not. He has no wives. What would he want with a wife? He's not looking for an heir."

"So what are you telling me?"

"The servants here, they all live at the palace, in the harem."

"And he allows it?"

"He wouldn't care in the least, if he knew. And I like it this way. No outsiders. Between here and the palace they go, and nowhere else. Except your girl. I'll have the keys to the new apartment dropped by your office tomorrow."

"You're serious?" Rubyan threw his hands up. "Oulezandur, even after forty years, you still surprise me."

***

Destlar settled back into the cushions and watched the news. The main item concerned a pleasure cruiser that had been hit by a freak wave in the middle of the Consluminous Sea. The reporter was happy to announce that all of the passengers had been saved, though there hadn't been enough time to get the entire crew off the ship before it went under. Next up was an unexpected development in the Assembly, where the decision to cut state funding to schools and universities by eight percent was vetoed by the First Advisor. Destlar was a little surprised. He considered having a word with Luckran about it in the morning.

The news continued, each report more prosaic and tiresome than the previous one. But it left Destlar happy because there was no mention of the ranting magician. Perhaps Luckran was right when he said the man was no threat. He was about to switch off the television when a beautiful young woman with long dark hair appeared on the screen. She was laughing, her arms about a handsome and equally happy-looking young man. The reporter informed the viewers that the newlywed couple had just won a large sum of money in the state lottery. It was one of those light-hearted reports that were often tacked on to the end of a newscast. Destlar usually switched off in disgust, but this time he was captivated. The groom lifted his bride and swung her about. She squealed and laughed as he hugged her close and kissed her on the lips.

Destlar pressed pause. The woman was looking directly into the camera, her white teeth and deep brown eyes sparkling. The man was looking at his wife adoringly, bewitched.

Destlar smiled back. He reached for the bell rope.

Moments later, the Emperor's valet entered the room softly. "Your Majesty?"

Destlar pointed at the television. "Bring them to me."

The valet looked at the screen, then turned to the Emperor and bowed. "Yes, Your Majesty."

***

The crowd gathered at the end of the pier. A heavy grey sky promised snow. The magician stood with his back to the sea, arms raised. His wife aimed a camera. More footage for tomorrow's news. "Today it begins!" he shouted. "Today we take the first step in our walk to freedom." The townspeople nudged each other and smiled, wondering what kind of entertainment was in store.

No one paid particular attention to the rumble of the jet. Every three days, the Imperial fighter screamed in from the East, across the town and out over the ocean. It had been doing so for years. Whether it was part of some training exercise, or just a reminder of who was boss, was anybody's guess.

The magician stopped talking. His audience thought he was simply waiting for the plane and its loud engines to pass. But then he clasped his hands together and tracked the jet across the sky, like a child aiming an imaginary gun. A few people laughed at the image.

Suddenly, a blinding bolt of white light shot from the magician's hands. Everyone except the camerawoman flinched. They half turned away, shielding their eyes from the barrage of photons, while she did her best to track the crackling stream as it raced towards the jet.

The pilot saw it coming and tried to manoeuvre the plane out of the way, but the light bent towards him. It struck the tail, tearing it from the fuselage. The plane spun like a sycamore seed and smashed into the sea. It was all over in seconds.

The magician staggered. He gripped the railing, then slowly turned and sat with his back to the timber. He dropped his head and closed his eyes, elated but too exhausted to show it. His wife continued to film.

The townspeople were stunned. They'd never witnessed such a devastating feat of magic. They stood in silence, fearfully wondering what form the Emperor's retribution would take.

***

"You said not to worry about him!" Destlar shouted. "Then, like that," he continued with a snap of his fingers, "he destroys one of my jets. What's next? An attack on the palace?" Standing in the middle of his living room, the Emperor towered over Luckran, clenching his fists in rage. "I want this fucker dead! Now!"

"Troops have already landed in the town, but he's gone into hiding."

"Bomb them. Wipe them out. They're the ones hiding him. They deserve it."

"But he may not be there any more. I expect he got out quickly. However, I'm sure someone there knows of his whereabouts. We'll find him."

"You'd better! And I want that wife and child brought to me."

"Yes, Your Majesty."

"Leave me!"

Luckran bowed, then left the room and quickly made for the elevator, one that only he and the Emperor's valet had access to. He tapped a card against the sensor beside the golden doors and they immediately slid apart. He stepped inside the mahogany-panelled car and pressed the button for the basement. It was only a few hours since the attack that had taken him completely by surprise, and yet he was afraid too much time had passed. He knew the magician would be exhausted after such an awesome effort, and Luckran wanted to catch him before he had a chance to regain his strength. He didn't fancy sending his troops against a man who could tear fighter jets out of the sky.

The spectacular images were all over the news, and the people were frightened. Those in the temperate latitudes, living in relative comfort, were scared of the barbarians in the North who, if it wasn't for the might of the Emperor, the Velkren, would come pouring south like a plague of locusts. Those same people in the North were terrified of the Imperial response. It would be better for all concerned if this was dealt with quickly and decisively.

The doors opened. Luckran stepped out, turned to his left and walked along the bright corridor to the communications centre. Inside the small, dimly lit room, one soldier sat at a console, headset in place. Behind him stood a general, looking at a large screen on the wall. The general turned as Luckran entered. "We have him, My Lord."

Luckran looked at the screen. The unstable images, obviously from a camera perched on a soldier's helmet, showed a small house, nestled amongst a group of fir trees. The light was fading, the soldiers' shadows stretching far across the snow in front of them.

Three soldiers ran up to the house. One of them kicked the door in. Seconds later, there came the unmistakable crack of automatic machine-gun fire. Two quick bursts. "That's it," said the general. "Easy."

The camera entered the cabin and panned about. In the middle of the floor sprawled a brown-robed figure. The chest was covered in blood. The camera focused on the face, the wide lifeless eyes staring at the ceiling. Then it turned as a soldier approached, escorting a terrified woman and boy. "Target eliminated, General," the soldier spoke to the camera. "And we have the wife and child. What shall we do with them?"

The general turned to Luckran. "Your orders, My Lord?"

Luckran considered. It would be merciful to execute the woman and child now. He could tell the Emperor they'd been shot when the soldiers stormed the hideout. He could have the video footage edited so that there was no mention of the wife and child. There would be little chance of the deception being discovered. However, it wasn't worth the risk. The Emperor's trust was far too valuable. "Bring them here, unharmed."

***

"I would advise against it, Your Majesty," Luckran said. The day after the attack on the jet, he stood again in the Emperor's living room with Destlar towering above him, fists clenched.

"I don't care!" Destlar's anger still had not abated, despite the torment he had unleashed upon the dead magician's family.

Earlier in the day he'd forced the woman and child to repeatedly watch the news report featuring images from the cabin. Finally, when the footage once more reached the stage where the dead magician's eyes stared out of the screen, Destlar had frozen the picture and went about raping and mutilating the mother. The seven-year-old boy had whimpered in the presence of a trinity of dreadful faces: his father's in death, his mother's in anguish and his tormentor's alive with hatred and... something else. His young mind did not recognise sadism.

After torturing the woman for three hours, Destlar finally grew tired of her. An attractive woman, he'd noted with glee when she'd been brought before him, she lay crumpled on the floor with her tongue sticking out one side of her mouth and her face and neck bruised purple. Destlar turned away in disgust.

He fixed his attention on the boy sitting in the corner with his hands over his eyes. Did he think he was hidden? Had his mind regressed to early childhood? "I see you," Destlar called in a playful voice. The boy retreated further into the corner. The Velkren approached and stood over him. The terrified child kept his hands over his eyes. His body shook as he cried. "You poor thing," Destlar soothed, then bent down to rub the blond hair. "To have such a father. A criminal. A madman. What kind of life would you have had anyway?" He then closed his eyes and felt the tingle in his guts build in intensity until it was almost painful. "You will go quickly, with ease." The fire moved up through his chest and out along his outstretched right arm.

But at that moment, he reconsidered. He removed his hand from the boy's head. The fire dwindled and died. Destlar turned to the mother and reached out to her with his mind. She wasn't dead, not yet. Smiling, he looked down at the boy. "Actually, I think I'll send you two to the dungeon. Why end the fun now?"

Half an hour later, with the woman and child safely in the hands of a trusted pair of talented and discreet doctors, the Emperor sat on his couch and dreamed up activities for the two, which would begin as soon as the mother was revived and revitalised. This entertained him for a while, soothing his anger. But he grew impatient. He didn't want to wait days, or maybe weeks. By the time Luckran arrived, he was pacing the room.

"I want every town and city in Rustletov that received that madman destroyed," the Emperor commanded as soon as his First Advisor walked into the room. He wasn't in the least bit sentimental about the country that once had been his home.

But the diminutive figure in the green robes was presently not inclined to follow orders. "The people of Rustletov are Your Majesty's loyal subjects," Luckran said. "To kill indiscriminately would be seen as unfair and might encourage others to join the radicals. And the Church would find it difficult to explain such actions from the Velkren."

"You dare defy me?" Destlar shouted.

Anyone else would have quailed in fear. But Luckran was well used to the Emperor's outbursts. Safe in his indispensability, he stood firm. "I exist only to serve Your Majesty. But my position as First Advisor compels me to always and ever provide the very best advice. That is what Your Majesty charged me with, all those years ago."

Destlar gritted his teeth. For a moment he looked like he might argue further, but then he waved Luckran away. "Leave!" he commanded.

"Yes, Your Majesty." Luckran bowed and quietly left the room. He'd saved Rustletov, but he was experienced enough to know that the Emperor's fury, like a bolt of lightning, would ground somewhere.

***

The woman stumbled down the stairs, her baby in one arm, her son held about the waist with the other. She ran to her friend's apartment and hammered on the door.

Many people, especially those in underprivileged areas, abided by the one-child law, because it was difficult to care for more than one, and because every so often younger siblings died horribly. Everyone knew it was Destlar's work, but what triggered the cull, and why particular areas were chosen, were mysteries. And there really was nothing a parent could do, other than ride it out and hope that the icy presence passed harmlessly by. Two decades earlier, it was rumoured, a community on the far side of the world had responded by bringing all the children together, in an effort to fool the Emperor. An enraged Destlar had responded by killing them all.

While most of the authorities, both secular and religious, remained uncomfortably silent, some defended the Velkren's actions. They said it was harsh but essential punishment for those who flout the law. Strict population control was necessary for survival. They pointed to the fact that the Velkren never targeted older siblings, conveniently ignoring his many mistakes.

The woman uselessly grappled with the door handle, then pounded on the wood once more. Inside the apartment, her friend ran to the door. "No!" the husband shouted, dragging her back. "There's nothing we can do."

"Please! She's my friend," the wife cried.

"If she was your friend, she'd leave us alone. We have to look after our own." The two adults looked across the room at their frightened teenage daughter, standing by the kitchen table with her hands to her mouth, face pale, eyes wide.

"It's the will of the Gods," the man said.

"Then the Gods are cruel," responded the woman, "to put us in the care of such a monster."

"Shut up!" the man hissed.

In the corridor, the woman went to her knees, pulled the boy towards her and pushed the baby against his chest. Confused, the boy pushed back.

"Mammy," he cried.

"Stop it! Move your hands!" She squeezed her children together, making them one.

"What's the matter?" an unfamiliar voice spoke. She looked up at a man in the sky-blue robes of the Order of Lurg, the God of Light. "Is the child sick?"

"Take the boy," she pleaded, pushing her son towards him. "Please. Take him away."

The priest frowned. "Why? I don't understand. What's the matter?" he reiterated.

"Take him!" she yelled. The baby started to choke. "No!" she screamed. "Please, no!" In horror she looked down at the little face, the eyes screwed up, the tiny mouth opened, pointy tongue protruding as the little one struggled for breath. She could actually see the neck tightening. "Please," she whimpered. "Don't. Please."

A terrible croak emanated from the delicate creature before the little head lolled to one side. She cradled her daughter's head in the crook of her neck and stroked her hair, rocking back and forth and crying till her throat cracked. The boy took a step back, whimpering. The priest didn't move.

***

Less than an hour after beginning, Destlar got bored. It never quite lived up to his expectations, probably because the victims were remote and their reactions blunted by distance. And yet he kept repeating the act, as if somehow it would be more rewarding this time.

He lifted himself from the couch and crossed to the corner of the room to pull the heavy velvet rope. In years gone by, the rope was one end of a complex system of cables that ran through walls and floors and terminated in a brass bell in the kitchen far below. But that system had been superseded; now the rope activated an electronic transmitter that communicated with the Imperial Valet's personal phone.

The valet, never too far from His Majesty's quarters, arrived within minutes. "Your Majesty?"

"Bring two girls."

"Yes, Your Majesty. Any particular types?"

"No. I'll leave it up to you."

"Very good, Your Majesty." The valet bowed, retreated, then headed straight for the harem. Considering the Emperor's current demeanour, he suspected the girls, whatever pair he chose, would not make it through the night.

Chapter 3

The first person Jeseque saw upon entering the office suite was the idiot Ferist Kryslor. She couldn't believe it. He'd been in her class at the academy, totally inept, and yet somehow he'd managed to graduate. What could he be doing here? Surely he hadn't been selected as well.

She had spent two years maintaining the orbital fleet. The first year had been tough; she had to work much harder than her male colleagues and she couldn't have afforded a single mistake. But her perseverance eventually wore down her workmates' prejudices and she was finally accepted as a valued member of the team, though not as a friend.

Then one day, to her utter amazement, she was reassigned to the ancillary staff for the construction of a new space station. It was totally unexpected, especially since there had been no indications that another space station was in the offing. Many people thought there was little need for the one that already existed. Why a second? Jeseque had her suspicions as to what its true purpose would be, which made the new post even more exciting.

And yet a nagging worry lingered. Doubts as to why she'd been chosen. Of course there would be junior engineers on a project of such magnitude, and she wouldn't be one of those going into space. She was young and inexperienced, but she was also a very good engineer and she learned quickly. Why wouldn't she be chosen?

Because it's out you're going, not in, said a little voice. This was rejection, not acceptance. Her current colleagues couldn't get used to working with a woman, even if they hid it well. Her commander had probably used his influence and was relieved to be rid of her.

So it was with mixed emotions she arrived at Hightower, Astronautics Headquarters in Wesmork. She was excited but apprehensive too and full of doubt. Discovering Ferist Kryslor added dismay and confusion to the mix and confirmed her fears that making this team wasn't so difficult after all.

Noticing her, Ferist jumped up, eyes wide. He wore the same dress uniform as she: dark blue jacket and trousers, white shirt and navy tie. He removed the blue peaked cap and shoved it under his arm. "Jeseque!" he smiled, displaying two rows of perfect teeth. They were his best feature. Though a few inches taller than Jeseque, he was chubby and his fair hair was already thinning on top. "What a surprise. Sit down," he offered. She sat, thinking she didn't need his permission to do so. He sat beside her. "Have you been assigned to the space station too?"

"Yes," was her curt reply. He was looking at her the same way he always did. A sort of timid hungry look. Right through school, she knew he longed for her but never had the courage to do anything about it.

"Oh fantastic! I was worried about not knowing anyone. How nice this is. Imagine being thrown together again like this. It'll be great to work with someone you already know, won't it?"

We don't know each other at all. That's what she wanted to say, but she simply kept quiet. He'd be well able to do the talking for them both. Whenever she'd been unlucky enough to be partnered with him in the laboratory, he'd spent the entire two hours talking all sorts of nonsense. None of it ever had anything to do with the task in hand. She guessed it was his way of covering up for his inadequacies, of hiding his anxiety.

A door opened. "Second Lieutenant Jeseque Debrone?"

Jeseque stood smartly to attention. "Sir!"

"This way."

She followed the major into his office.

***

Jeseque walked down the wide corridor, dazed. Just before Ferist entered the office as she came out, he'd suggested she wait for him. Normally she would have ignored the request, but she had to know what news Major Tavenar had for him. So she waited by the window at the end of the corridor. Standing with her hands behind her back, she looked out at the empty lawn that stretched to the high stone wall a hundred yards away. Reflected in the glass she could see the many blue uniforms bustling about behind her, each with an important task to see to, no doubt. No one seemed to notice her. She sighed, turned from the window and walked to the wooden bench by the grey brick wall. She sat down heavily, took her cap off and rubbed her forehead. She wanted to complain to someone, but she knew no one would listen.

Except Ferist, of course. Eventually he came, his steel-capped heels clicking on the plastic-covered floor. He was in no position to do anything for her, but at least she could vent to him.

"I still can't believe this," he said as he reached her, smiling. "I'm really looking forward to working with you again." He sat down beside her, a little too closely. She was glad her cap was between them.

"So you've been assigned to the space station?"

"Yes."

"Then we won't be together, because I haven't. It seems there was some kind of mix-up. I'm for the IP manufacturing facility."

Ferist's smile disappeared. His head dropped as he looked at the floor. "I'm sorry." He almost sounded guilty.

Jeseque shrugged. "It's hardly your fault."

His head snapped up. "But it's not right!" Then he softened. "I mean, to get your hopes up like that. It's so unfair." They were silent a moment. "Are you staying in Wesmork?" he asked eventually.

"No. It seems my belongings are already on their way to IP." She took a piece of card from her inside pocket. "Train ticket."

"What is IP?"

"Imperial Protector. Strange name for combat jets. Anyway, there's a new model ready for production."

"Sounds interesting."

"I suppose," Jeseque reluctantly agreed. "Though not as exciting as your work will be."

"Yeah. I'm sorry. If they'd let me, I'd trade places." Jeseque wondered if he meant it. Well, it made no difference either way. Right, she thought, that's enough of that. She was about to say farewell when he plunged in.

"Would you like to go get something to eat, before your journey?"

"No, I think I'd better be on my way." But as soon as she said it, she reconsidered. She may have missed out on a wonderful opportunity, but now another was presenting itself. She looked at Ferist. He had just been included in a most exciting project but was crestfallen because the girl he got hot and bothered over when alone in bed had just turned him down. "Actually," she said with a smile, "I'm not in such a hurry. And I'd love to catch up."

***

Rubyan rode in the back of a government limousine. He'd spent the day at Hightower, and it was now after sunset. The six-lane boulevard leading to the palace was relatively quiet at that hour. The rain had stopped, but the thick-foliaged maple trees lining the centre continued to shed their heavy collection of water. At the top of the street stood the palace, the building's base covering more than three acres of ground. The chauffeur stopped outside the large steel gates that were ornamented with loops and swirls in a way that imitated the wrought-iron works of old. A uniformed security guard with a machine gun slung casually across his shoulder held up his hand. Rubyan lowered the window and handed out his identification. The guard waved to another, and the gates silently opened. They had been expecting him.

The floodlit limestone building sat 200 yards inside the fence. The ground floor, stretching for almost 300 feet on either side of the main portal, was perhaps 60 feet high. Between gigantic pillars, windows rose from just above the plinth to the pillars' lintel far above. There were three floors above that, each one a third the height of the ground floor and with matching windows.

Above the roof line the silhouettes of trees in His Majesty's garden could be seen stirring in the wind. In the middle of this garden rose a square tower, 100 feet across and four storeys tall. His Majesty's private quarters.

Between the floodlights reflecting brilliantly off the white limestone and the windows radiating a soft yellow glow, the building sparkled like a gargantuan jewel perched upon the knuckle of the highest hill in Wesmork. Nothing could compete, not even the 60-floor structures miles away in the city centre.

The palace was also the seat of government, with His Majesty's ministers and viceroys meeting in the Imperial Assembly, housed in the east wing's ground floor and presided over by the First Advisor.

The driveway split in two as it curved around a large pond in the middle of the garden and the car took the left branch to pull up at the base of the wide steps that led to the main entrance. It was a long flight of steps, enough so that the first basement was entirely above ground, and Rubyan was breathing heavily by the time he reached the large entranceway at the top. The magician looked up at the huge keystone archway and the throne within the ring of fire that was carved in the stone above the large gold-handled doors. A doorman held the way open for Rubyan as he entered an enormous foyer, fabulously lit by spectacular crystal chandeliers hanging from the ceiling so far above. Bustling about the foyer was everyone from ministers and their secretaries to porters and caretakers.

A guard approached and Rubyan handed him his identification. The guard pointed a small device at the card. The device beeped. He then spent a few moments comparing the photograph with Rubyan. Eventually he seemed satisfied. "Very good, doctor. Would you please empty your pockets, remove your watch, then step through the metal detector."

"Of course." Rubyan placed his watch, keys and wallet in a small plastic container. As it was passed through a scanner, he walked through the metal detector.

Another guard met him on the far side. "Thank you, doctor," he said, while a third handed him his belongings. "Do you know where you're going?"

"Yes."

***

Though the small medical facility was located in one corner of the east wing's top floor, Destlar liked to think of it as his dungeon. Apart from the two doctors employed there, he was the only one with access to the brightly lit area. Not even Luckran could enter here.

"Are they ready?" Destlar asked the on-duty doctor who approached as soon as he stepped through the sliding door.

The doctor bowed. "Yes, Your Majesty."

"Begin," Destlar commanded as he settled into the brown leather couch against the wall. He fixed his robes about him.

The doctor took a few steps along a corridor to Destlar's left, entering the first door on the right. The silence was misleading. One might mistake the place for an ordinary hospital ward or recuperation centre. But the people in the rooms were captives, not patients. It was so unlike the dungeons in his old palace in the North, where the prisoners howled and screamed and threw themselves at the bolted iron doors. Here, it was much more elegant. The prisoners spent most of their time in dreamless sleep, only to be awoken whenever Destlar wished them to perform.

Today he looked forward to a very special performance.

Destlar could hear the doctor moving about. Through the open door he could see a person lying on a bed, covered in a white sheet. Long dark hair spread out on the pillow. He knew there was another bed behind the door which contained the second and final cast member in this, his most splendid production. He wished he'd had the couple placed together in a double bed. That would have been deliciously ironic.

Muted beeps testified to the doctor's operation of unseen equipment. The woman in the bed stirred. The doctor came into view. He helped her out of bed. Dressed in a white gown, she padded across the tiled floor. The doctor, gently holding her elbow, escorted her from the room and helped her into a matching armchair on the Emperor's left. She looked around, dazed. Destlar watched her intently, awaiting recognition. A smile crept across his thin lips.

Her eyes began to focus. Destlar reached out with his mind, entering hers. He could feel her awaken. He could see her memories pop to the surface. She turned to look at him and as her eyes opened wide, lightning lashed through her brain. She gasped, then whimpered. Destlar took a deep breath, savouring the moment.

The doctor returned, this time guiding a man to the chair on Destlar's right. The woman's mind erupted violently once more when she recognised her darling husband. The Emperor's lip twitched, his eyes sparkled.

The young man fell into the chair and looked about, his head wobbling like a drunkard. Destlar tried to catch the wandering vacant eyes but failed. Growing impatient, he was about to tell the doctor to wake the man properly when, by chance, the wife's weakly smiling face came into the husband's field of vision.

The man woke with a jolt. His blue eyes snapping into life. The woman's eyes filled with tears, but with great effort she kept her smile in place. Her husband smiled back. It was the moment Destlar had been waiting for.

The man's lips stretched wide and his mouth opened, revealing long steel teeth, each one sharpened like a canine. The woman wailed, covering her face with shaking hands. The man lifted his hands to his mouth, his fingers tentatively exploring the unfamiliar set of fangs he found himself mysteriously endowed with. His sobbing was drowned out by his wife's hysterics.

"Quiet!" Destlar roared. The woman jumped in the chair, shocked into relative silence. "That's better," the Emperor continued softly. "It's almost time for the second act. It's a pity there's been such a protracted interval, but the props department needed time to get the teeth in place. However, I think you'll find it was worth the wait. We could have attached false teeth to the originals, but that would have been cheap. Much better to pull out the old and embed those beautiful steel blades into the bone. I think the doctors should be congratulated for doing such a magnificent job in such a timely manner."

Two sets of eyes stared at him, two minds attacked from opposite directions, the past and the future. They struggled to keep painful memories at bay. They tried in vain to ignore imagined futures that were dominated by shiny teeth. And the moment was suffocated by the consuming presence of the dark one. Though they knew the room was bright, the frightened pair could not convince themselves of the fact. The walls and floor reflected the ceiling lights brilliantly, and yet they were surrounded by darkness, as if they were enveloped in a thick cold fog.

Their brains were ill-equipped to deal with such contrasting images. They were overpowered by the combined weight of the past, present and future and they sought sanctuary in the only available refuge: sleep. Destlar sensed their attempts to escape into unconsciousness. He was amused to see them slip into slumber, in unison, as if marriage truly had transformed the two into one. "There's nowhere to hide," he whispered with a smile as he reached further into their minds and shaped their dreams, turning them into nightmares.

The couple lay naked together on warm sand, waves hissing and foaming across their feet. They kissed. Something ran lightly across her shoulder. She thought it was his fingers at first but looked down to see a little black spider scuttle along her left breast towards her nipple. He flicked it away. But it was followed by another. And then another. Soon there were hundreds, tiny feet prickling across their damp skin. With a yelp, they tried to get up, but before they could move there were thousands, crawling through their hair, across their faces, into their mouths.

Together they awoke with pitiful cries. "Please pay attention," Destlar admonished mockingly. "You just got out of bed and are already falling asleep. Shame on you.

"Now, I shall not be performing this time. You two will have the stage to yourselves. But before we again raise the curtain, it might be nice to review the first act. I would like to hear your opinions. Perhaps you think there are some aspects that could have been done differently."

Destlar nodded to the doctor. On the other side of the small room, opposite the couch, a wide television screen came to life. The lights dimmed and the chairs either side of the couch turned to face the screen. "Leave us," Destlar commanded.

The doctor bowed. "Yes, Your Majesty." As he headed for the exit, the screen showed Destlar welcoming a handsome man and a beautiful woman into his private quarters.

***

"Please, come in," the Emperor said with a smile. The young couple, astonished to find themselves in the presence of the

Velkren, hesitated on the threshold. The valet was forced to give each a little nudge in the back. They stepped inside. The man bowed and the woman curtsied. She wore a pale blue strapless dress. He wore a dark suit.

"I believe you just got married," the Emperor said.

"Yes, Your Majesty," they answered, as the valet quietly closed the door from the outside.

"And you also won quite a sum of money. The Gods look upon you favourably, which is why I have chosen you. I understand you had just retired to the bridal suite when my representatives arrived."

"Yes, Your Majesty," they repeated. They had been frightened by the two men who had presented them with official-looking documents that said they were to be taken to the palace immediately. With no alternative, they had got dressed and had then been escorted from the hotel by the incommunicative Palace agents. Stories of arrest, interrogation and imprisonment on the back of erroneous information and false accusations came to mind. They wondered if someone was jealous of their sudden wealth.

But their worry turned to astonishment after the agents delivered them to the Emperor's valet and he took them to the tower to land them in the presence of the divine emissary.

"I am sorry to have interrupted," the Emperor continued, "what I'm sure would have been a very special moment for you. And I don't wish to deny you any longer. Please, follow me." He escorted the perplexed couple to his bedroom. "Continue," he said with a smile as he indicated the large bed.

They looked at each other, frowning. The woman laughed nervously. The man turned to the Emperor. "You mean here? Now?"

The Emperor drew himself up to his full height, and his voice became heavy. "You will address me in the appropriate and proper manner!"

The man bowed low. "Please accept my apologies, Your Majesty. I forgot myself."

A nervous silence followed. The woman could not look the Emperor in the face. His small dark eyes scared her. The tension grew, and the Emperor's impatience became apparent.

"The Gods watch you make love. They rejoice in the union. You do not object to this. You, simple base creatures, are honoured even to be noticed by the Ultimate Ones. I deserve and expect the same kind of worship, and yet you dare deny me!"

The couple looked at each other and came to unspoken agreement. Reluctantly, they made their way to the bed. The Emperor sat in an armchair to one side. The husband undressed his wife, while she reciprocated. They lay together on the bed, awkward and self-conscious, trying to pretend they were alone, but failing.

Destlar's heart thumped. It wasn't the act itself that excited him, but the activity within the protagonists' minds: embarrassment and fear, coupled with sexual arousal.

The woman seemed to be enjoying the situation more than might have been expected. Perhaps an exhibitionist streak lay hidden within her, one that was missing in her husband. Or maybe it was simply the fact that she was being watched by a member of the opposite sex. Whatever the reason, she was certainly becoming more excited and less afraid and ashamed than her husband. Destlar took this as his cue. He stood up. "She deserves better than that, boy," he shouted. With a flick of his wrist, he threw the man across the room.

Limbs flailing, the man landed heavily against an ornamental table, toppling it. The wind was knocked from him. He gasped, then winced at the sharp pain in his ribs. Propping himself on his elbows and looking up at the bed, he was astounded to see the Emperor climbing onto the mattress. "Come here, my sweet bride." The Emperor grabbed a handful of long black hair and pulled the woman towards him. As she was being dragged across the bed covers, she looked across at her husband. Emboldened by her imploring eyes, he struggled to his feet and charged. But just as he was about to reach the bed, he slammed into an invisible barrier and crumpled to the floor, blood pouring from a broken nose. Lights flashed in his head, and he felt himself sinking. However, welcome sleep was snatched away by something repulsively alien reaching inside his head and dragging him back. His body was picked from the floor and thrown into the armchair beside the bed, where he was afforded a perfect view of his wife being savagely beaten and raped. He tried to close his eyes, but they were no longer his to command.

***

"Excellent!" Destlar applauded. The television showed a still image of the woman lying on a bed. The white covers were stained with her blood. Her nose bled, her eyes were swollen and her face and limbs were heavily bruised. Her broken right arm lay twisted by her side. Deep cuts were slashed across her abdomen and breasts.

During the distressing recording, the couple had tried to turn away from the television, but their heads had been held immobile by an impalpable but irresistible force, as if the channel linking the neck muscles to the brain had been severed. They tried closing their eyes but found they couldn't even blink.

"Young lady," Destlar continued, "you should be proud. A stellar performance. Your husband may be disappointed he didn't have as important a role, but he shouldn't worry, for it will be made up to him in the next act." It didn't bother Destlar that his words were not really penetrating the minds of the stupefied couple. "Now, my lady, please stand up and remove your gown."

As if hypnotised, the woman immediately obeyed. The gown slid to the cold tiles. Destlar admired her sensual curves. "So preoccupied with your husband's new teeth, I neglected to congratulate the doctors on the wonderful work they did in restoring your beautiful body. The canvas has been wiped clean, ready for another's work."

He turned to the husband. "Which brings us to the artist. Please, imitate your wife by undressing."

The man stood shakily, and let the gown fall from his shoulders. The couple stood facing each other, only a few feet apart, but perceiving nothing. Destlar watched them with interest, a tiny smile on his lips. Their brains' higher functions were shutting down, almost as if they were in a waking coma. Unable to face reality, they had retreated into a featureless wasteland. Upon this virgin territory, Destlar built an alternative reality.

The man's face lit up like a light bulb. He stepped forward and took his wife's hand. Holding her at arm's length, he looked her up and down, his eyes sparkling. "You look fabulous," he said.

The woman giggled. "You sound so funny." She reached out and touched her husband's front teeth, then giggled again. "Can you kiss me with those?" He pulled her close, caressing her. He tried to kiss her, but she pulled away, laughing. "You have to get rid of those teeth. They're so ridiculous." He pulled her close again. She stroked his chest, kissed his neck. He cupped her breasts, squeezed them. She sighed with pleasure.

Suddenly there was a change. His body stiffened. He let go of her breasts. She frowned. He stood back. His expression altered, darkened. "Gods, I'm starving!" he said. He gripped his stomach, groaning.

"Oh come on," she said. "You're acting like you haven't eaten for days." Her laugh sounded forced, nervous.

The pain in his guts was intense. He'd never been so famished. He looked at his wife with predator's eyes. She took a step back. "What's the matter?" He sprang at her, knocking her to the floor. Her right elbow cracked against the hard tiles and she cried out, in pain and bewilderment. For a fleeting moment, when his cheek brushed hers and his mouth sought her neck, she thought he was playfully trying to kiss her. But then he sank his teeth into her throat and she screamed.

Blood fountained, splashing on the tiles and across her husband's face. She would have been dead in seconds if Destlar hadn't kept her alive. Her husband lifted his head and looked at her, his mouth and metalwork covered in her blood. She didn't recognise the savage face as he grinned at her. He dropped his head, this time to her left breast. She screamed again as he took a huge bite.

Destlar luxuriated amongst the neural spikes in the mind of the terrorised and traumatised woman whose last moments were spent watching her ravenous husband feast upon her flesh.

The man stopped chewing. Something left him, something that had warped his reasoning and confused his senses. Realisation dawned. With a horrendous cry he spat out the meat and desperately shuffled across the floor, away from the bloodied carcass. His wife's lifeless eyes stared at him accusingly. He vomited. He howled. Destlar sighed.

The Emperor settled back on the couch and closed his eyes, relishing the moment. Sometimes the games he devised did not live up to expectations, but this one had. It was all very pleasing. He listened to the whimpering figure at his feet. "Well played, young man," he said. "You I will certainly keep. I'm sure there are one or two girls in the harem you would like to have for dinner."

He started to laugh at his own joke, then stopped when a slight but distinctive sensation invaded his mind. His eyes shot wide and he bolted upright. Someone was practising magic.

***

Rubyan wandered about the foyer. He thought the feeling would intensify, once he was inside the palace, but it didn't. He wondered if perhaps the Emperor was absent.

For about three months he'd been regularly meeting with General Meckreen as they worked out the logistics for the installation of the MatScan equipment in the villa in the Swutland mountains and eventually aboard the spaceship. At the same time, he was weaving the spell, layer upon layer. When complete, it would be ready to protect the MatScan system from any form of attack. But it was demanding work and Rubyan was surprised by his own stamina.

In fact, he was puzzled. He no longer felt tired in the evening. Instead, the work left him invigorated. Often, he would spend the night with his young lady in the apartment provided by Luckran, his excuse to his wife being that he was extremely busy on a task assigned to him by the Emperor himself. He expended quite a bit of energy those nights but was always fit and eager the following morning.

Then he noticed the magic. It was just about detectable, like something seen out of the corner of his eye. It disappeared as soon as he tried to focus on it. At first, he thought he was imagining it. But as time went by, he became convinced he was somehow enveloped in a magical field. Rubyan had hoped entering the palace and getting close to the Emperor would intensify that field. But he was wrong. The feeling was as elusive as ever.

As Rubyan ambled about, wondering what to do now that he'd made it inside, he noticed an area of the foyer that was cordoned off with purple velvet ropes. On the wall the other side of the ropes was a large canvas in a gold frame. Of course, *The Vanquished*. He'd forgotten Tchamilla's most famous painting was displayed in the palace. He wandered over to the ropes.

Though Rubyan had always wondered what it was about the painting that generated such excitement and admiration, he had to admit it was impressive. About 20 feet across and eight feet high, it depicted the famous sea battle and subsequent razing of the city of Mazeran 400 years earlier. Awash with golden light, from the setting sun in the background and the burning city in the middle distance, it was both soothing and distressing.

Its most intriguing aspect was the line of ships on the horizon, the defeated Mazeranian fleet. For centuries the debate had continued over whether the ships too were burning. Some people were convinced they were, others equally sure it was the play of the setting sun on the sails. Being a contemporary piece, the painting was also embroiled in historians' arguments over the details of the battle. One side claimed that the inferior enemy fleet was sunk by the Emperor's more heavily armed ships. The other side believed that, to the contrary, the haphazard and poorly disciplined Imperial fleet was trounced by the smaller and more nimble enemy, forcing Emperor Destlar, aboard the lead ship, to save the situation by setting fire to the Mazeranian ships with nothing more substantial than his will.

Some Church orders expounded the most accepted version of events, at least amongst the faithful. They taught that the Mazeranians were in league with evil spirits who summoned a sudden and ferocious storm that battered the Imperial fleet alone. But the Velkren Emperor calmed the seas, banished the evil spirits and sank the enemy ships in flames. He then sailed into port and destroyed the heathens and their repugnant city.

Rubyan could see why the debate had raged for so long as he couldn't decide whether the ships were on fire or not. And he understood why this would be interesting to artists and art critics, but historically, it was irrelevant. Tchamilla, though he was alive at the time of the battle, was far from accurate in his portrayal. Everyone agreed that the Mazeranian fleet was at the bottom of the ocean by the time the city was alight, whether it was sunk by Imperial cannon or the Emperor's flames. And yet, in the painting, the ships were still visible while the city burned.

Rubyan was a lot more interested in the figures in the foreground, standing on a hill looking down upon the conflagration. Accompanied by magicians and clergymen in elaborate robes was one figure in black: the Emperor. The artist had very accurately captured the thin features, the long nose, the pale skin. Rubyan wondered what it would be like to stand and look upon a picture painted centuries earlier and say, "I was there. That's me in the picture."

Rubyan focused on the Emperor's dark eyes. Even from a distance, and though he knew they were nothing more than dabs of black paint on canvas, he was held by those tiny piercing eyes. He supposed that was the mark of the master painter, capturing so well the Emperor's most enthralling and frightening features. Rubyan wondered how Tchamilla did it. Without giving much thought to his actions, the magician bent the light reflecting off the painting, giving him a closer view of the Emperor without needing to cross the ropes.

Moments later he tensed, his hands involuntarily forming fists so tight his nails dug into his palms. The air was alive with electricity and the sounds in the foyer were suddenly attenuated. He looked about. No one else seemed to notice.

His chest tightened as he became enveloped in a terrifying and alien darkness. He could see the people, the deep red carpet, the velvet ropes, the painting, the dazzling chandeliers, all in perfect clarity. And yet, at the same time, he felt as if he were being closed into a dark and tiny space. His ears popped. Sound returned, then amplified. The chatter in the foyer became a roar.

Rubyan reeled. He staggered towards a pillar and hung on. He felt as if he were in two places at once. Blinding light and roaring sound. Shadowy silence. Into the dark charged the creature. Indistinct. Black upon black. Radiating anger, hatred, fear.

Rubyan slid to the floor. His heart pounded against his chest and his head ached as the dark one focused his malevolence upon him. People gathered about him. He could only see their legs. Someone crouched down and spoke to him. He couldn't make out the words. He wondered where he was and why it was so dark. Just before he passed out, he saw green robes swishing towards him.

***

He woke in a dimly lit room. The head of the bed was tilted so that he was half sitting up. The sheets were crisp and white. There was a plastic tube attached to his left arm. The other end of the tube went into a small machine by the bed. The machine had little green displays and red lights. It beeped and clicked. Through the blinds on his left, he could see the city lights reflected off heavy clouds.

He frowned. Hospital? Had he been in some kind of accident? He could remember going to the palace and admiring the painting of the Emperor.

All of a sudden, like turning a corner, the entire episode opened before him with frightening clarity. His eyes widened and his heart raced.

When he woke again the sky was less cloudy. This time he approached the traumatic episode more carefully, glancing at dark memories.

The Emperor had attacked him. No, that wasn't right. It wasn't an attack. The Emperor had…looked at him. Yes, simply looked at him. But with an intensity so full of hate it had put Rubyan in hospital. He had been terrified. He thought he was dying.

But the shock was wearing off. He was miles from the palace, safe. And, he had to admit, a little excited. Proximity to such awesome might was intoxicating. It produced a fear that was at the same time exhilarating. It reminded him of riding through the narrow city streets on his motorcycle, all those years ago.

No helmet, wet streets. One false move, leaning too much into a corner, and that could have been the end of him. Such fear was the attraction.

But there was something else. Perhaps his mind was playing tricks with him, but he had the feeling there was another facet to the Emperor's gaze. Not just enmity, but also...fear? Why would one so powerful be afraid?

Rubyan was confused by his own feelings. He should be angry. What had he done to deserve such a reaction from the Emperor? But he wasn't angry. Instead, he felt privileged to have been in the presence of such magnificence. To have caused such a strong reaction. He couldn't escape the feeling he'd been considered a threat.

***

Rubyan finished the last few pieces of fruit and placed the bowl back on the tray with the rest of the dinner plates. The door swung open and in walked Luckran. "Finally you're awake," the First Advisor said as he sat down beside the bed. His mouth formed a thin line.

"You're not going to ask me how I'm doing?" Rubyan ventured.

"I'm sure you're perfectly fine," Luckran answered sharply. "In body, but not in mind. What possessed you to go to the palace? How did you even gain access?"

"Someone at the club arranged it for me." Rubyan decided he would not give a name, unless he was pressed.

"But why go there? Are you insane?"

"Why is it such a big deal?"

Luckran's eyes opened wide. "Because magicians aren't allowed," he answered loudly, thumping the arm of his chair. Rubyan was surprised by the outburst. Luckran was seldom angry. And even when he was, it was normally the quiet and dignified variety. "Destlar went crazy," Luckran continued, his voice still raised. "He wanted you found and killed. I've had to tell him you were taken away and will be executed tomorrow morning."

"He can't just—"

"Of course he can. Who do you think you're dealing with? And let me tell you, anyone else would be executed. You're safe only because I need you."

"You can't be serious."

"I am very serious. Don't you ever do that again."

"Take it easy."

"Don't tell me to take it easy. I can't afford to take it easy. So stupid! Do you think magicians are kept away just for the fun of it?"

"I thought it would be all right since no one knows I'm a magician."

Luckran's anger dissipated. "Ordinary people can't spot it, but he's a magician. He sensed you, felt your magic. And magic terrifies him, any but his own."

"He really was scared? I can't understand why. He's invincible."

"I know he is. But the most powerful are often the most paranoid." Luckran eyed Rubyan piercingly. "What were you doing there? What were you hoping to gain? If you believed it wouldn't be a problem, you'd have asked me to get you in."

Rubyan lay back on the pillow and stared at the ceiling. He searched for the spell and was surprised he could find it more easily this time. It seemed stronger than ever. "I think he's keeping me alive," he said, eventually.

Luckran frowned. "What are you talking about?"

Rubyan turned to look at his old friend, the immortal First Advisor. "I mean I've joined the club," he said quietly. "You're not the only one His Majesty feels he can't do without."

Luckran let forth a short mirthless laugh. "Don't be daft."

"You're the one who keeps telling me how important my work is. And the spell to protect MatScan will take years to finish."

"But he doesn't know about the spell."

"Maybe he does."

"No, Rendal. He doesn't!"

Kubyan leaned across and stared into the other man's eyes. "Oulezandur, I can sense it. You can't feel him regenerating you because you're not a magician. But I can." Then he lay back on the pillows. "I don't know how to explain it. I just know I'm not ageing, not any more."

***

The following day, towards noon, Kubyan was anxious to leave the hospital. He felt perfectly well, but the doctors were concerned. Of course it was his age that worried them. And he made the mistake of telling them he had a lot of work to do, which made them more determined to keep him in bed. His wife, who'd visited the evening before, was on the doctors' side. To argue would have been pointless, so he'd had to endure one more night of being woken periodically by over-anxious nurses who wanted to take his temperature and ask him how he felt.

Recalling his wife's visit and how concerned she'd been made him wince inside. He felt guilty that he'd hardly spared her a thought before she came through the door. Instead, he'd been thinking of the young woman in the secret apartment, wondering if she was thinking of him. Was she worried about him? Did she miss him?

He was at it again. He'd begun with his wife but then quickly moved on to his girlfriend. Shaking his head in disgust, he banished the beautiful creature from his mind. He should be focusing on more important matters, like his recent brush with death. How ironic, he thought, that the source of his newfound youth had almost killed him. Or was he exaggerating? The incident had not been near fatal; it had just felt that way.

How he would love to have been able to talk to his father about his experience. His father, an experimental physicist at Wesmork University, had been incensed by the ban on research into magic. He might have experimented himself, quietly, if he hadn't been missing the most basic ingredient: magic. Without a magician, there was nothing to experiment on.

Until his son came along. Rendal was a late bloomer. His rare abilities did not manifest themselves until he was in his teens, when he began to show interest in his father's work. Sometimes when he was in the lab, finely calibrated instruments would behave erratically. And then one evening, as the family sat down to dinner, his mother toppled a glass. A pool of water ran for the table's edge and was about to cascade when, without moving, Rendal pulled it back. For a moment he held it. Then it was gone, over the edge and onto the floor. His mother yelped. His father smiled.

Ignoring his wife's protests, Rendal's father decided to take advantage of this unexpected development. He persuaded his son to keep his nature secret, which wasn't difficult as Rendal didn't want his friends to know he might be a magician. Magicians were feared and mistrusted. Many people thought they were mad and attributed their unnatural abilities to engagements with evil spirits. Most magicians, whether male or female, ended up living lonely hermitic lives, talking to themselves, therefore giving credence to the demons theory. Magicians seldom went to college, and they most certainly were not allowed to study science. Rendal wanted to follow in his father's footsteps.

Which he did. It was a proud day for the Rubyans when Rendal joined his father on the faculty of Wesmork University. As they had done all through Rendal's time at school and college, father and son continued to work together at home, trying to unravel the mystery of magic. It was Rendal's father who discovered the magical field.

But there were rumours. It is difficult for magicians to at all times hide their abilities. Eventually, Rendal became very adept at controlling his reflexes, but by then it was too late. The police came calling, and it looked bad for the Rubyans. They were taken to the palace. How different Rendal's entrance had been that day, all those years ago. They did not walk through the main portal, with the carving of the Velkren above the doors. They were not respectfully welcomed. That day, father and son were escorted through some basement door, into a small white room with a steel table and chairs in the centre.

Their prospects were not good, with long jail sentences awaiting. When the First Advisor walked through the door, their fears increased. However, it wasn't keys to a cell he arrived with, but money. Any amount of it. And a directive. "Continue to study magic. Report directly to me and keep the nature of your research secret." Then he looked directly at the younger Dr Rubyan. "Don't let anyone know you're a magician." He set them up in a laboratory in the Centre for Advanced Technologies, saying they should equip it in whatever manner they wished.

Before long they convinced the First Advisor he had chosen wisely. They combined the magical field, which had eluded all of science until then, with the electromagnetic field in a very precise and delicate manner, producing what they called the self-perpetuating spell. It was at this point the First Advisor began to direct their research, and Project Deep Sleep was born.

As he sat in the armchair, waiting for one more visit from the doctor, Rubyan felt the stab of guilt. Shortly after Project Deep Sleep was initiated, his father was diagnosed with pancreatic cancer. Within months, he was gone. He'd been proud of what they'd achieved, but was disappointed that, even though they'd found the magical field, they knew nothing of the means by which some people, magicians, manipulated it. He used to complain about them spending too much time making gadgets for Luckran. "We're not scientists any more," he'd lament, "we're engineers."

Since then, nothing had changed. Rubyan was still playing the part of engineer, on yet another project for the First Advisor. But the work was so important the Velkren was holding him ageless. There would be time. There would be plenty of time. "I promise you," he whispered, "I will return to science."

Chapter 4

Jeseque set the glass of pineapple juice down on the ornate white metal table with a clink. She sat back, shuffling a bit to try and get comfortable. The antique lawn furniture may have been beautiful, but it wasn't very practical, especially the chair backs with their elaborate swirls that shoved metal balls into the occupant's spine.

Jeseque, Ferist and Ferist's mother had just finished a lunch of fruit, cheese, bread, juices and coffee. Real coffee! Jeseque felt a bit guilty for enjoying such wonderful fare. The amount of food still on the table would feed an ordinary family for a week. But it would have been unwise to make a fuss. She had a role to play, and it wasn't her fault if her taste buds enjoyed it so much.

Jeseque looked out across the lake. With the sun high in a cloudless sky, the water shimmered, sparkled. It was a hot day, as most were, so close to the southern tropic, but the large umbrella over the table and the breeze off the water provided some respite. The lazy lapping of the waves against the stony shore was hypnotic, so much so that Jeseque almost didn't hear Ferist's mother speak. She must have asked what kind of work Jeseque did, because Ferist answered, "I told you, mother. She's an engineer. We studied together."

"Oh. I didn't know girls did that. I thought she was just attending the same campus as you, learning to type, or something like that."

Ferist sighed.

"Do you like that kind of work, Jeseque?" his mother continued. "Getting all covered in dirt and grease."

"Oh for the love of the Gods, mother! She doesn't fix cars. She's building the latest supersonic fighter jet."

"Really? Well that sounds interesting."

"It is," Jeseque finally spoke. "Though not as interesting as Ferist's work."

"Nonsense," Ferist retorted.

"Well, we wouldn't know," replied his mother. "We're not allowed to ask." Though she tried to decorate her voice with pride, Jeseque couldn't help but feel the woman didn't really care.

Jeseque and Ferist had been together for three years and this was the first time she'd been invited to the family estate. Ferist seldom talked about his parents, which suited her fine, as it meant she didn't have to reciprocate. He'd asked about her mother and father only once and her curt response had been designed to give the impression they were dead. She was relieved Ferist hadn't delved further, though part of her was surprised, perhaps even annoyed, that he hadn't wanted to know more.

Ferist's mother was something like Jeseque had expected, her mental picture assembled from little pieces he'd said about her, plus the fact that she was rich and always had been and was married to a member of the Assembly. She was in her mid-fifties but looked younger. A lot of money, time and effort had been put into keeping the body in splendid shape, the breasts firm, the face free of wrinkles and the hair blonde and always in style. Like the furniture, Jeseque guessed her main purpose was show.

Ferist's father, the Viceroy of Zervnia, had been held up by some matter at the Assembly and had not yet arrived from Wesmork. When Ferist had reluctantly told Jeseque his father was ruler of the little country famous for its expensive wine, she hadn't been surprised. It explained a lot. Ferist's graduation, despite his incompetence. His acceptance on the space station project in her place. His never-ending supply of money. It angered her. Why should she be dumped aside just because his father had influence? But she buried her feelings, determined to continue to cultivate her contact, certain that it would eventually bear fruit.

And yet, so far, he'd proved unexpectedly stubborn. Ferist and his colleagues must have been subjected to some highly effective lectures on the need for secrecy, and on the punishment awaiting those who leaked. Despite her efforts, Ferist kept quiet. But she hadn't yet decided to give up.

In the meantime, her revolutionary aspirations were satisfied somewhat by her transmission of every piece of information she got on the IP jets to NALO. She wasn't sure if any of the information would ever be useful, but at least she was doing something.

"Ah, here he is," said Ferist. Jeseque looked up the hill towards the villa. A heavy man walked towards them. She looked at Ferist as he stood up. He appeared nervous. "Father!" he called. "You made it."

"Of course I did," came the reply as His Highness, Prince Carlden IV, walked up to the table. The expensive grey suit did a lot to compensate for the dumpy figure. He had a fat red nose and very little hair.

Oh dear, thought Jeseque, this is what Ferist will look like.

"Later than I should be," the prince continued, "thanks to those idiots who want to tax us out of business."

"Please," interrupted his wife. "No Assembly talk. Let me introduce our guest."

"No need," he replied gruffly as he sat down and poured himself a cup of coffee. "I've heard all about her. Ferist, are you trying to impress us with this? Are you so desperate to finally bring home a woman that you grabbed the first one who didn't tell you to get lost? A female engineer. What next?"

"Carlden!" his wife cried.

"Be quiet! It's your fault she's here. If you'd told me they were coming, I would have put a stop to it." He turned to Jeseque as he plastered a slice of bread with strawberry jam. "Young lady, you are not welcome here. Ferist may play about with you in Wesmork, for a time, though it embarrasses me somewhat. But I won't have you coming about here and getting comfortable, getting ideas. You are not the type of woman we want for Ferist. Please go up to the house. I wish to speak with my son."

Jeseque was amazed. She was used to being ridiculed for her choice of profession, but it was seldom put so bluntly. She had to admire the man's direct approach. No dancing about the issue with him. She supposed he was accustomed to getting his way, at least in Zervnia. She was also struck by the contrast between him and his son, who sat quietly throughout, head down, staring at the table. Father's looks, but mother's brains. Ah, she thought, if a suitable heir is what you were after, you should have been more concerned about the intellect and less about the tits.

Jeseque stood. "This is your house, so I will do as you ask. But let me say this: I pay no heed to the opinions of one who was born with everything, one who gained nothing on merit." She turned and walked away, delighted to have put the arrogant prick in his place, while at the same time wishing she'd kept her mouth shut. A good agent doesn't allow emotion to overcome logic.

***

"Insolent as well," the viceroy said as Jeseque walked off. "Never bring her here again."

Ferist remained silent, staring at the table. Carlden looked at his son and sighed. "You can stay for the night, since you wouldn't make the evening flight now anyway. But first thing in the morning, she goes. You can go with her or remain here. It's up to you. You'll soon have to dump her anyway. I don't mind you playing around with her for a while. She's sort of attractive, and you could do with the experience. Your younger brother is way ahead of you. I just don't know why you can't catch a decent woman, a man in your position. I suppose I'll have to take care of that for you too.

"Now, I'm pulling you out of the military." Ferist looked up, surprised. "You're making no progress. I got you on that space station project but you're going nowhere. You're a nobody. It's time you came back here. You've a lot to learn."

***

Later in the evening, Jeseque and Ferist walked between the trees beside the lake. She'd expected him to be embarrassed and ashamed after the encounter with his father, but he behaved as if the girl he supposedly loved hadn't been insulted and banished. What a hilarious piece of theatre. She felt like laughing out loud. "Doesn't it bother you?" she asked.

"What?"

She looked at him. He genuinely didn't know what she was talking about. "The way your father treats you. The way he pushes you about."

Ferist shrugged. "He knows what's best for me. I owe him a lot. He fixes things."

"Yeah. Even me."

He stopped short, stared at her. "You knew?"

Jeseque frowned. "Knew what?"

"That he…What did you mean just now?"

"I'm out. Apparently, I'm not princess material."

"Oh."

Jeseque continued to frown. "What did you mean?"

"Nothing."

"No. You were going to say something."

"I just thought you meant something else."

"Like what?"

He started walking again. "Honestly, it's nothing."

Jeseque stamped her foot. "Ferist!"

He stopped, looked at her, then out at the lake. "You'll get angry."

"Only if you don't tell me."

He glanced at her, then became very interested in the state of his perfect fingernails. "Father had you switched to IP," he said quietly. He glanced at her again.

Jeseque felt her blood boil. She had suspected as much, but to hear it confirmed enraged her. She wanted to shout at Ferist. To tell him he was a spoiled brat, pathetic and unworthy. And the way he came out with it, as if he was admitting to something slightly embarrassing, like his mother bought his clothes for him.

With effort, she held back, channelling her fury, sensing an opportunity.

She took a deep breath. "Your father," she said coldly, "had me taken from the space station project. You were put in my place. Is that what you're telling me?"

Ferist nodded, still looking at his hands.

"And you never told me." She let her voice rise. "All this time, you never told me!"

"I wanted to."

"No, you didn't. I had to drag it out of you. You're a pathetic little shit, Ferist!"

"Jeseque, please. I'm sorry."

"You do everything he says. I bet you've told him everything about the precious project." She wondered if she'd thrown that in a bit too soon.

"I certainly have not."

"But if I asked," she continued, ignoring his protestation, "you'd tighten like a guitar string. Oh no, Jeseque, that's top secret."

"I would tell you, Jeseque."

"Bullshit!" It was indeed bullshit. She'd tried before and got nowhere. But this time she sensed weakness.

"No, it's true," he said. "I trust you."

She made a show of trying to calm herself. Then she smiled. "You trust me? Really?"

***

Ferist regarded the beautiful face, the freckled nose and the blue eyes with the fire about the pupil like the corona of an eclipsed sun. Even when she was angry, a tad scary, he adored her. How could he leave her? Reject the girl he loved and who loved him, just because his father told him to? His stomach tightened at the very notion of living without her. Damn it! It wasn't right. He was tired of being ordered about.

"Why should I be keeping secrets from you?" he said in a righteous tone.

Because, a little voice warned, these aren't the typical secrets you might have, like nipping to the pub on the quiet.

He hesitated, but only for a moment. "Listen, though. You cannot speak of this to anyone. I could get into serious trouble."

"Oh no, Ferist," Jeseque said, "it's OK. You don't have to tell me. I just wanted to know if you would. Of course if you did, I wouldn't say a word. I mean, who am I going to tell? You're all I have."

Ferist smiled. "No, I want to. Truth be told, I've been dying to tell someone."

They started walking again. Jeseque wrapped her arm about his. "This is so romantic. So tell me, why all the secrecy?"

"Well, first of all, we ancillary staff don't know the whole story, because the craft was in fact built by the Imperial Engineering Corps, and no one gets any information out of them."

"Imperial Engineering," Jeseque whispered. "They're only used for the most delicate operations."

"I know. Anyway, we've figured out some of it because we order all the parts. It's nuclear powered. And it has a missile-launching system."

I knew it, Jeseque thought. A weapons platform.

"But there's more. A lot more." He stopped again, looked her straight in the eye. "We think it's a spaceship, not a space station."

She frowned. "You think it is. Why?"

"It was built for standard gravity. But it's not designed to spin, so it's not a centrifuge. And the only other way you can have gravity in space is when the craft is under acceleration, which means it has to be a ship, not a station."

Though she was irked by his inaccurate statement, which implied there was no gravity in space, she resisted the urge to correct him. "Designed for standard gravity. How?"

"All ordinary furniture. Beds, tables, desks. The toilets are ordinary toilets. The same with the showers. Well, there are slight differences. The furniture is designed to be bolted to the floor, and the toilet is not exactly like the one you'd have at home. All the plumbing is designed to contain the water during free fall. But it's not designed for use during free fall, which suggests the ship will spend most of its time under acceleration."

"Or deceleration," Jeseque added. "But it doesn't make sense. Eventually it'll get to wherever it's going, and then it will be in free fall. What then? Unless the intention is to land somewhere. Was it designed for re-entry?"

"We can't be sure, but we've seen nothing to suggest that."

"A nuclear-powered spaceship carrying missiles and not designed for prolonged free fall," Jeseque summed up. NALO will love this, she thought.

"Yes," Ferist agreed. "It certainly is a puzzler." They strolled on.

***

Jeseque and Ferist woke to a rapping on their bedroom door. "Who's there?" Ferist called as he switched on the light and climbed out of bed.

"Second Lieutenants Kryslor and Debrone," came a voice through the door. "You are to report to Major Tavenar immediately. He's waiting downstairs."

Ferist turned to look at Jeseque sitting up in the bed, his eyebrows raised in surprise and confusion. Jeseque returned a frown. "Tavenar?" Ferist said. "What's he doing here?"

"The name is familiar," she replied.

"You don't remember? He's the major who interviewed us at Hightower."

Jeseque felt a tightening in her belly. Could they somehow have discovered Ferist's indiscretion? Surely not.

They both got dressed quickly and went downstairs. The captain who had spoken to them through the door was waiting at the bottom. "Come with me," he ordered. He escorted the two through the main door and into the back of a waiting car. Jeseque and Ferist silently watched him go around the front of the car and climb into the driver's seat. The captain's face remained impassive as he turned around and held out his hand. "Phones," he commanded. Ferist handed over his phone immediately. Jeseque hesitated, but only for a moment. She knew it would be pointless to refuse.

***

Major Tavenar stood in the middle of the spacious office. He was sandy-haired, small, but fit and lean. Prince Carlden sat behind a large desk. The lamp on the desk provided the only light and it shone outwards, illuminating the major's face while keeping the prince in semi-darkness. Tavenar noted the cheap trick, designed to make him uncomfortable, uneasy, and to ensure his host's expressions remained hidden. He also noted the prince didn't offer him a seat.

This wasn't going to be easy. Tavenar wondered if he should have waited for an opportune moment to snatch Lieutenants Kryslor and Debrone and avoid this meeting altogether. But he'd been too nervous. He wanted to deal with the potentially explosive situation immediately. Damn it, he thought, why had he let himself get into this mess?

"Your Highness, earlier today your son divulged secret information to his companion, Second Lieutenant Debrone." There was no response. Tavenar wondered if the viceroy realised how serious the situation was. "Though your son and his colleagues are not aware of it, we monitor all their conversations through their phones. The computers are programmed to listen for specific words and phrases. A flag went up today, alerting us to the security breach. Luckily, my superior was not present at the time and the incident was brought to my attention instead." General Meckreen was in the Swutland mountains, for which the major again silently thanked the Gods.

"Don't worry about it," the prince finally replied. "I've decided to keep him here anyway. I'll make sure he speaks to no one else about his work. As for the girl, I'll take care of her too."

Tavenar guessed that meant Debrone would receive a bullet in the head and a trip to the bottom of a lake, or some such.

"It's not that simple," he said. "If I report your son's breach, not only is he in a lot of trouble, but our little arrangement comes to light. My superior will want to know how he got on the project in the first place."

"Which is why you're not reporting it."

"Yes. But if I don't and the girl goes to the media, then the First Advisor will have our heads."

"I told you I'd take care of her."

"I'm afraid that's not good enough. I also have to consider the fact that your son might leak information again."

"Are you threatening my son?" The tone dropped menacingly. "I could easily take care of you instead."

Tavenar smiled. "When you paid me to have your son take Debrone's place, I had a feeling the day might come when you would want rid of me. So I have it all arranged. I disappear; the First Advisor becomes aware of our transaction."

"I see," Carlden replied gruffly.

"I've read the thrillers. Anyway, you're assuming the worst. You may be comfortable with dealing out death, but I'm not. My solution is kind and simple. I will take your son and his companion inside the project completely."

"That's all you need do to make the problem go away?"

"Yes. It'll be a little bit tricky with the girl, but I'll manage it. However, there's a snag. Though your son will be perfectly safe, and living in comfort, you will not see him again for decades. He and Debrone will be cut off from the outside world."

"Completely?"

"Yes."

"For decades?"

Tavenar nodded. He was expecting an argument, but he didn't know how unhappy Carlden was with Ferist.

***

Prince Carlden's second son was everything he'd hoped Ferist would be. However, though a man in his position could flout the one-child law, he would not get away with nominating the younger child as heir, unless the older died.

Now, Tavenar was offering the perfect solution. Prince Carlden's heir mysteriously disappears. A major investigation and search begins. There would be grief and sympathy. Eventually, Ferist would be declared dead and the family's future would be placed into capable hands. And of course Ferist wouldn't actually be dead. He'd be off somewhere, enjoying life with his weird girlfriend.

"No chance of him paying us a visit?" he asked the major.

"I'm afraid that would be impossible."

"Fine. Take him away."

Tavenar's eyes widened. "Really?"

"Yes. I assume this project, whatever it is, is related to the space station and will be adventurous and exciting."

"Indeed it will."

"Then good. It's a wonderful opportunity for him. I'm sure he'll be delighted."

***

Tavenar got into the passenger seat. He turned to look at Kryslor and Debrone. They appeared confused and frightened. "Leave us for now, Captain," he said to the driver.

"Yes, sir," the captain replied as he got out of the car.

"Do you two have any idea," Tavenar said, "of the trouble you've caused?"

"Actually, Major, I don't," Debrone said.

Tavenar sighed. "He knows," he said, indicating Kryslor. "Tell your sweetheart here what you were told would happen, in the event of a security breach."

"It would be reported directly to the First Advisor," Kryslor said quietly.

"And what do you think the First Advisor would do with you two, if he found out?" The couple didn't reply. "I can see you're scared. Good. At least you have that much sense. But I have good news for you. I can avoid reporting this matter to the First Advisor, if you do as you're told and you don't question my decision.

"You will be kept in seclusion until I can arrange for transport to the SpaceExpress launch complex. There you will join the crew of the new craft in orbit. I'm sure there are many questions you'd like to ask me already, but I don't have the time to deal with them. For now, just be thankful I'm not taking you to the palace."

There was shock in the back seat. Kryslor looked stupefied, but there was something about Debrone that made Tavenar uneasy.

"Why are you doing this for us, Major?" Debrone asked.

She was intelligent, Tavenar was dismayed to see. She'd managed to focus on the salient fact, that his actions appeared to be designed to save their lives. And she wanted to know why. For a moment he considered taking her from the car and putting her in Carlden's hands.

"Didn't I just tell you, Lieutenant," he said, "no questions. Not another word, from either of you."

The major faced front and stared through the windscreen, his mind racing. Captain Abrim would not want a woman aboard his ship. And he sure as hell wouldn't want a couple.

He turned around and looked straight at the two frightened lieutenants. "You don't know each other," he said. "If you wish to survive this, you must behave like you've never met."

***

Major Tavenar sat at the head of the table in the conference room at the SpaceExpress launch complex. The door opened and Captain Abrim walked in. He was a tall, handsome man and, not for the first time, Tavenar wondered why such a man would agree to a mission that would eventually put him 30 years out of step with the rest of humanity and might even result in him never returning home at all. Like the rest of the crew, Abrim had no family. Even so, it was hard to imagine there wasn't something or someone to tie him to Earda. But apparently there wasn't, otherwise he wouldn't have been selected.

"You wished to see me, Major?" Abrim said.

"Yes, Captain. Take a seat."

Abrim removed his cap and sat down.

Wondering how to approach this meeting, Tavenar had decided it would be best to pretend he was simply the messenger. "Good news. You've been assigned two extra engineers."

"Really?" Abrim looked surprised but pleased. "I thought my requests had been ignored."

"No, we listen," Tavenar said with a smile. "Now, one of them you might know already. Or at least have heard of him. Second Lieutenant Ferist Kryslor."

Abrim frowned. "I don't think so."

"Oh you must have. Of the ancillary crew. You'll recognise him when you see him. He's one we've been keeping an eye on. Top notch."

"What's his specialty?"

"Avionics."

Abrim nodded. "Good."

Tavenar gritted his teeth. That was the easy part. The ancillary crew had been specially chosen, with the criteria extending beyond their professional expertise and prowess. It was the psychologists who had the final say, as they looked for people who might be likely to accept a position on the interstellar craft, should one arise.

Debrone had fit the bill, somewhat. She wasn't religious, but she had nothing tying her to Earda. However, she never would have been chosen for the mission itself, because of her gender. Someone had ignored that, either on purpose or by mistake. Whatever the reason, it made it somewhat easier for Tavenar to replace her with Kryslor, back when the project was in its early stages.

But now she was back. And he had to get her on the ship, one way or another. It was either that or hand her back to the viceroy. Tavenar was tempted, but he couldn't bring himself to do it. The girl had done nothing wrong. She didn't deserve to die.

"The second choice is a little strange," Tavenar continued in as casual a tone as he could muster, "though she was in fact originally assigned to the ancillary crew."

"She?"

"Yes. Second Lieutenant Jeseque Debrone. Gifted engineer. Stellar references from her time at IP."

Abrim stared at him. "You can't be serious, Major. A woman aboard my ship?"

"These are my orders, Captain. You know it wasn't easy to find a crew for this mission. Lieutenant Debrone is the most qualified and is willing to go."

"I don't care if she's willing to go. We're going without her. I'm very happy with the crew I have and I'm delighted to take on an extra engineer. But we can do without the woman."

"Captain. These are your orders."

Abrim shook his head. "Ridiculous. Who's running this show? Isn't there someone I can talk to?"

"I knew you wouldn't be happy and I explained that. But all I keep hearing is that Debrone is the most qualified and the most suitable."

"It's the damn psychologists. Isn't it?"

"It doesn't matter who made the final decision. The decision is made. I know you don't like it, but what can you do? Disobey a direct order?" Tavenar sat back. "Take her aboard, Captain. You can always simply ignore her."

Abrim sighed. "Since I have no choice," he said.

Tavenar nodded. "You're dismissed."

Abrim stood up, put on his cap and saluted. "Sir."

As the captain left the room, Tavenar let out a long slow breath. Though he was relieved to be done with the meeting, he was still nervous. Abrim might try to go above him, although the major didn't think he would. Military personnel might grumble, but they seldom questioned orders, especially when dealing with the Imperial Engineering Corps. All the same, Tavenar would not be able to relax until the spaceship left orbit, taking Kryslor, Debrone and Abrim with it.

Chapter 5

Hervan Willkob, priest of the Order of Lurg, stood outside the church, dressed in his sky-blue robes. He had arrived in Wesmork earlier that morning for a scheduled meeting with Prelate Magnez, a man in the upper tiers of the hierarchy and one Willkob had come to admire and respect during his years of study in the Capital.

While the Church was divided into six orders, representing the six Gods, the Order of Lurg held authority over all, and the building Willkob now stood before was its official and spiritual centre. Like all churches of the God of Light, its plan was a perfect circle. Concentric semicircles of stone steps led to the main entrance. Wrapping around the building in both directions were narrow stained-glass windows, each one at a slightly odd angle. Between the windows, coarse yellow brick rose 150 feet to be topped by a green-domed roof.

Willkob climbed the steps, reminiscing about his innocent acolyte days, when each morning before sunrise he and his classmates would enter the dark building. The site had been chosen a century earlier, on top of a hill with the main entrance facing south. Though in the meantime the city had spread and buildings had grown taller, no construction was allowed to block the rays of the rising and setting sun. In the morning, the students would make their way inside and along the right wall to kneel before the windows just before the day's first rays filtered through the stained glass, the shifting patterns of colour a proclaimed source of humility and meditation.

Willkob always found the meditative state much more accessible in the privacy of his room, but he had enjoyed the morning ritual and its evening equivalent for its predictability and for the beauty of the multicoloured windows.

He walked through the glass doors and into the large open space. Even though the sun was already climbing the sky, the windows to his right still dappled the floor and seats with the filtered sun. Before the windows knelt a dozen or more of the faithful, heads bowed.

The rest of the church was empty, the daily pilgrim caravans not yet given access. The altar at the top formed a segment one quarter the area of the floor. The back of the church was filled with pews arranged in concentric semicircles. In between these two areas were more pews, half facing east, the rest facing west. The very centre of the church was a sunken basin, 20 feet in diameter with a stone rim, a gold-tiled floor and filled with the clearest of water. In the roof far above, an arc of clear glass was centred upon the entrance and arranged in such a manner as to allow the Northern Solstice sun at its zenith to shine through and sparkle off the golden basin.

Willkob turned his eyes heavenwards to admire once again the beautiful mosaic. From above the altar, gold tiles radiated outwards, six rays in all, one for each of the Gods. These rays were mirrored by the marble aisles between the concentric seating below. On the ceiling, between each ray, was a depiction of a God, garbed in elaborate robes, each one a male figure with very pale skin. From left to right went Water, Wind, Fertility, Death and Magic. Willkob craned his neck as he followed the rays to the back of the church, where they blended into the deep red that surrounded the picture of Lurg, the God of Light, in all his majesty. His robes were simple white, except at the cuffs and hem, where they were splattered with random colour. Above his head was a halo of gold and below his feet, in dark robes, sat the Velkren upon his white throne.

Willkob turned around to look at the actual throne, in the centre of the marble altar, upon which Emperor Destlar seldom sat. Willkob, normally a cheerful-looking man with a round face, bushy eyebrows and lively blue eyes, was pensive this day.

He approached the marble chair with confusion in his mind, very unlike the conviction of his early years. In those days he had spent hours before the altar, gazing in wonder upon the seat of Lurg's Emissary. The being whose eternal governance and protection was testament to the benevolence of the Gods and to their love for their devout children.

"Hervan," a voice whispered in the silence. "How good to see you."

Willkob turned from the altar, a little startled. In his soft-soled shoes, the Prelate's approach had gone unnoticed. "Prelate Magnez," he replied with a bow. "Thank you for taking the time to see me."

"No need for thanks. I always enjoy meeting my past pupils, especially one as bright as yourself. Come, let's go to my office."

After a short stroll down the hill and along a winding path between ash trees, they arrived at a large two-storey house that had once been the home of a wealthy banker, but which had later become the central administration building for the Order of Lurg. The Prelate escorted his guest up the wide stairs and into a large office with long windows reaching to within a few feet of the high ceiling. Ignoring the oak desk, the Prelate instead offered a leather armchair to Willkob while he lowered himself into its partner on the other side of the coffee table. Before they were even settled, an old woman came into the room. "Coffee, please," ordered Magnez. On the way to the office the two men had chatted about Willkob's uneventful journey from the North. But now it was time to get to more serious matters. "So, young man, what is it you wish to speak to me about?"

For a moment Willkob hesitated. He'd never before spoken aloud his concerns. Should he do so now, to one so highly placed in the Church? Yet this was a man he respected, a man he trusted. "I will admit to you, Prelate," he said tentatively, "I have been studying the discredited texts."

"Indeed? Well, that's something we strongly discourage amongst the laity, but I don't see anything wrong with an educated man like yourself reading such books."

"But some of these texts claim the Velkren stole the Frandomian Empire a little over seven centuries ago."

"There is disagreement amongst scholars as to the date, but it was probably around about then."

Willkob was surprised. He had expected the old man to denounce such claims. "Then you don't believe the Velkren was appointed by the Gods?"

"Hervan! Don't be ridiculous. Of course I do. The manner in which it was achieved is of little concern, except as a historical curiosity. We cannot pretend to understand the ways of the Gods. Perhaps seizing the Frandomian throne was the best way to do it."

"But there are other texts that claim the Velkren had no interest in the Church whatsoever, when he first rose to power. That he simply used it as a means to stabilise his position."

"Now those beliefs belong to the unfortunate misguided. We make strenuous efforts to keep writings such as these from the ordinary man. You and I can safely read them, because we see them for what they are."

The beverages were served. Magnez heaped two spoons of sugar into his cup, then added a splash of milk. Willkob wasn't very fond of coffee. And he couldn't see the point in covering its bitter taste with milk and sugar. Why bother drinking it at all? However, for the sake of good manners, he took a sip.

His eyes opened wide. He'd never drunk anything like it before. It was sharp but not sour and felt heavy and smooth on his tongue. And with the taste came the aroma. He inhaled deeply through his nose. It was intoxicating. He couldn't describe it, or compare it to anything else, because it was like nothing he'd ever smelled before.

"This is the first time you've tasted real coffee," Magnez remarked.

"Yes. It's quite remarkable." Willkob wondered how the Prelate could bear to destroy it with sugar.

"I simply cannot abide the fake stuff." The old man reached forward and selected a cream pastry from the plate which had been deposited along with the coffee. Willkob noticed the bulge around the middle of the dark blue robes. The robes themselves were of a very high quality. He wondered if the embroidery at the edges was real gold thread. It seemed his mentor was growing fond of his luxuries in his old age.

"What exactly is all this about?" Magnez asked. "Why the interest in the Velkren's origins?"

The images of the hysterical woman with the little boy and the lifeless baby flashed into Willkob's mind. The horrific death sounds were as clear now as they had been on that terrible day, three years earlier. "He dishes out extreme punishments. In some cases, it's hard to see how the victims could be guilty of anything."

"There are times when it seems the Velkren acts in a manner that is not in keeping with our teachings of love and forgiveness. But He is not one of us. He is not subject to our laws or morals. He carries out the will of the Gods. We are not capable of understanding their methods. Everything happens for a reason. It may seem like the Velkren is being harsh, but perhaps that's what is needed, from time to time.

"You must understand that without the Velkren, the true Faith would not have spread to all parts of the world in the way that it has. Millions of people are awaiting eternal salvation, thanks to His presence, to His authority. And His control of the planet ensures stability. Can you imagine the chaos if He wasn't here, to keep the heathen anarchists subdued, to prevent us, weaklings that we are, from killing each other over food and resources? We are to be eternally grateful to the Gods for sending us the Velkren, and we should not question His ways." He reached for another pastry.

"Perhaps you are right, Prelate."

"Of course I'm right," Magnez concluded, clearly believing nothing more needed to be said. "Soon I must go, as I have a meeting to attend. Sit. Please, sit back and finish your coffee. I don't need to rush off just yet. I just wanted to say I have booked a table for us at a very fine restaurant this evening. I hope you can make it. We can talk more then."

"I have nothing planned. Thank you, I would be honoured."

"Very good. You'll enjoy this place. Excellent food. I usually go for the pheasant."

***

Willkob sat at the back of the church, deep in thought. He was disappointed with the changes he perceived in his old teacher. Real coffee! When most people found it hard to put food on the table. When his own community in Gernaturov, the capital city of Rustletov, was concerned with keeping the heat on during winter.

He had come to Wesmork looking for reassurance. But all he had received were empty phrases. Ignorance of the ways of the Gods could be used to justify anything. He had hoped to press harder, to open his heart completely, but when the time had come, he'd felt it would have achieved nothing but arouse suspicion and condemnation.

Now he was more convinced than ever. The leading hierarchy had become too comfortable. The Emperor's ruthless and despotic control suited the wealthy, and there could be no doubting the wealth of the Church. They would never allow themselves to even consider the possibility the Emperor might be a fraud.

But he was a fraud. He had used the Church for his own selfish gains. Seven centuries were long enough. It was time for change.

Chapter 6

I was the first to meet Arnelius, after he escaped his body, escaped the prison built for him by Destlar. He rightly deduced he was not alone and instantly called out, his 'voice' propagating through the universe in a manner that is difficult to explain to those who have not experienced the grid.

Picture him arriving unexpectedly in the foyer of some enormous mansion and shouting "hello," hoping someone on the upper floors would respond.

I was the one to respond. Many others heard him too, but I was the one who bothered to come downstairs and welcome the latest member of our exclusive club.

I'm glad I took the time to meet Arnelius, for he is one of the most interesting characters I've encountered during my six billion years of roaming. The story of his leap beyond the physical is truly astounding.

There are many different ways of joining the Grid Riders, but it all boils down to evolution in the end. I belong to a species that paralleled humanity's journey for a few million years. We evolved to a state of self-awareness. We started to ask questions of the universe, and slowly we uncovered its secrets. The more we learned, the more sophisticated our technologies became. And the better our technologies, the more we learned. Eventually, we realised it was possible to exist beyond physical form. After that, all our efforts were put into making the theory a reality.

That's how I came to be as I am now. Other species manage the jump without artificial aids. Their transfiguration is as natural as the caterpillar to the butterfly. Some of these entities look down on me and my brethren. They believe we cheated. That we sneaked into the club through the back door. I find it quite depressing that beings as ancient and wise as the Grid Riders are not immune to such petty prejudices.

There are many intelligent species that never make the jump, except for maybe one or two in their entire history. Creatures that somehow, upon physical death, join us, despite the fact that none of their fellows ever manage the trick. Such beings are extremely rare and impossible to predict. They themselves can't explain how they did it.

The Necrophobes are obsessed with these beings.

When Arnelius began to relate his story, initially I thought he might be one of these extraordinary individuals who blindly leap. But he's not. His leap was anything but blind.

***

"I was full of confidence when I set out to destroy Destlar," Arnelius said. "I was proud to be ridding the world of a monster who was terrorising simple, innocent people. I was arrogant and complacent. And to my utter surprise, Destlar got the better of me.

"But not to the extent he thinks. I'm sure he believes I'm dead. It's ironic, but his chosen method of torture actually gave me the time to find my way here. He enclosed me in a void, and inside this void he slowed time. Aeons of darkness drove his other victims crazy. But for me, it simply gave me the chance to learn.

"First, I examined my own mind, chasing along pathways that were forever changing in response to my own thoughts. I delved into my memories, delighting in the ability to retrieve any instance from a long life, forgotten events relived with absolute clarity. I was amazed to find my brain held every detail of every moment of my existence.

"While studying the brain and its functions, I probed ever deeper, until I began to play and experiment with the fabric of space-time itself. At infinitesimal distances, I discovered matter doesn't exist, that it is nothing but the reverberations of twisted knots of space-time. Ages I spent in this fantastic territory, until I found I could manipulate this grid pervading the universe. Experimenting, I organised a tiny portion into a specific pattern, then moved it about through the higher dimensions. Encouraged, I went about constructing a replica of my mind, a task that was accomplished with surprising speed, once I'd mastered the employment of multitudinous nodes in the grid, all performing their recording task concurrently.

"Upon completion, all I had to do was imbue the pattern with energy and it became me, or I became it. And so here I am. According to my personal clock, centuries have passed. But for Destlar, it's only been minutes. I imagine he's down there still, trying to see inside my head."

***

An awesome feat. Arnelius went from utter ignorance of the grid's existence to such a complete understanding of its nature that he was able to copy himself into it. I took to spending time with him. I thought it might be interesting to hang about with one so unique.

Many years later, he took me to a planet with rolling oceans and shifting plates and a staggering variety of life; an evolutionary playhouse. He'd promised me something unique but, as beautiful as the place was, I couldn't fathom what that might be. I told him so.

"Though I never tire of this magnificent universe, it seldom surprises me any more. I can't imagine what we could find here that I haven't seen already."

We were standing at the edge of a steep cliff. Waves crashed against the rocks far below. I turned my head to the left to follow the cliff edge as it swept around and down in a broad arc. The land dropped to the sea, then rose again into blue-purple mountains on the far side of the water, forming a wide bay. The sea reflected a cloudless sky.

Our black robes whipped about in the wind. I had waited for Arnelius to materialise on the cliff, so that I could see what form he took. He'd been very insistent that I copy him.

"I didn't mean you should look exactly like me," he'd complained when I popped out of nothingness. We were both tall, broad-shouldered, fair-skinned and dark-haired. "Alter your appearance. You're making me uncomfortable."

My chin and nose became pointy, my ears large and floppy. "That's enough," he sighed, not taken with my attempt at humour. I started to make my eyes bigger. "Leave the eyes alone!" he snapped.

"Calm down," I said. "I'm not changing their composition. 'Observe with the same eyes as me, and nothing more.' How many times have you said that?"

"I don't want you spoiling the surprise."

I looked around again, at the sea and the cliffs and the sky. "What surprise? It's a fine scene, but hardly unique."

"Nothing's unique. But it can still be awesome. Haven't you noticed it's getting darker?"

I frowned. "Ah, yes. Now that you mention it."

"Look at the sun." Together we looked at the white ball in the blue sky. "Human eyes couldn't do this," Arnelius informed me. "They'd be blinded. I modified the make-up, adding dynamic filters. Now, can you see it?"

Of course I could. There was a bite taken out of the sun. "Arnelius, surely you don't expect me to be amazed by a solar eclipse."

"This one will astound you," he replied with a smile.

The moon moved from the bottom left of the sun to the top right. As the minutes passed, more and more of the sun was covered. The sky darkened and the stars began to show. The temperature dropped dramatically.

It didn't take long for me to realise this inner rocky planet had a relatively large moon. "This is unusual," I said once it looked like the sun might be covered completely. "But I have seen such before."

"No," Arnelius replied without taking his eyes from the sun. "Not like this."

As the moon continued across the face of the sun, I wondered what could possibly be different about this eclipse. Then suddenly it became clear. "It's the same size!" I exclaimed.

Arnelius glanced over at me. He smiled. "Exactly the same size."

The minutes passed. As the moon slid into position, the bright ball of light in the top corner got smaller and smaller. It seemed to get more intense as it shrank, as if fighting for its life. I imagined it screaming as the black hole covered it, smothered it, extinguished it.

It was gone. The moon, as if designed for the task, sat perfectly on top of the sun. I could see prominences dancing on the circumference. And all about was the halo, bright and pulsing, like a timid child that flourishes in the sudden and unexpected absence of a rambunctious sibling.

"Magnificent," I said, not taking my eyes away for even a second. "Truly amazing. Thank you, Arnelius."

We stood together in silence, heads tilted back. The stars glittered. And the perfect eclipse continued. It was as if the moon had got stuck, like it had slotted into position and was going to stay there forever. Then a thin arc of light appeared along the bottom left of the black circle. A second later it exploded into life. The sun was reborn. Slowly, it reclaimed the sky.

Altogether, it took about two hours for the moon to completely traverse the sun. "Of course it's perfectly natural," I said when the moon finally disappeared and the day returned to normal. "In a universe so vast, the laws of probability dictate it must happen somewhere. More than once, in fact, but so rare I never stumbled upon it."

"When I lived here, I believed the gods made the moon just the right size," Arnelius said. "To me, it was art in the heavens. I was proud that I wasn't afraid of the eclipse, because I knew what it was, unlike the ignorant peasants who were terrified. And yet, I was no better. With my education and knowledge, I should have been able to deduce it's simply a fluke."

"The most beautiful fluke I've ever seen," I replied.

***

This was Arnelius's home planet, Earda. Hundreds of years later he made practical use of the perfect eclipse, during his search for a sister planet. His reasoning was that another world at an almost identical moment in its evolution would also orbit a yellow dwarf star and have one gigantic satellite, with their sizes and distances from each other just right. He initiated the search by sending a ripple through the grid that sought out these perfect eclipses. The eclipse was only one of many criteria, of course. But it was a start. And it worked.

As he knew it would, eventually. A universe this big runs out of ideas and has to repeat itself. Over and over but gradually dissipating, until entropy reaches a maximum and there's nothing left but emptiness. When that happens, I wonder if I'll go insane, like Destlar's victims trapped in endless nothingness. I think about that sometimes, but not too often. There's not a thing I can do about it, so what's the point?

The Necrophobes seem to think there is a point. As fellow Grid Riders, they're immortal. There is absolutely nothing in the entire universe that could ever cause them harm. And yet they're not happy, because it's the end of the universe itself they dread. It just goes to show you, no matter how good some people have it, they can still find something to worry about.

***

Arnelius was happy to be home. I was a bit surprised at how nostalgic he was. I've never felt any desire to return to the planet I grew up on, even when it still existed. But I suppose it was different in my case. For me, that planet was nothing more than a branch to cling to while awaiting maturity and my transfer to the grid. There was nothing special about it. My species wasn't even indigenous to it, so we felt no real affinity. Whereas Arnelius had never expected to leave Earda. He had not even realised there was anywhere else to go. It had literally been his whole world. Once I thought about it, I realised his feelings for the place were quite normal.

Thanks to the eclipse, I was a little enamoured too. So I decided to accompany Arnelius on his tour. I'm glad I did; it was the beginning of the best bit of fun I've had in a million years.

**

We strolled along a quiet street on a bright but cold morning, wearing long dark woollen trousers into which were tucked white linen shirts. Over the shirts we wore heavy coats and on our feet were strong leather boots. We looked like a pair of wealthy merchantmen.

Our clothes were not actually made from linen, leather and wool. We simply kneaded matter into forms that imitated the local apparel.

The sun had just risen and the city was still very much in a slumber, though we could hear movement in the houses on either side of the street. "The square is just down here, towards the river," Arnelius told me, pointing to the end of the narrow street. Moments later we emerged into a wide-open space.

Arnelius stopped, looking about. "It's changed quite a bit. Not surprising, really; it's almost three hundred years since I've been here, by local counting." We left the dirt-street and walked across the cobbled square. Arnelius pointed to a large building directly opposite. "That's the new customs house." Four storeys were topped with a copper roof. "Or it was new back then. The roof used to be brown." He stopped, then turned full circle, examining the other buildings that bordered the square. "The rest is different." We walked off to the right, into the shadow of a two-storey inn. "There was a row of houses here, the school in the middle." He moved to the left side of the inn. "It would have been about here. A narrow structure, with rickety stairs rising three floors." He smiled, for a moment lost in his memories. Then he turned around and looked across the roofs to the hill overlooking the square. Atop the hill, a large grey structure dominated the city. "The King had us placed right in the middle of the city, not far from the castle."

"What about the statue?" I asked. In the centre of the square, on top of a stone pedestal, a green man sat on a green throne. They were green not for artistic reasons, but because they were made from copper, just like the roof of the building behind the seated figure.

"That's new as well," Arnelius said.

We made our way over to the statue, which I judged to be about one and a half times normal size. The man was robed and cowled, but his features were visible. I was about to say something when I felt the shock emanate from my companion. I looked over to see his mouth hanging open, his eyes wide. "What is it?" I asked.

"It's him."

"Who?"

"Destlar."

***

We sat next to the hearth in the inn. The innkeeper, a thin little man with grey hair, riddled the ashes with a poker, then gathered the glowing embers into a pile. "You'll be wanting breakfast," he said as he built a pyramid of sticks about the embers.

"No, thank you," Arnelius said. "Two mugs of ale will do fine."

"Very good," he said, trying to hide his disappointment. He finished with the fire, then made his way behind the bar.

Arnelius shook his head, smiling. "Destlar. What a surprise."

"That word in the inscription: Velkren. What does it mean?" On the pedestal was written *The Eternal Emperor — Velkren of the Gods.*

"It means angel, or seraph. It looks like Destlar hoodwinked the people into believing he's divine. And immortal."

The innkeeper returned with two brown mugs filled with a dark liquid. I took a sip, smacked my lips and sighed.

"It's quite a large inn you have here," Arnelius said to our host. "You receive that many guests?"

"Usually we do. A lot of pilgrims, you see. They come to worship the Velkren."

"And they can afford such luxury."

The man swelled with the compliment. "Oh no, good sir. Most camp outside the city. But the wealthy stay here. However, there aren't many pilgrims at the moment, because His Majesty has departed with the fleet."

"Ah. That's a shame. We were hoping to meet him."

"Not wanting to be disrespectful, but I don't think you'd be allowed to see him anyway. No one does, except his closest advisors."

"I see. Tell me, if one were to meet him, how would one address him?"

The innkeeper was surprised by the question. "Your Majesty, of course."

"One wouldn't call him Destlar?"

Startled, he took a step back. "Good heavens, no. I doubt if even the magicians would dare to be so disrespectful." He walked away, shaking his head.

"What do you think of that?" Arnelius asked once we were alone.

"I've seen this many times," I replied. "When the monarch dies, those closest to the top decide it might be easier, for them of course, to pretend he still lives. And this fits in nicely with the idea that he's some kind of agent of the gods. You heard the man say no one actually gets to see him. How would they, since he's long dead? It's a nice trick, if you can pull it off. The people with the real power can get on with their business quietly and without fuss or fanfare. And the citizens worship someone who isn't there."

"But he must have been Emperor at some point." Arnelius shook his head. "He's the last person I would have expected to sit on the throne."

"You knew him well?"

"We studied together. The King created a school for magicians, and boys who showed promise were enrolled. I was in its very first class, and so was Destlar. It was a small school in the beginning; there were only seven of us altogether.

"We were unfair to Destlar, right from the start. He was from Rustletov, a principality to the north. We thought it was a backward place and that its inhabitants were rough and stupid. Of course we were the stupid ones, but we were merely boys. Things only got worse for Destlar, because he wasn't very good at his studies. Our teachers, mostly magicians themselves, were not in the least bit sympathetic. Destlar had no imagination. He could copy others, and even then, not very successfully. We made fun of him. We would cast spells. Of course I now know they weren't spells, and all the hocus-pocus was unnecessary. But we would cast spells that would send him sprawling in the wet and mucky street outside the school. Or we'd turn his hair bright orange. Or sometimes we'd make him sneeze continuously in class until the teacher lost his patience and threw him out. Destlar would try to retaliate, but he couldn't get the spells right. Sometimes they would rebound on him, which sent us into hysterics."

"Little shits."

"Indeed. We quickly learned, though, not to push him too far. One day we surrounded him in the corner of the classroom. We pinched him and poked him and thumped him, all without laying a finger on him. I think it maddened him even more that we could do it all so effortlessly, and that he was reduced to flailing about with his fists. Then all of a sudden, he seemed to give up. He crouched down, put his hands to his temples, screwed his eyes shut and screamed.

"I'll never forget it. My brain was slammed with pain. It was as if I'd been simultaneously kicked on both sides of my head. I staggered back a couple of steps, tripped on my own feet and fell on my backside. Dazed, I looked about at the others. They hadn't lost their footing like me, but they were all holding their heads and grimacing."

"The drowning man's grip," I said.

Arnelius nodded. "Something like that. We were wary of him from then on. Under pressure, he was dangerous. As the years went by, he became a more accomplished magician, though always a step or two behind the rest of us. And then he finally got the better of me, years later. Though I've never forgotten the piercing headache he gave me that day in the classroom, I ignored the lesson. When I attacked him that final day, outside the peasant's shack, I was again backing him into a corner. I should have expected him to strike back."

"Do you think that maybe your behaviour shaped him?"

"Aren't we all shaped by those about us? But still, there had always been something inside him that enjoyed torturing defenceless creatures, and I don't think we can be blamed for that. We disliked him because he was a foreigner, but that wasn't the only reason. During our third year at school, there was a lot of hushed talk amongst the children down Coopers Lane. They spoke of a mysterious child, a ghost, that cried in the night. My friends and I went to investigate. We sneaked out of the school on a moonlit night. We were excited, but a little scared too. Coopers Lane was down the hill from the school, so it didn't take us long to get there. We were laughing and joking, wondering aloud what it was the children had heard. Suddenly it came, low and pitiful at first, then rising to a scream before terminating abruptly. We stood there, eyes wide.

"An upstairs shutter to our left opened. 'Did you hear it?' a little voice said. 'A baby crying.' A rougher, older voice answered. 'It's just a cat. Go to sleep.' The shutter slammed closed, breaking the spell. Suddenly as wise as the rough voice, we explained to each other how much a cat's cry can sound like a baby's. We made our way further down the street, to a gap between two houses, from where the sound had come. The gap became a lane that led down to a small stream that joins the river further on. We made our way quietly down the lane, keeping close to the bushes. Noticing the hunkered figure by the moon-dappled water, we crouched down to watch, edging closer. On the ground before the figure lay a small animal with bright eyes. The cat.

"Then we sensed the magic. I gasped, for I knew instantly it was Destlar. The cat started to cry. A most horrifying squeal that would rob anyone of hope. Destlar was tormenting it, playing with it. Not with his hands, but with his mind. Though I was sickened, I also remember feeling contempt for him. He wasn't even doing it right. He lacked the necessary dexterity. Rather than strangling the unfortunate creature, which I'm sure was his aim, he was squeezing its entire body. He was incapable of focusing upon the throat alone. Instead of a rope about its neck, it was as if he had the cat in a vice.

"The cat continued to scream and cry, like before. Then it started to choke, as Destlar finally got hold of its neck. Abruptly the noise stopped and the cat lay still. We thought he'd killed it, but no, it was still alive.

"Destlar repeated the dose perhaps three times more. The last time, he held on until the cat was truly dead. Then he rose to his feet and walked upstream. We wondered where he was going, but none of us felt like following. We returned quietly to the school and went to bed."

"And as he got older," I concluded, "cats weren't enough."

"I lost track of him when we finished school. Years later, reports started coming in from Rustletov of a depraved magician terrorising the countryside. One story I particularly remember, about a farmer and his wife. I interviewed a merchant who happened upon the scene. He told me how he stopped his wagon outside a boggy field, intrigued by the sight of a tall dark-robed figure standing over a fallen woman. As the dark one waved his hands in the air above her, she cried out. When the farmer went to his wife's aid, they were all assaulted by a clap of thunder much louder, the merchant said, than any he'd ever heard. It echoed off the hills. He let go of the reins to cover his ears and his horse bolted. His ears rang with pain for hours afterwards, he said. And the last thing he noticed before the horse panicked was the farmer crumpling to the ground, blood flowing from his ears.

"I had already suspected it was Destlar, but the merchant's description of the pale-faced magician confirmed it. By this time, the King was dead and his son, having annexed Rustletov, had decided it was an empire he ruled and not a kingdom. I was Emperor Neiron's chief advisor, and I convinced him I should remove this despicable monster from his realm. I never once considered helping Destlar. Perhaps he wasn't beyond hope."

"Would he have let you?"

"Probably not. But I should have tried." For a moment Arnelius was lost in thought. Then he shrugged. "One should never regret. After all, I wouldn't be here now with you if I hadn't attacked Destlar."

"And after disposing of you, he moved up a level, to regicide."

"We don't know that for sure."

"Most likely. After all, he'd robbed the Empire of its most brilliant advisor and protector. Neiron was left defenceless."

Arnelius smiled. "You're probably right, about him usurping the throne, that is."

The innkeeper came over to add fuel to the fire. "Are you sure you won't have breakfast?"

"No," I answered. "But we'll have more ale."

"Of course." And he shuffled off.

We sat there for a few moments, listening to the crackling and hissing timber. Arnelius was again lost in thought. I still had not got used to the level of feeling he obviously had for Earda and its people. "Does it upset you?" I asked.

Arnelius looked up from the flames, surprised by the question. "Of course not. It's just that he's not the type of person one would like to see on the throne." There was another moment's silence. "It wasn't his fault," Arnelius continued, eventually. "He couldn't help himself. It's not as if he was evil."

"There's no such thing."

"He behaved the way he did because that's the way his brain was wired."

"These people are little more than animals," I stated. "They possess only an illusion of free will. One person is loving and kind. Another is cruel. Why? Genetics and environment, nothing more. The cruel man should be reproached no more than the dog that bites. Nor should the kind man receive praise. They are actors, following a haphazard script."

"Are we any different?" Arnelius wondered.

"The Grid Riders have wandered the universe for ten billion years, and still we don't know the answer. Unlike matter at the quantum level, there's nothing random about the grid. Our choices have nothing to do with chance. But we can't rule out determinism. Perhaps we're entirely predictable."

"And therefore no more free than Destlar? I believe it's an unanswerable question." Arnelius took another sip of ale, then pushed the mug aside. "I feel like taking a wander about the castle. Do you want to come?"

"No, thanks. I'm enjoying this," I said, lifting my mug.

Arnelius frowned. "It's stale."

"Really?" I took another mouthful. "Maybe it's meant to be."

***

While Arnelius nipped off to the castle, I sat by the fire and waited. The innkeeper arrived with yet another mug of ale. "Will your companion be returning?"

"In a little while," I replied.

I could feel the alcohol's effects on my brain, and it gave me an inkling of what it might be like to be intoxicated. However, the body sitting by the fire was not really me. It was only a puppet and I, still wholly within the grid, the puppeteer. I could experience everything through the puppet with absolute fidelity: sight, sound, touch, taste and smell. But the physical brain was only a channel for these sensations. Alcohol might bend and twist that channel, but it could have no effect upon my true being. What a shame I hadn't discovered this amazing substance before entering the grid.

I wondered if I could simulate drunkenness, perhaps by slowing down the signals passing between the grid's nodes, the ones that constitute my mind, and therefore me. But I was reluctant. What if I was too inebriated to undo it? I might never sober up.

I gasped. I was afraid to try it. Fear! How magnificently invigorating. I hadn't felt fear since...well, I don't recall ever feeling fear. Of course it wasn't a terrifying thought I'd just had. It was more like what a man might experience while standing on a bridge, looking down at the water as it foams its way between the rocks far below and imagining jumping in, even though he has no intention of actually doing so. But consider such for one whose personal safety has never been in question. Even a minimal threat, and self-induced at that (which also made me wonder if perhaps a Grid Rider could commit suicide…maybe it actually happens), was an unexpected savoury delight. A bit like the ale itself.

I took a sip of the latest sample and held it in my mouth for a moment, noting the marked difference in taste. "You should come back," I said to Arnelius. "I think he opened a new barrel. It tastes fresher." I was speaking through the higher dimensions. Naturally, I didn't vocalise, and the innkeeper heard nothing.

How can I describe this form of communication that comes so naturally to me and my kind? It's a bit like an inner voice. I form the thought in my mind, then send it. I can direct my messages, or I can broadcast, like Arnelius did when he first entered the grid. That's something like shouting, and it can be heard for many light-years, if so desired. But eventually it peters out, lost in the background noise. It's impossible for a single message to reach every point in the universe. (And a good thing too, or we'd all be deaf.) We Grid Riders are not omnipotent. We must obey the laws of the universe. It's just that we're very well versed in those laws.

"Just a few more minutes," Arnelius answered. "I'm reading about their ships. Fascinating."

True to his word, about five minutes later the door opened and in walked Arnelius. Before he made it to the fire, the innkeeper was on his heels, once more suggesting victuals of a more solid variety.

"No, thank you, ale will suffice," Arnelius responded as he settled back into his seat. The innkeeper hurried off. "It's not a castle any more," Arnelius said to me. "It's an enormous palace. And the sense I get from everyone there is that it really is Destlar."

The sense I get. For a moment I didn't know what he meant. Then I realised he was observing the people from the outside. Arnelius believed it was immoral to look inside a creature's mind, to peek at their memories. It was yet another peculiar trait that set him apart. And yet he was to later discard this particular principle, in spectacular fashion.

"But," Arnelius continued, "I find it hard to imagine he could live to such an unnatural age."

"Biological entities, those that have not found their way to us, have been known to perpetually avoid death. The most common method is where they produce an electronic facsimile of the brain."

"Which is obviously not the case here," Arnelius interjected. "They don't have the technology."

"True. So it would have to be some other method. If he is still alive, then he's somehow regenerating his body."

Arnelius shook his head. "Sophisticated. I can't see Destlar coming up with something like that. And yet, the impression I got in the palace..." He let the sentence die.

"There is the possibility he copied the technique from someone else."

Arnelius clapped his hands. "Instead of discussing the possibilities, why don't we go and find out? He's supposed to be with the fleet. And anyway, I want to see those ships for real."

"Fine. But wait until you've had more ale. I think you'll like it this time."

***

"The Empire certainly has expanded," Arnelius said as we raced across a blue sky above a green sea. "According to the palace records, the fleet set sail from Emidelwea last month. The King of Emidelwea is a loyal vassal to the Emperor. It's a centuries-old kingdom about six hundred miles south of the palace, and we didn't even know it existed when I lived here."

Arnelius gave me a copy of the naval documents he'd read at the palace. He didn't actually hand me anything, as we were not in physical form. He simply transmitted what he'd seen to me. Basically, I was reviewing an excerpt from his memory.

According to the documents, the fleet travelled along the northern shore before turning south for the city of Mazeran.

It was a war fleet, and its purpose was to bring about the end of the rebellious, sacrilegious and self-proclaimed Republic of Mazeran. The fleet consisted of 27 double-decked ships, rigged with fore, main and mizzen masts, each one carrying 40 broadside cannons together with two bow chasers in the forecastle. "I've no idea what any of that means," I complained.

"Keep going. There are drawings. I hope the Mazeranians put up a fight; I'd like to see those ships in action."

Moments later we spotted the Imperial fleet. From our vantage point, the ships looked like insects on a pond. We dived towards them.

I shot along the hull of one ship, then across the water and through the snapping canvas of another. I rose into the air and looked down upon those floating trees. "They haven't yet figured out how to make iron float."

"Don't be so derisive," Arnelius shot back. "These ships are a marvellous feat of sophisticated engineering."

And of course he was right. Though I can move about in space with no more effort than deciding to do so, I'm always amazed by the ingenuity of the vast majority of the universe's sentient creatures who are forced to accept action and reaction of matter as their only method of locomotion. And these ships were a wonderful example. The sails bulging with the wind, pulling upon their stout timber masts. The hulls smacking and pounding through the water, rising and falling with the waves. The ropes creaking and the men shouting as they moved about the deck and scampered along the rigging, all with purpose and surety. It was a delight to watch.

"It's him!" Arnelius shouted.

"What?"

"In the lead ship. I just checked. It's really him."

"Are you sure?"

"Positive. No one could mistake that nose. He's hardly aged. I can't believe it. How is he doing it?"

"You don't sense anything?"

"No."

"Me neither. Whatever it is, he must perform it only on occasion, perhaps when he feels age creeping up on him. Oh, I'm looking forward to this. It's a long time since I witnessed a biological regeneration."

"I wonder should I talk to him."

"You want to?"

"Perhaps. I'm not sure."

"But not as yourself."

"No, of course not. How would I explain that?"

"Then you'll have to come up with a story."

"I'll wait till he comes ashore. There's the city now." The walled city of Mazeran wrapped itself about the arms of a wide bay in the south-east corner of the small sea.

"And there are the other ships," I said. Just then, the Imperial fleet, which had been heading south towards the city, turned right and sailed towards the setting sun. "Here comes your battle, Arnelius. The Mazeranians are trying to escape, but I don't think they'll make it." I dropped through the air to get a closer look at their ships.

***

The Mazeran fleet numbered only ten ships. They were much smaller than the Imperial vessels, with varying numbers and types of cannon. They sailed in single file and, with the wind behind them, were soon crossing the path of the larger fleet. Destlar's ships were without formation, but those in the vanguard began firing from their bow chasers as soon as they were within reach.

When more of the Imperial ships were within range and their missiles were finally inflicting damage, smashing into the rigging of the smaller ships, the Mazeranians opened fire. What had looked like an attempt to flee turned out to be a masterful tactical manoeuvre. With Destlar's ships sailing towards their enemy, only their forward-facing guns were being brought to bear. Whereas the Mazeranians were rapidly launching their starboard stones, smashing them into the hulls of their surprised adversary. Three ships went under quickly, the confidence of the Imperial fleet sinking just as fast.

Unbeknownst to the Mazeranians, the Emperor went down with the lead ship. Taking no part in the battle's orchestration, he was below deck when the hull was breached in three separate locations and in quick succession. The vessel was going under before anyone could react.

With his arms and legs flailing, Destlar's tiny black eyes darted about in terror, pale lips clamped tight, lungs about to burst. But just as had happened centuries before, when Arnelius had been about to kill him, blinding light shot from his outstretched arms to pulverise the tiny cabin's walls and ceilings and the main deck above. The Emperor shot up through the water like an ice cube released from the bottom of a glass. He broke the surface completely, twisted about so that he faced the sky, then splashed back into the ocean like a sporting dolphin.

A line was thrown from a nearby ship and in less than a minute the sopping Velkren stood on the quarterdeck next to the captain. Though the Imperial fleet was about to panic, with stones smashing through many ships with uncanny accuracy, those next to the Emperor were much more frightened by the palpable fury, standing in a puddle of sea water.

The captain tried to look away but found it impossible. The Velkren's hood had slipped from his head, making the encounter all the more unusual and frightening; normally the Emperor's face was hidden in shadow. The eyes were seldom seen, and the captain wondered if the Emperor did this in order to preserve his subjects' sanity. Unable to tear his gaze from the tiny circles of raging darkness, he felt his stomach tighten. His fingernails dug deep into the palms of his hands.

Finally the Emperor looked past the captain and focused on the nearest Mazeranian ship. The captain staggered, as if released from enchantment. Breathing deeply, he turned to look at the enemy ship and saw a small fire catch hold in the bow. Efforts to put it out were futile, as the bizarre blue tongues were impervious to both water and sand. They licked their way through the forecastle and onto the main deck. In less than a minute, the whole structure, including the rigging, was engulfed, as if the ship had been dipped in naphtha. Sailors went screaming into the water, many with their clothes on fire.

The smaller fleet was utterly destroyed, one ship after another, by the Velkren's flames of retribution.

***

Late that night the stars, like a billion horrified eyes, witnessed the destruction of an ancient noble city and its people. Destlar stood on a hill to the west, basking in the glow of the conflagration that was a reflection of his own internal rage. His officers and prelates huddled to one side, filled with fear and awe. They were hardly more surprised by his potency than he was himself.

That evening, the Imperial fleet had dropped anchor beyond the range of the city walls with their heavy bombards sitting atop. Destlar and a small contingent, consisting of magicians, clergy, commanders and seamen, had rowed from four separate ships across the sheltered bay to the sandy beach where General Demurdle and a cavalry troop awaited. With right fist held aloft, the general saluted the Emperor before escorting him to the white pavilion atop the hill.

General Demurdle then formally presented himself with greetings from the Queen of Arbadesea, sovereign of the land to the west of Mazeran. He also brought welcome news of a 20,000-strong Arbadesean army camped on the other side of the hill. The queen hoped her display of loyalty to the Empire might result in an expansion of her realm. Destlar was happy to have her rule both lands, in his name, of course.

"Shall we attack at first light, Your Majesty?" Demurdle had asked.

"No need," was the reply. Destlar then took a few steps in the direction of the city. In the dwindling light, warming fires could be seen along the walls and in the interior.

Destlar focused his attention upon a fire on the wall nearest him. Instinctively he reached across to caress the flames, to supplement them with the same occult qualities of the brethren he'd brought forth earlier in the evening, out to sea. Then with a flick of his wrist, he whipped little balls of light from out of the flames and set them sailing on the wind. Some landed on stone and died. More landed on timber roofs and walls and started to feed.

The Emperor repeated the process with fires upon farther walls. Within minutes, the ferocious flames were spreading through the city, cracking stone, melting iron and burning through wood and flesh. They roared through the screaming and panicked heathens, the wrath of Lurg sending all into the arms of Kerl.

With no escape seawards, the citizens of the self-proclaimed republic fled through the southern gate. "General," the Emperor commanded. "No prisoners. None are to be left alive."

General Demurdle was not pleased with having to fight in the dark, but he nevertheless moved instantly to obey.

***

Prefect Prunsios, the magician chosen by the Mazeranians to lead them against the Empire, had removed his people from the surrounding countryside to this haven by the sea, believing the city could withstand any army thrown against its 50-foot walls. However, though he was a talented sorcerer himself, he could not have foreseen the scale and brutality of the mystic attack that would be launched against them that night.

The Prefect, leading a small group of frightened citizens from the city, was met by a troop of Arbadesean cavalry, armoured in leather and mail and swinging their heavy broadswords indiscriminately. Before leaving, Prunsios had filled his pockets with small round pebbles, taken from a gravelled path in the city's beautiful park, its giant oaks already in flames, the smoke stinging the eyes of the crying children.

Taking a handful of these stones, the magician threw them in the air. As each one reached its apex and began to fall, it shot forward faster than lead from a musket. Many struck flesh, be it horse or man, and in each case the victim went down screaming. Another handful came quickly after, followed by another, until the remaining horsemen retreated, quickly realising they were up against a formidable and exceptional foe.

As the heavy smoke was blown in their direction by the southerly wind, accompanied by the strangely alluring aroma of burning timber, the Prefect whispered to a captain of the City Guard. "Take them as quickly as possible."

"Yes, sir. To Ram's Horn?"

"Yes. Whoever escapes will gather there. The women and children will move into the valley and the forests beyond while you hold the pass."

"You're not coming with us, sir?"

"No. I will face this monster. I fear I am not his equal, but I must try."

"Then allow me to assemble a company to aid you."

"No. We wouldn't get anywhere near him. I will go alone and attempt to sneak upon him. Now go, before more cavalry arrive."

Prunsios left the sobbing children and followed the path westwards by the base of the wall, guided by the flickering light, the death throes of his beloved city. Shrouded as he was in the swirling smoke, he escaped notice for much of his journey. Eventually, though, he was forced to leave the relative safety of the wall and cross open ground towards Sunset Hill and the lighted camp atop.

He stopped in the middle of the field below the hill, listening. Hoofs pounded the earth, off to his left. The darkness swirled, then gathered together in the form of a horse and rider. Out of the smoke they came.

Prunsios shot his hands into his pockets but found them empty. Snorting, the horse galloped straight at him. The soldier drew his sword and, in the flickering light, Prunsios saw his eyes narrow, his mouth close to a thin line. The hoofs struck soil, the sword was raised.

The horseman gasped as the sword was snatched from his hand. His eyes widened as he watched it shoot through the air to be deftly caught at the hilt by the magician.

A large man himself, Prunsios took a tight grip with both hands, then quickly slashed the blade across the horse's chest. Down the beast went with a high-pitched scream, but the rider expertly jumped clear. He rolled and was almost on his feet when the Prefect swung the blade again, dishing out the sentence that had been meant for him.

Prunsios was a unique individual, and he knew it. Magic could not be taught to those lacking in innate ability. It was a gift very few were born with. And even amongst magicians, some were more skilful than others. Not many could imitate his tricks with the stones and the sword, and perhaps no one else could do so in the moment and under pressure. Most magic was brought about through intense concentration for minutes at a time. Instantaneous magic was extremely difficult and tiring. The enchantment over the pebbles, and later the sword, left the magician exhausted and in no fit state to face Destlar. His enemy's display with the unstoppable flames was a frightening testament to his talents. There was no knowing what else he might be capable of, or how indefatigable he might be. And there were no guarantees he would be as tired from his labours as Prunsios was.

So Prunsios had used the darkness to get close to the tyrant. Now he would sleep. He crept around the hill and into a copse where he hoped to spend the night undiscovered, then strike in the morning.

***

The wind died and the smouldering city sent columns of grey smoke straight into the cloudless sky. The stars disappeared as morning approached and the sun lifted its orange face above the dark mountains in the distance. Prunsios, peering out from amongst the trees, wondered how many of his people had made it to safely. And would it matter in the end? Would the Arbadesean army hunt them down and enslave them, or kill them?

He dismissed such thoughts. There was nothing he could do about that now. It was time to concentrate.

One large white tent, surrounded by several smaller ones, was evidently Destlar's pavilion. The camp was quiet, with most of the soldiers gone into action. A few were left behind as guards, but their body language suggested they felt their presence was more routine than necessary.

Prunsios prepared a spell, one that would isolate the pavilion so that no sound from within would escape. He wanted to be sure he and the Emperor would not be disturbed while they battled, for Destlar was a man without honour. He was not the type who would agree to single combat and would be more than happy to have his men greet Prunsios with arrows.

Though the silencing spell was easy to conjure and required little concentration to maintain, the Prefect hoped it would remain unused. Perhaps Destlar was asleep. If so, Prunsios could run into the tent and take his head off before anyone knew what had happened. For this reason, he would not drop the spell across the tent until he stepped inside. Activating the spell any earlier would be unwise as it might in fact wake his target. Some magicians, especially those as powerful as Destlar, were quite sensitive to the machinations of others of their kind.

When all was ready, Prunsios picked up the sword and ran for the tent, coming from the side opposite to the ineffectual guards who'd wandered far enough away from the opening for a magician, adept in the art of going unnoticed, to reach the entrance.

***

Destlar slowly descended through freezing water, the light from above growing ever fainter. For ages, he fell, his teeth clenched tight, holding off death as it grappled to gain access, to flow into his burning lungs. His body was screaming for air, his heart almost exploding through his chest. At last, he succumbed. Water surged down a throat that was gasping for something other...

He woke with a whimper. Then his eyes focused on the white canvas roof and he realised with embarrassment where he was.

For a few minutes, the Emperor sat on the bed with his feet on the rug, waiting for his heart to return to normal. The dream had frightened him. It reminded him of how close he'd come to death. His desire to deal with the Mazeranians in person had almost cost him everything. And yet he'd survived, had even become stronger. Must he forever be conflicted?

He jumped to his feet as a man wielding a broadsword ducked through the flaps. For a moment the two men held eye contact, then the intruder looked to the roof. Destlar felt the spell come to life and instantly he knew it would be pointless to call out. He felt fear as he realised the man before him was none other than the sorcerer, leader of this ungodly city.

Without a word, Prunsios leaped forward, swinging the sword high, both hands tight on the hilt. Destlar stumbled backwards, raising his hands to guard his head, an instinctive move that, for most people, would have achieved nothing. But with Destlar, it produced the familiar searing light. Though he had turned his face from the blade as it whistled through its arc, the bolt from his fingers sought out the metal and enveloped it, heating it so quickly that Prunsios dropped the sword with a cry.

Blinded momentarily, it was the Prefect's turn to retreat, raising his hands to shield against the imminent strike. This time the stream of light broke against an invisible barrier, one instantly conjured by the Prefect. The stream crackled loudly before it was channelled to the ground and disappeared.

Prunsios fixed his eyes upon the abandoned sword, lying on the rug behind Destlar. He snatched at it with his mind and, almost faster than the eye could track, it silently flew through the air at shoulder height. Warned by his keen senses, Destlar ducked just in time. The blade passed only inches above his head, to be caught by Prunsios, who gritted his teeth against the slowly dissipating heat in the hilt and repeated his initial attack.

Destlar's response was also similar, but this time the Prefect was prepared and he bent the light away from the blade. Once again, the light sizzled and died upon his invisible shield. Unrestrained, the sword descended upon the naked skull and Prunsios' heart jumped as he anticipated the blade crunching through bone. But just as it was about to reach its target, it disappeared in a shower of dust.

It was a spectacularly swift reaction from Destlar. The Prefect staggered back in shock, only just getting his mystic barrier raised before it was swathed once more. Had it not been for the silencing spell, the crackle and boom would have woken the entire camp.

But now the spell unravelled as an exhausted Prunsios sank to his knees. Raising the barrier for a third time had taken its toll. He looked up at the pale face, the eyes burning with hate, the thin lips twisting into an ugly grimace. All the despot needed to do now was call for help.

But he didn't. Believing he had already won, the Emperor played his favourite game, cutting off the fallen magician's senses and slowing his personal clock.

***

Arnelius and I watched with interest as Prunsios rattled the cage. But quickly the Prefect realised he would not gain freedom through strength. Calmly, he examined the spell.

Meanwhile, Destlar tried to see inside his captive's mind, but failed. He was reminded of a time, hundreds of years earlier, when he'd first taken on a fellow magician. On that occasion, the vanquished brain had also proven opaque. Yet he had performed this torture on many magicians since, and none until now had denied him the pleasure of observing a mind, trapped in emptiness for eternity, descend into madness. It was very irritating.

Darkness! Sudden and complete.

Destlar collapsed to the floor as all sensation was abruptly lost. It took him a few seconds to realise what had happened. He screamed, silently.

Prunsios had spent decades of his time studying the spell, then amazingly turned it upon his jailer. One moment Destlar was outside the bars, looking in. The next, he was on the inside, looking out. Only there was nothing to look out at. He was in total darkness, cut off from the world. He was alone with his thoughts. With the memories of how others had been driven demented by an eternity of nothing. The Gods had turned on him. They were using the heathen to spin his own magic against him. They would imprison him forever, just punishment for his ill-use of the divine arts. Destlar panicked.

As sudden as it went out, the light returned. Destlar found himself in an unfamiliar position, looking down from the roof of the tent. His inert body was directly below, with Prunsios staggering about only feet from it.

Having stumbled into the grid alongside Arnelius and me, Destlar was as confused and frightened as we were astounded. Desperate to revert to an ordinary existence, he grabbed hold of his own spell and tore it apart. Instantly he was back inside his body. He jumped to his feet and ran from the tent. "Kill him!" he roared at the startled guards. They looked at the Emperor in shock and confusion. "In there. The Prefect. Kill him!"

The guards leaped through the flaps. Despite his heroic efforts, Prunsios lost his head to a broadsword after all.

***

"Incredible!" I said. "To actually witness an instinctive leap. I've met some who've done it, of course, but I've never actually seen it happen, in person."

I waited for Arnelius to respond, but he was strangely quiet.

"They're so rare," I continued, "these creatures who unwittingly join us. And impossible to predict. What an amazing creature this Destlar is. When he's under serious threat, instinct takes over. It happened when you attacked him. And we saw how he escaped the sinking ship. And then that bit with the sword. I bet he's never even tried anything like it. And yet, in desperation, he disintegrates a piece of metal that's moving towards his unguarded head at a significant velocity. Marvellous!"

Still nothing from Arnelius.

"Don't you think?" I prodded. "And when he gets caught in his own trap, rather than succumb to madness, he leaps into the grid. Pop! There he is, right beside us, and without a notion of how he did it. He didn't even realise what he'd done, otherwise he surely would have stayed."

"Yes," Arnelius replied at last. "He retreated to where he felt secure."

"It's truly baffling. His mind appeared in the grid, instantaneously. How? Normally, it takes millions of years to develop a path. Either evolution does the whole job, or it goes so far and technology does the rest."

I was babbling, because I was excited and because Arnelius was so withdrawn.

"How is it that these single entities, unique amongst their species, find a way?"

"He's not unique."

"Of course! How could I forget? Though your situation was different. You didn't leap blindly. You spent centuries of your time figuring it out. Quite an achievement, but not as stupendous as what your old friend just did. What an amazing place this is. The home of two extremely unusual Grid Rider births. Though Destlar's was short-lived. He may have missed his chance."

"Perhaps."

"Aren't you interested in any of this? Don't you find it astonishing?"

"Maybe I should try to help him?"

"What do you mean? Help him join us? But how?"

"No. I mean I could try to cure him."

"Of what?"

"You don't think he's a sick man? After what he did to the city and all its people?"

"He's not sick. He's just an animal. It's what they do."

"I was an animal too, once."

114

"What's the matter with you, Arnelius? We were all animals once. Some of us were lucky enough to mature, others not. Destlar almost made it. And maybe he will yet. But I don't see what you can do about it. Or why you should want to."

"He doesn't have to be like this. It's all due to fear."

"I fear you're losing your mind."

"Leave me for a while, please. I need to think."

Chapter 7

A pallid sun found Hervan Willkob loading bags of coal into a box on the back of an agricultural tractor. With a grunt, he dropped the latest wet sack into the box. It landed on top of another with a heavy thump, then rustled as it rolled off the hump and slid into a corner. Willkob turned and walked over to the coal pallet, thankful it was still more than half full; the sacks were much easier to lift when they were still at waist height. He recalled the day, not long after taking the job in the fuel yard, when he'd used the forklift to elevate an almost empty pallet and move it next to the customer's vehicle, simply because he'd found it so difficult to haul the dead weight up from down around his ankles. The yard owner had come running out of his office, squawking and flapping like a panicked hen, shouting about the cost of fuel and how it was inexcusable to waste it in such a lazy manner. Willkob had learned his lesson.

Wrapped up in a heavy coat with a deep hood, and wearing padded gloves, the ex-priest carried his burden with accustomed ease. He'd discovered that grasping a lump of coal in each fist, in a corner of the bag, gave him a sound grip and reduced the chances of the woven fibre slipping from his grasp and onto the gravel.

When he'd first begun working in the yard, he'd found the freezing conditions almost impossible to endure. He had not been accustomed to spending so much time exposed to the wind and rain and sleet and snow. That, together with the heavy work that was too much for his soft and coddled body, had taken him to a sad and dispirited place, where he viewed himself as pathetic and useless. A place he had considered leaving, to return home. But the thoughts of such an ignominious journey were more despairing than the prospect of day upon day of ice, snow and sacks of coal. He stuck to it.

That was in the past. Now he found the job invigorating and rewarding. Though it was exhausting work, he ended each day feeling good about himself. He couldn't pinpoint the day the change had come about. It was gradual. He'd grown tough, and he accepted the work as just penance for his years of opulence within the Church.

He'd left his post and gone north, little more than 200 miles, hoping to somehow become involved with NALO. Living in Rustletov, even that far from the equatorials, he'd been presented with a very clear picture of the northern terrorists. On television and in the papers, they were portrayed as a group unwilling to live within society, who would rather kill and steal than work as honest men. A people to be feared and despised. However, a little research revealed all this to be nothing more than Palace propaganda. The truth was very different. NALO saw itself as the real government of the North, with ministers for education, welfare, defence and so on. They looked upon the Empire's police and military as an occupying force. Their manifesto promised the protection of the people of the North (a conglomeration of ethnic and religious groups) and the assassination of Destlar the Defiler. They stole from the South in order to provide for their people, who otherwise would find it impossible to survive.

The fuel yard where Willkob found employment was, he was pleased to discover, a perfect example of NALO's fine work. In small towns throughout the region, people did not earn enough money to heat their homes during the long vicious winter. Therefore, NALO bought tons of coal, gallons of oil and had it delivered to yards such as the one in which Willkob worked. The people of the town, and many of the poor farmers in the surrounding countryside, bought the fuel using vouchers distributed by NALO's department of welfare. These vouchers could only be used to buy necessities such as fuel, food and medicine. Shop owners were not allowed to make more than set profits, as no one was supposed to get rich off the scheme.

And it worked. True, it wasn't perfect. There were a few who exchanged vouchers for alcohol or other vices, but overall it was a marvellous success. Even so, there were some within NALO who believed the welfare system provided the absentee landlords with an easy way out. These official owners of almost all property within NALO's domain continued to charge rents above what their tenants were capable of paying. And the vouchers, proclaimed the dissenters, facilitated this extortion. But though they complained, the dissenters never seriously considered ending the scheme. The correct solution was the removal of the landlords, but even NALO couldn't accomplish that without a bloody revolt.

As Willkob carried another bag to the box, he was watched by two people. One was the owner of the tractor, the other was best known about town as the seller of NALO's newspaper, *Northern Lights*.

"He's been asking questions," the newspaper woman said. "Says he'd like to get involved."

"What do you know of him?"

"He arrived here on the bus about a year ago. He doesn't say much about his past. All I know is that he used to live in Gernaturov. He looked about for work and within the week he started here. As part-payment, he gets to stay in a room above the shop. He goes to the pub a couple of times a week, getting to know people. And people like him. From talking to him, you can tell he's an educated man, but he's not arrogant."

"Educated." They watched the little man carry the last sack to the tractor; only his broad nose, glistening in the cold, and his bushy eyebrows could be seen within the hood. "Perhaps we can make better use of him."

***

Four months later Willkob walked along a quiet street on the outskirts of Gernaturov. Alongside him was a grey-haired man with sharp features, the leader of the group of five. Two more approached from the opposite direction while a fifth sat in a parked van across the street. They were dressed in nondescript grey suits. They all carried small guns in their pockets, which made Willkob nervous. He wasn't used to this. He had to suppress a laugh when suddenly an image of the priest in blue robes formed behind his eyes, looking aghast upon this unrecognisable self with a firearm in one pocket and a black mask in the other. The leader glanced across at him, frowning.

The approaching pairs met at the door to the bank and quickly pulled woollen masks over their heads. They took the guns from their pockets and rushed through the glass doors.

"Everyone on the floor!" the leader shouted. As they had specifically chosen a quiet time of the day, there were only three customers and two tellers present. The customers, two middle-aged women and an old man, called out in alarm and tried to move towards the doors. They were roughly pushed to the floor by one of the raiders, a large beefy man, while the other went behind the counter with the leader and forced the tellers to the floor. Willkob stayed by the door, as planned.

The leader went into the back to get the manager and have him open the safe while his associate behind the counter filled a sack with money from the cash drawers. They moved quickly but seemed very relaxed about the whole thing. The large man kept an eye on the customers. Willkob held his gun by his side, looking nervously about. It was his job to handle any customer who happened to come in. He was hoping no one would.

When the cash drawers were emptied, the raider stood over the tellers, reminding everyone to remain calm, that it would all be over in minutes. For what seemed like an age, nothing happened. The only sounds were light whimpers from the floor and some muffled shouts and door slamming from the back. But eventually the leader re-emerged. Willkob's heart thumped, but he began to feel a little more confident as he knew the time had come for them to leave. He held open the door as his two comrades came out from behind the counter, carrying sacks full of money. The large man, standing above the three customers, also made for the exit. As he did, the old man started to get up. The raider turned around and punched him in the face. The old man cried and fell back onto the tiled floor.

"Leave him," Willkob said. "Let's go."

But the giant wasn't listening. He started to kick the old man. He kicked him in the ribs and the gut and the face. In seconds, the fallen man's face was bleeding profusely, his nose smashed.

Willkob stood frozen, horrified. Then something made him move. Later he supposed it had been his sudden conviction that if he remained inactive, he would have been involved in a brutal murder. He knew he was no match for the giant, so he did the only thing he could. From within another dimension, the priest in the blue robes looked on, amazed as the new Willkob stepped forward and pressed his gun against the madman's head, just behind his right ear. "Stop," he said, quietly but firmly. He was surprised by the steadiness of his voice.

They stood together, unmoving. Again, time seemed to slow. Willkob wondered if the giant was considering calling his bluff. He wondered how he himself would react. He never got to find out as the door shot open and the leader shouted at them both to hurry up. The scene disintegrated as they all raced for the waiting van.

As the van accelerated away, the giant pushed Willkob down onto the floor. "This fucker tried to shoot me!"

"No I didn't," Willkob croaked. The giant's forearm was pressing down on his windpipe.

"Get off him," the leader commanded. The giant got up with a grunt, kneeling heavily on Willkob's inner thigh in the process.

Willkob moaned through clenched teeth, then slowly got into a sitting position, massaging his neck with one hand and his leg with the other. "He's crazy," he explained to the leader.

"He was about to kill that man." Everyone except the driver stared at him.

Without taking his eyes off Willkob, the leader addressed the brute. "The old man, covered in blood. That was your work?" He got no reply, which he accepted as an affirmative. "And what did he do to provoke such an attack?" Again there was no reply. "You may be thankful this man here was the witness," he continued with a nod at Willkob, "and not me, because I'd have put a bullet in your thick head. These people, leading their common lives, they're not our enemies."

Though the pain in Willkob's neck and thigh began to abate, Willkob remained uncomfortable under the leader's steady gaze.

***

The week following the raid, Zaybya the newspaper woman came into the yard. "I heard what you did in the bank. The Committee's impressed."

The Committee was the appointed local authority. Willkob knew little about it, other than that it was held in high regard.

"They've decided," Zaybya continued, "this yard is no place for a man like you. An educated man, a kind soul. Would we be right in thinking that in your past life, you spent some time teaching?"

"You would."

Zaybya nodded knowingly. "So here's the story. The Committee want you to take over from Elbmurc Dab. She's a great teacher. Taught me, in fact. But she's getting on in years and her mind's starting to slip."

"They want me to teach?"

"Indeed they do. Every man and woman in the right spot."

Willkob looked about the yard. Though he'd come to enjoy the work, he didn't think he'd miss the cold and the wet and the heavy loads.

Zaybya seemed to read his mind. "Say goodbye to this place," she said with a slap to Willkob's back. "From now on you work with a nice warm fire at your arse."

Willkob noticed he wasn't being asked. It was as if he was in the army and he was being reassigned. Well, it was an army he'd come in search of. "What about my other...activities?" he asked.

Zaybya shrugged. "There's nothing to stop you continuing in that role."

As Zaybya turned to leave, Willkob stopped her with a question. "I've been curious. Why doesn't the Palace do something about all this?"

"Do what?"

"Well, I'm sure it's within their capabilities to figure out who in the community are actual members, then arrest them?"

"And what would that achieve? For every one they arrested, there'd be a dozen outraged young men and women eager to take their place. No, old Luckran is quite content to leave things the way they are. And so is the Church, of course, since everyone here dutifully pays their rent." Zaybya spat in the gravel as she said this.

"Their rent?"

"Didn't you know? Most of the property here is owned by the Church."

Chapter 8

Major Tavenar entered Prince Carlden's office. This time the curtains were open and the sun streamed in. The viceroy sat behind his desk, in plain view. He didn't get up.

"We've got a serious problem," Tavenar said.

Carlden sighed. "What's he done this time?"

Tavenar frowned. For a moment he didn't know to whom Carlden was referring. "Oh," he said, when it finally dawned on him. "Your son didn't do anything." Second Lieutenant Kryslor was in hibernation aboard the ship that had kicked itself out of orbit eight years earlier. "No, it's the general. Somehow, he found out."

"You've lost me. General who? And what has he found out?"

"My commanding officer. He knows what I did. He knows I included your son and his girlfriend in the project. He's furious. Right now, he's on his way back to Wesmork and has arranged a meeting with the First Advisor."

Carlden shook his head, wishing he'd never got involved with Tavenar, conveniently forgetting how happy he was to be rid of Ferist. "When is this general due to meet Luckran?"

"He's arriving in Wesmork the day after tomorrow. He's scheduled to meet the First Advisor in the palace the following morning. He wants me there too, to explain myself."

"Has he given Luckran any idea of what he wants to discuss?"

"No. He won't talk about something like that until they're face to face."

"And if he's not around to make a fuss, will the problem go away?"

Tavenar had spent a day and a half dreaming of the general's plane going down in flames, taking all his worries with it. "Certainly." He almost sighed with the relief of passing the problem over to one who had the power and the will to deal with it. And why not? The prince had created the mess. He should clean it up.

"What's his name?"

Ingrained loyalty to the corps caused Tavenar to hesitate. He failed to notice his reluctance had nothing to do with the knowledge that to name the man was to issue his death warrant.

Carlden sat forward, his hands flat on the desk. "Do you want this sorted out or not?"

"General Meckreen."

"Meckreen," the prince said with a nod, as if he approved of the name. He stood up. "You should leave now. Don't worry. The meeting won't take place."

"You're sure?"

"Positive."

***

The sun set on Wesmork, painting the bellies of the heavy dark clouds a deep orange, as if in a futile effort to seal the water in. As General Meckreen prepared to leave his Hightower office, the rain began to spatter against the windows. Within minutes it was a downpour. He walked down the stairs in the middle of the glass cube that was the building's vestibule, the water drumming on the roof and running down the huge panes. Rivulets reflected the bright interior in irregular lines.

Looking to his right, Meckreen noted the light was still on in Major Tavenar's office. He'd just had a very brief and unsatisfactory meeting in that office. Standing to attention, Tavenar had informed the general he would present his case to the First Advisor. When the general pressed, the major simply reiterated. Meckreen had been tempted to charge him with insubordination right then. But he decided to give the man his chance. "Then I'll see you at the palace in the morning, Major," he'd replied. "I very much hope you have a damn good explanation."

Meckreen looked away from the window, shaking his head. He was surprised and disappointed to find one of his most reliable men had behaved in what seemed to be a very irresponsible manner. Why would the major place two young and inexperienced engineers aboard the ship? It made no sense.

The general reached the bottom of the stairs, then stood for a moment, looking out at the downpour. Realising it could be quite a while before the weather cleared, and anxious to drive the short distance home to a warm shower and bed, he strode out into the rain, pointing his remote key at his car, which was parked just beyond the manicured lawns. The locks popped open. A few more steps and he was reaching for the driver's door. Suddenly, four men appeared out of the darkness. Two of them jumped into the car, one in the back, the other in the passenger's seat. "What in the name of Kerl do you think you're doing?" Meckreen shouted, more annoyed than alarmed as he assumed they were brazenly grabbing a lift.

Another pushed Meckreen towards the back seat while he jumped behind the wheel. The fourth man shoved something hard against Meckreen's side. The general looked down, amazed to see a gun in the man's gloved hand. "Get in!"

"Don't be ridiculous."

"Just shut up and get in."

By sheer chance, a police car appeared. Meckreen shoved the gun away and waved energetically. The butt of the gun hit him hard on the side of the head. His legs buckled. On his way to the pavement, he lost consciousness.

***

The assignment was not proceeding in the manner the kidnappers had anticipated. "Drag him into the back," the gun wielder yelled. He then turned to face the police car as it stopped with a screech of tyres and the doors opened. He pointed his gun at the car, then hesitated.

The police didn't. He saw a flash, heard the dull crack. The pain in his thigh was sharp and sudden. He screamed, but as he went down, he managed to fire off a few rounds. The flunkeys crouched for cover, which allowed the others to drag Meckreen into the back and race away.

The driver joined the city traffic, narrowly avoiding a bus. Through the mirror he could see the stopped police car with the flashing lights reflecting off the wet tarmac. He could just make out the shape of his fallen comrade on the ground, one of the flunkeys standing over him. Then the scene disappeared behind the traffic and the rain.

"Hey!" shouted the man in the back. "What about Bram? We can't leave him."

"What can we do?" the driver replied. "They have him." He thumped the wheel. "Damn it! They had to show up. Just our luck." He thumped the wheel again. "The bastards had to show up."

***

Luckran and Rubyan sat either side of the fire in the warm and cosy lounge. A waitress approached, carrying the house phone; personal phones were discouraged in the Governors' Rooms. "Excuse me, My Lord. There is an urgent call for you."

Rubyan frowned. To be disturbed while in their favourite retreat was unusual. Luckran glanced at him as he accepted the proffered phone. "Lord Luckran speaking."

Rubyan could hear the voice on the other end but could not make out the words. But whatever was said, it rattled the First Advisor. Shock flickered in the old man's eyes, brief but unmistakable. Rubyan was intrigued.

"You're sure it was him?" Luckran said quietly.

Rubyan watched Luckran's self-assuredness quickly return as he listened to the speaker on the other end. "Chief," he said, "this is a code seven-twenty! Enact Operation Zero. Stop at nothing. Understood?" He listened some more, then shook his head and grimaced. "Is there no discipline in that force of yours? Get on to the hospital and have them call me immediately." He then switched off the phone with an angry stab of his finger.

"What's going on?"

"Meckreen's been kidnapped. That was the police chief. One of the kidnappers was apprehended, but those idiots he puts in uniform nearly beat him to death, which leaves him difficult to interrogate."

"How did they know of Meckreen's importance? It's all so secret. Does anyone even know he's commander of Imperial Engineering?"

"Very few. The chief knows he's important, but he doesn't know why. And there's Tavenar, of course."

"Who?"

"Major Tavenar. He and Meckreen were supposed to meet me in the morning. I wonder if that has anything to do with this." Luckran picked up the phone again and dialled. "Find Major Tavenar," he ordered. "Bring him to the Governors' Rooms immediately."

He put down the phone. The two men sat in silence, sipping their brandy. Rubyan could see Luckran was troubled. A moment later the phone rang and Luckran jumped to answer it. "Yes! How is he?" The answer was short. "Damn!" He slammed the phone down. "He's dead."

Rubyan raised his eyebrows. "Meckreen?"

Luckran rolled his eyes. "If only; that would be the end of it. No, the kidnapper. The stupid flunkeys kicked him to death. Now, if the others get away with Meckreen, it might be difficult to find them."

Again they sat in silence. The fire hissed and spat. Presently, Luckran sighed. "This could be serious, Rendal. Meckreen knows so much."

"The ship and its destination. By the way, are you ever going to name them?"

"You don't name that which doesn't exist. Anyway, it's the villa in the mountains I'm more worried about. If that secret is revealed…" He trailed off, then thumped the armrest again. "Damn it! We must find him."

"But what about his oath?" Rubyan argued. "Even if his kidnappers somehow know he has valuable information, he'll not give anything away."

Luckran laughed. "The oath prevents the corps from tattling to pretty girls in the hope of getting laid. But those men have never been seriously tested. A broken finger or two and Meckreen will squeal."

***

Less than an hour later, Luckran and Rubyan were gently interrupted by the housekeeper. "My Lord, Major Tavenar."

Rubyan turned to see a small man in uniform standing over by the doorway to his left. The major walked up briskly and saluted. "My Lord. You summoned me."

"Yes, Major," answered Luckran. "Pull up a chair."

"Thank you, sir."

Rubyan could see the man was nervous, but most people were during an interview with the First Advisor.

"General Meckreen has been kidnapped," Luckran said.

"Kidnapped? Why?"

Even Rubyan could tell Tavenar's show of surprise was fake and Luckran was suddenly on the hunt. He leaned forward to look Tavenar closely in the eye. "It would be for the best if you told me everything. This kidnapping has something to do with the reason the general was so keen to meet with me." It was delivered as a statement, not a conjecture.

"I'm sorry, My Lord. I'm afraid I don't know anything about it." Rubyan felt sorry for the man. He was visibly sweating.

"Dr Rubyan," Luckran intoned as he stood up. "Please excuse us while I escort the major upstairs."

***

The two men left the lounge and walked up the wide stairs to the top floor. Tavenar's legs almost gave out as he climbed.

"Sit down, Major," Luckran commanded upon entering a vacant bedroom.

Tavenar trembled as he lowered himself into the armchair by the large bed. He felt like crawling under the bed. Luckran leaned over and stared into his face again. The green eyes, which Tavenar noticed matched the robe, were terrifying in their intensity. The man didn't blink, which made Tavenar's eyes water.

"Tell me what's happening," the First Advisor demanded as he stood over him.

"I don't know," Tavenar stammered.

With speed and strength that belied the frail figure, the First Advisor snatched up the major's left hand and snapped the index finger. Tavenar howled. He gritted his teeth, doubled over with his right hand tightly grasping his left wrist. He rocked back and forth, whimpering.

Luckran crossed the room and sat down, patiently waiting for the younger man to somewhat regain his composure. In a minute or so, the whimpering stopped and the major took a few deep breaths, then sat back. His face was shiny and pale.

"You have something to tell me?"

"Prince Carlden," Tavenar gasped. "The viceroy. He kidnapped Meckreen."

Luckran hid his surprise. "Why?"

Tavenar took another deep breath. He let his head rest on the back of the chair and stared up at the ceiling. He began to talk. It was actually a great relief to unburden himself. Not until that moment did he realise how much stress he'd been under, how much he'd worried ever since he'd foolishly accepted Carlden's money. He knew he would later pay, perhaps even with his life, but at that moment he didn't care. "He persuaded me to assign his son, an avionics engineer, to the ancillary team building the ship. His son then leaked information about the ship to his girlfriend, also an avionics engineer. I was frightened. I didn't know what to do. I considered doing nothing, ignoring it, but I was afraid he'd tell her more. And then she'd start telling others. Carlden wanted to kill her. I'm not sure what he was going to do with his son. But I couldn't allow that. I'm not a murderer."

"I don't care what you are, or what you think you are. Tell me what you did."

Tavenar dropped his head and stared at the carpet. "To ensure neither of them would be a further security risk, I put them on the ship itself. That way they would be isolated completely from the public."

"You put them on the ship," Luckran reiterated incredulously. "The most important project in history, and you throw two random people aboard the ship, just to get them out of the way!" Luckran got to his feet. "You're a pair of bumbling fools!" He walked out, slamming the door behind him.

***

Unnoticed, Meckreen's car stopped at the back of an unused warehouse on the south side of the city. With a lot of huffing and cursing, the general's inert bulk was heaved into the boot of a second car which had been parked there that morning by the kidnappers. The driver slammed the boot and as the others turned to jump aboard, he put his hand on the nearest man's shoulder. "The flunkeys will be looking for three men. You'll have to find your own way back. But first, see what you can find out about Bram."

The kidnapper nodded. "Will do," he said.

"Be discreet."

"Of course." He turned to go. "Good luck, you two."

"We'll need it," the driver replied as he jumped behind the wheel. He drove around to the front of the building and entered the city traffic. The heavy rain was keeping people off the streets, except for some who seemed to have been caught unawares and were standing under shop awnings, waiting for the rain to ease.

Within half an hour, the traffic lessened as they reached the city limits. Shops were hidden behind strong metal barriers, some dented, some with enigmatic messages scrawled across them in purples and reds. Scattered amongst them was the odd deserted building. Litter was pasted to the footpaths in the downpour and clogged the drains so that some intersections were already impassable to pedestrians. The rain continued to hammer on the roof of the old red car. Suddenly, above the noise could be heard the chopping of a helicopter. "Another one," the driver said as he and his companion in the passenger seat searched the dark skies. It was hard to tell what direction the noise was coming from.

"Can't see it."

"Be thankful. If they spot us, we're done."

"We don't know they're looking for us."

"Of course they are. Our man's more important than we thought." The street climbed rapidly as they approached the mountains, a natural barrier to the city's expansion. They were heading for one of the less frequented routes, a road that grew narrow as it passed through a tight fissure in the rocks. Suddenly the streets and houses and shops were behind them as the driver dropped a gear to allow for the steepening incline.

At the brow of the hill was a junction with another road running east–west. "Shit!" Red lights were flashing. "Keep your gun hidden for now."

A policeman stood in the middle of the road, waving them down with a flashlight. "What's the trouble, officer?" the driver asked politely as he pulled up.

The flunkey stood with shoulders hunched and eyes squinted, as if that somehow lessened the effects of the rain. "Where are you coming from?"

"Visiting relatives in the city," the driver replied, wondering if his voice sounded neutral. He glanced across at the squad car with its spinning lights. A second policeman sat inside.

"And where are you going?"

"Home. Just an hour's drive across the mountain."

The policeman bent down to shine the light into the face of the man in the passenger seat, who tried to smile through a squint. The light was then moved to shine on the empty back seat. Detecting nothing suspicious, the policeman faced the driver again. "I need to search the vehicle. Open the boot."

The driver got out while the other stealthily placed his hand on his gun, hidden between the seat and the car door. "This old boot," the driver explained, "the lock is dodgy. I don't know when I last opened it." He inserted the key only partway. "Damn thing is a pain in the arse to open," he complained, fiddling with the key.

The wind picked up, whipping the policeman's light coat about him. He wasn't properly dressed for the weather. Though it had hardly seemed possible, at that moment the rain got even heavier. "Go on. Get out of here!" the policeman shouted as he ran back to his car.

Moments later the kidnappers were through the intersection and heading higher into the mountains.

"He just let you go?" the passenger asked incredulously. "I can't believe it. The stupid bastard, he had us. I was all psyched up to shoot the other one as soon as you opened the boot."

"Survival of the dumbest. What else would you expect from the flunkeys?"

The passenger laughed. "Well, we're home and dry now."

"Yeah. Except for Bram."

***

The search was called off in the morning's early hours as Luckran believed the kidnappers had escaped and therefore his only hope was Prince Carlden. The viceroy had been absent from the capital, so Luckran had sent a plane to fetch him. His Highness arrived in the early afternoon and was deposited unceremoniously in a holding cell in the palace basement. There was nothing in the brightly lit room but a steel table and two matching chairs.

Luckran walked in with Tavenar before him. It was the first time Carlden had seen the major out of his smart military uniform, and the grey shirt and trousers accentuated the picture of misery. Carlden was shocked by how defeated the major appeared. He stood inside the door with his eyes on the floor, absently fidgeting with the metal splint upon the index finger of his left hand.

Luckran sat down in front of Carlden, fixing his robes about him. "Where have they taken General Meckreen?"

The prince was surprised by these words, and though he did his best to hide it, Luckran noticed. "You told them to kill him, didn't you? But instead, they kidnapped him. Now you will tell me who they are and where they live."

For a moment, Carlden didn't answer. Luckran's summons hadn't surprised him. He'd expected the First Advisor to put two and two together and quickly suspect Tavenar. And of course Tavenar would point to him. How he would love to have had the major shot as well, but the little shit had his insurance policy.

Carlden's plan had been to deny everything. Since there was no proof, it would have been his word against Tavenar's. A major against the Prince of Zervnia. He had imagined himself laughing it off.

But Luckran had dragged the prince, upstanding member of the Assembly, into this interrogation cell in the basement of the very building where he'd always felt so powerful. What a kick in the teeth that was. It showed how little the First Advisor cared for the fact that this was Prince Carlden Kryslor sitting before him, fifteenth in a direct line of Kryslors to wear the signet.

Carlden considered his options. He didn't have many, so it didn't take him long to come to a decision. "You made a mistake, My Lord, bringing me here," he said with a tight smile as he indicated his surroundings. "You couldn't have sent a clearer message. Whether I cooperate or not, I'm finished. I'm already dead. So why should I bother?"

Luckran smiled back humourlessly. "It was no mistake. I expected you to be difficult." He produced a small electronic screen from within his robes and set it on the table before the prisoner. "I'm sure you recognise that villa. It'll soon be dark in Zervnia, but you can still make out the man sitting on the patio. Your son likes to relax there with a glass of wine, after a long, arduous day."

Carlden's mouth went dry. The camera was on the hill opposite his house. Luckran let the images sink in for a moment, then took out his phone and made a call. "Show His Highness who we have keeping a watchful eye on his son."

The camera panned and onto the screen slid a close-up view of a sniper, rifle resting on a grassy bank, shoulder to the stock, eye close to the telescopic sight. Carlden imagined what the eye could see. Light rebounding from his son was entering that firm and resolute pupil. Suddenly the eye seemed to exist independently of the head and body in which it resided. It was its own entity, and it fed off the light from his son's forehead. It blinked, as if to swallow. With a single word from Luckran, that sinister creature would send something in return, something small and hard and fatal. Carlden could not tear his own eyes away from the terrifying monster before him.

***

General Meckreen sat on the rough timber floor inside a one-room cabin, which was bare except for a table, a few chairs and a stove that gave off little heat. The kidnappers stood above him. A darkening sky could be seen through a small window.

He had regained consciousness in the boot of the car the night before. Persistent kicking had alerted his captors, and they'd taken him out and put him in the back seat. The passenger had relocated to the back too, to keep an eye on him. By dawn they were well into the mountains and the road was covered in a sprinkling of snow. They drove for hours more. By early afternoon, they arrived in a small one-street town. The general had been pulled from the car and shoved into the cabin.

Meckreen looked up as another man entered the cabin, carrying a tray with three steaming bowls. A much older man followed him. They were all dressed in dark heavy clothes. Meckreen's mouth watered at the aroma and his stomach twisted and groaned. The kidnappers took a bowl each; the third was handed to the general. He propped himself up against the wall, took the bowl and started spooning the stew into his mouth. He wasn't sure what type of meat it was, but it tasted great.

"Why are we feeding him?" someone asked in an angry voice. "We should kill him." At this, Meckreen stopped eating, his hunger forgotten. He looked from one man to the other with wide eyes. "That's what we were contracted to do," continued the driver. "If we'd just walked up to him and shot him outside Hightower, like we were supposed to, Bram would be here now."

"It was Bram's idea to kidnap him," answered the man who'd sat in the back with Meckreen. "A stupid idea."

"No it wasn't. Someone wants him dead, which means he must be valuable to another alive. We might be able to negotiate. If it doesn't work, we lose nothing. We can kill him then."

"Way too risky," said the old man, speaking for the first time. He looked directly at Meckreen. The general searched for compassion, for sympathy in the weather-beaten face. He found none. "It was idiotic of Bram to change the plan on a whim, and he paid for it with his life."

Everyone went silent for a moment. Meckreen recalled the man who'd pressed the gun against his ribs. He felt no sorrow at hearing of his death.

"We know nothing about this man," the old man continued, "except that he's a general. And we don't get the rest of the money until we prove he's dead. Kill him. Now."

The driver took out a gun and walked towards the general.

"No," he pleaded. "I have information. Valuable information."

"We don't care," the old man said.

The gun was aimed at his head. "Wait!" Meckreen shouted, raising his hands before his face. "I'm the commander of the Imperial Engineering Corps."

The gun was lowered. There was silence for a moment. Then the old man spoke. "Go on."

"I know the location of every Imperial villa. NALO will pay for this information."

"How do we know you're telling the truth?"

"I'll show you. Are you on the network?"

"Of course we are," the driver answered indignantly. "You think we're barbarians?"

You're about to kill a man for money, Meckreen thought. What else would you be? "I'll log into my military account. That will prove it."

***

Luckran left the prince and the major together in the cell and walked down the hall to the security control centre. A computer technician was halfway out of his chair as he walked in. "Lord Luckran," he said, settling back down. "I was about to go find you. Someone just accessed General Meckreen's account."

"From where?"

"We don't know, yet. Whoever it is, he's trying hard to hide his location, which is unusual, but not unheard of. The path is convoluted and will take some time to unravel."

"Check the network in a place called Cararuishk."

"Yes, sir." The technician turned back to the computer.

Luckran turned to another man, General Hurfinkle, Air Force commander. "I believe I know where they are, General. A village about two hundred and fifty miles east of here."

"You wish to land troops, My Lord?"

Luckran hesitated. Keeping the villa hidden was of paramount importance. If word got out, there was no telling what might happen. His mind conjured an image of a tenacious investigative reporter crossing the mountains with the help of a talented magician. The magician senses magic in the villa's basement. Destlar finds out.

It was an unlikely scenario, but not impossible. And there were sure to be many other situations that he wasn't picturing right then but that could arise. Some might involve the ship too.

There was one thing that was absolutely certain: he did not want to end up looking back on this moment, wishing he'd been more resolute.

But were Meckreen's secrets worth the lives of innocent people?

"Lord Luckran," the technician called. "You are correct. That's where the account is being accessed from."

***

"So you know I'm telling the truth," Meckreen said. He and the four men had left the cabin and gone into a house down the street. It was modest, but comfortable. As they entered, a little girl ran up to the driver, obviously her father. Her delight turned quickly to disappointment as he pushed her away. "Take her out into the garden!" he called to the woman in the kitchen. The woman hurried into the living room, picked up the child and ran out.

It had taken the driver quite some time to connect to the network through an old computer. For a time Meckreen had been very worried he would fail. But eventually the man had stood up and offered the seat to the general. A moment later Meckreen had his photograph displayed on the screen, along with all his particulars.

"When you take me back to Wesmork," he continued, "I'll give you the locations of the villas."

"No," the old man responded. "You're logged in. I'm sure we can find the information ourselves."

Meckreen turned quickly to the keyboard, but before he could log out the two younger men grabbed him and threw him out of the seat. The driver sat down and began navigating through the account. "A fine-looking mansion you built there, General," he said. He raised his eyebrows. "In the Swutland mountains. Interesting."

"What's that?" the old man asked, pointing at another area of the screen.

The driver clicked on it and frowned. "A spaceship?"

"You mean the new space station," Meckreen's back-seat companion said.

"No. It says spaceship."

A message appeared across the centre of the screen.

"Damn!" the driver said. "I lost the connection. Give me a second to open it again." He typed a few keys, then frowned.

"It's gone. I've no access at all." He turned to his fellow kidnapper. "Pick up that phone," he said.

The man complied. "Nothing," he said.

"He's found us," Meckreen said in a frightened whisper, sitting on the floor.

"Who?"

"Lord Luckran. The First Advisor."

The younger men argued over whether they should wait for the network to return or kill their captive immediately. The old man pondered.

Meckreen sat on the floor. He was certain Luckran had found him, and that he would dispose of him and his captors. The First Advisor knew him better than he knew himself. He knew he would betray the corps. He, commander of the Imperial Engineering Corps, could have died with his oath intact. Instead, he would die a coward, a failure, a disgrace.

He was jolted from his private recriminations when the door burst open. "Planes! We can hear planes." Already? He wondered how long he'd been sitting, staring at the floor.

Everyone ran outside into the night. Meckreen got slowly to his feet and followed. He looked up. It was dark, but he could see the lights and hear the jets. The villagers thought they would land and deploy troops, but he knew better. As the planes passed overhead, he listened carefully. He could hear the bombs dropping.

Chapter 9

Jeseque stepped off the treadmill, walked across the blue-grey carpet and through the glass doors to the narrow corridor beyond. To her right were the double doors leading into the hibernation centre. She looked to her left, her eyes running along the closed cabin doors on both sides of the corridor, all the way to the far end, to the lounge on the right, the kitchen on the left. With the rest of the crew in bed for the night, no light shone from either of the open portals.

Jeseque let the gymnasium door swing closed behind her and stepped through the frosted counterparts opposite, her presence automatically snapping the washroom's ceiling lights from slumber. White tiled surfaces and steel fixtures sparkled in their pristine youth. Diagonally opposite to her left, beyond wall hooks for towels and clothing, a row of six shower heads bowed to the concave floor. To her immediate left, six basins gripped the wall below a long mirror while beyond them the only areas of privacy were provided by five toilet cubicles.

Obviously, the designers of the nameless ship had not expected a female aboard. In the morning of the crew's first day out of hibernation, Jeseque had naively walked headlong into a scene of communal ablutions, a profusion of skin, hair and appendages. Quickly she'd backtracked, thankful she'd gone unnoticed. For most of the day she'd stayed in her cabin, bothered by no one. Captain Abrim had made his feelings about her very clear.

"Well isn't this a pretty sight," he'd said upon meeting her for the first time. "A female engineer. You should be in a museum. Not aboard my ship!" he'd spat, shaking his head in disgust. "Just stay out of my way, Debrone. That's all I ask. Is that clear?"

Jeseque was happy to oblige. She was like an owl, coming out at night when everyone else was asleep. She liked having the entire gymnasium to herself, or quietly eating a meal in the kitchen while considering her options. And of course it was the only sensible time to use the washroom.

She wondered how Ferist was getting on.

She walked past the wall hooks and through a door to the right that led to the laundry room. On metal shelves there were sets of clothes for the crew, arranged in different sizes. Grey knee-length shorts and matching short-sleeve tops. The bottom shelf held packets of disposable underwear and socks, again in different sizes.

A separate rack held black robes for the five magicians who were also aboard. Jeseque tilted her head. She couldn't get used to seeing those robes. It was baffling to find magicians aboard a spaceship. But then everything about the mission was mysterious. However, she was determined to unravel that mystery. It gave her something to do. And while on the treadmill, she'd come up with an idea that would help her get started.

Jeseque quickly got undressed, wrapped a towel about herself, then grabbed her dirty clothes from the floor and threw them in the hamper that sat beside the washing machine. She left the laundry room and crossed to the wall hook nearest the showers. She glanced at the door into the washroom to see if anyone was coming. After a moment's hesitation, she removed the towel and hung it on the hook. Someone might walk in, but there was nothing she could do about it.

She stepped under the shower head. There was a quiet click and the water came, warm and gentle. She closed her eyes and put her face beneath the cascade. The water massaged her skin like a million tiny pinpricks. She lowered her head and let it run through her hair. Her breathing was deep and contented.

She reached for the soap dispenser on the wall, filled her hands and rubbed them together. She washed quickly, eager to wrap herself in the towel once more. As she was rinsing, she turned around and put her head back, letting the water run through her hair and down her back and legs.

The door opened. She dived for the towel and held it before her. A crewman walked in and headed for the toilets. "I'm not looking," he said, with his right hand cupped to the side of his face. Jeseque stood still, the towel held in her armpits. "I'll only be a second," he called as he disappeared into a cubicle. She could hear the amusement in his voice. He urinated. It seemed to go on forever, but eventually he emerged, this time with his left hand to his face. He turned to the sink and washed his hands thoroughly, almost in slow motion. He looked at her through the mirror, then winked. Jeseque looked away, refusing to let herself be embarrassed or intimidated. "You're wasting water," he said. Jeseque glared at him. He smiled back as he rinsed his hands, wrapping one hand about the other, over and over. He wasn't at all concerned about the amount of water he was using. Of course there was no concern, since the water was recycled. But Jeseque knew he was hoping she would point that out, that she would argue with him. She ignored him. For a moment she wondered what she would do if he approached her, if he tried to grab the towel. Would anyone care if she was molested, even raped? But she forced such fears from her mind and again looked away from the intruder as he placed his hands beneath the dryer. She knew he was looking at her, but she was determined not to make eye contact again. Finally the dryer stopped and he headed for the door. "Don't forget to wash behind your ears," he said as he left.

Jeseque sighed with relief. She put the towel back on the hook, finished rinsing, grabbed the towel again and quickly dried herself while making her way back into the laundry centre. Moments later she was dressed in a set of the smallest garments available. Before launch, Tavenar had had someone provide her with female necessities, as he put it, but not clothes, other than underwear. She didn't mind; the men's clothes were comfortable, if a little big.

Jeseque returned to her cabin next to the kitchen. It was a tiny square room, as long as the narrow bed that was fixed to the wall opposite the door. To her right as she entered there was a small desk upon which sat a computer console. Jeseque sat down to type. She was a bit surprised Abrim had even bothered to give her a computer account. But it was at the lowest security level, giving her access to little more than the library of books, music and films.

Actually, there was something else: the operating system. Though she could make no changes to the system beyond her own account, she could learn how it worked, discover its weaknesses.

Since the craft was a self-contained unit, all data was stored in one central repository. When a message was sent from one person to another, the data itself did not go anywhere. Instead, the owner of the file was changed from sender to recipient. It was an old-style system, one she was surprised to find in a state-of-the-art spaceship.

Jeseque had almost skipped her shower because she was so eager to try out the idea she'd had while jogging. But time wasn't pressing on her and she'd figured it would be nicer to work on the idea while clean and refreshed rather than all sweaty.

She opened a new file and wrote a short computer program that would raise her status to what was appropriately known in computer parlance as control; it would give her complete control of the computer. She saved the file, then had the computer execute it. As expected, it politely informed her she did not have permission to execute the program.

Jeseque sent the program, as a message attachment, to Captain Abrim. She realised she was taking a chance; if Abrim was at his console right now, he'd see her message and wonder what was going on. But she was confident he was asleep. It was worth the risk.

Again, she asked the computer to run the program, and this time, as it belonged to the captain, the computer happily complied. A little excited now, Jeseque checked her account's status. The computer informed her she now had control. She sat back and smiled. Compared to the network on Earda, heavily secured, protected and monitored by the government, the security system on the ship was so basic as to be laughable. A locked door with the key under the mat. But of course the designers hadn't expected NALO to be aboard.

Thanks to her new status, the system menu was now heavily populated. Though she was tempted by the weapons subsystems, she moved past them to the virtual windows. A few seconds after launching the application, the screen was filled with stars. Controls allowed her to pan about, apparently accessing sensor arrays all about the ship. If the pictures were to be believed, they were in deep space.

But could she believe them? The sensor stream could be a fake. And if they were accelerating, how come she could pan all about and not see any rocket fire? Other than the stars, all she could see were the featureless grey walls.

The official explanation for the acceleration that provided a neat one gravity involved magic. It said so right there in the ship's documentation. Jeseque could hardly believe her eyes. Magic! It was preposterous. Magicians didn't work with engineers and scientists. They were an eccentric lot who believed in arm waving and words of power. Despite numerous accounts of their unnatural abilities, Jeseque never could bring herself to believe in them, filing them alongside ghosts and extraterrestrials.

That the sensor stream was fake and they weren't in space at all would be a far more likely explanation, if it wasn't for the fact that she clearly remembered going into orbit.

***

Jeseque strapped herself into the seat. The inside of the orbital looked very much like a passenger plane, except that it was turned on its end. A ladder ascended between rows of double seats. Jeseque sat in the bottom row on the left. Ferist sat across from her, on the other side of the ladder.

He had his eyes closed. His face was pale and his knuckles were white as he gripped the armrests. His excitement had dissipated as the moment of launch drew close.

She guessed he'd been fully briefed as he'd seemed full of enthusiasm while he mingled with his newfound crewmates. Jeseque suspected the crew were going out of their way to make it clear that he was very welcome, in order to highlight even more that she was not. And he was too stupid to realise it. He was also completely ignoring her and she was annoyed at finding herself feeling hurt.

Jeseque turned away from Ferist and tried to think. She was excited too, but also confused. She couldn't figure out why she was there. Somehow, it was for Tavenar's benefit, of that much she was sure. And Ferist's breach of security was most likely the catalyst. But no matter how much she pondered, she could not come up with a plausible theory.

The crew continued to come on board. As each man climbed the ladder, he looked over his left shoulder at her with disdain. Unable to endure so much attention, Jeseque looked down at her feet.

Her unexpected inclusion wasn't the only mystery. Where was the spaceship headed? And, if Ferist's descriptions were correct, why was free fall not part of the design?

Her ruminations were disturbed by a dark shape in her peripheral vision. She looked up and was flabbergasted to see a black robe moving past. She looked over at Ferist, to see his reaction, but he still had his eyes closed.

A second black robe climbed the ladder. Magicians? Surely not. She looked around. No one else seemed to be surprised by the unusually garbed astronauts, as three more filed past.

Jeseque smiled to herself. Not long ago she had been a frustrated and unappreciated NALO agent, passing on what was most likely useless information about fighter jets. Now she was about to go into orbit, to rendezvous with a curious spaceship, accompanied by five individuals who were either magicians or the entertainment troupe (she couldn't decide which was more bizarre). Suddenly life had become interesting.

The doors behind her hissed as they sealed tight. She watched Ferist squeeze his eyes shut and his breathing become heavy. With a rumble, the orbital began to shake. The noise grew to a roar. Jeseque was pushed hard against the soft-cushioned seat. At first it was only mildly uncomfortable, but within seconds she was finding it hard to breathe. For each intake she struggled to lift her leaden chest. However, despite the pain and effort, Jeseque was thrilled by the awesome power and acceleration that was firing her into space. Earda held her in a vice-like grip, like a jealous lover, but the relentless rockets battled on, setting her free.

The roaring and shaking ended abruptly. Jeseque arched her back as her lungs filled to capacity, then exhaled long and slow as her body rose from the seat, the straps preventing her from floating about the cabin.

She looked across at Ferist. He smiled at her sheepishly, then looked away. She noticed he was holding himself very still and was staring straight ahead. He didn't seem to be even considering looking out the window. She figured he was probably doing his best not to puke.

There was no way she was going to miss this opportunity. She undid her straps, anchored her feet beneath her seat and the one in front of her, then placed her face next to the tiny window. Patches of white cloud swirled across a curved blue ocean. One large circular bank of cloud, with a dark hole at its centre, was perched further above the water than its neighbours, as if it were on stilts. In the distance, the cloud and water disappeared in a haze. The edge of the world was a bright blue curve. Like a neon tube, the atmosphere was a striking contrast to the blackness of space. A delicate shell that protected the delicate organisms within.

To the right, the sun reflected blindingly off the enormously expansive icecap.

Absolutely beautiful. But space was diminishing with the encroaching ice. She wondered what would be left in a hundred years.

***

The windows across the aisle suddenly darkened. Jeseque craned her neck as she tried to catch a glimpse of the spaceship without, but all she could see was a curved grey shell.

She could feel the orbital making slight adjustments to its trajectory as it nudged itself towards its target. Moments later there was the bump, clunk and clank as the airlocks mated. Then came the hissing sound of the airlocks filling with air. A buzzer sounded and instantly the cabin was filled with movement. The black robes were the first to float by, followed by the captain and the rest of the crew.

Pointedly ignored, Jeseque waited until everyone else had disembarked. She unbuckled her straps and pulled herself along the ladder, around to the right and into the airlock.

The two sets of doors between the ships remained open and bright light spilled from the larger craft into the orbital. Though the pair of circular airlocks fitted together perfectly, the dividing line between them was obvious; every little scratch and stain on the old orbital was highlighted by the unblemished new craft.

As she crossed the divide, Jeseque noticed something strange: just a few yards further on, a padded mat was attached to the tunnel wall. Just beyond the mat, the tunnel became a rectangular corridor with very definite walls, ceiling and carpeted floor. The mat lined up with the floor. She also noticed the handholds, which she was using to pull herself forward, ended directly above the mat.

As Jeseque reached for the penultimate handhold, she felt a pull on her feet. She grabbed at the last handhold but lost her grip because she wasn't expecting to fall. She hit the padding with a thump. Laughter joined her from the end of the corridor. She lifted her head to see bright faces peeping around a corner for a moment before disappearing.

Jeseque got to her feet and stared at the floor. "It seems you were right, Ferist," she whispered. "Simulated gravity." She couldn't imagine how it could be achieved in free fall, other than making use of centripetal force. She looked back at the orbital. The ship wasn't rotating and she'd floated out of the orbital.

Another mystery.

She jumped off the padding onto the carpet, walked down the corridor and into the ship proper.

The captain was waiting for her. "Debrone," he said. "Remember, as far as I'm concerned, you're little more than a stowaway. Don't get in the way," he continued, delivering his earlier pep talk once more. "Become invisible. Understood?"

He didn't wait for an answer. He turned smartly and Jeseque followed him along a narrow corridor with closed double doors at regular intervals along the right. The surroundings were so ordinary that she felt she might be walking through a common apartment block or office building, except there were no windows.

The corridor turned right, then quickly left. Jeseque saw it extend many yards further, single doors advancing at regular intervals on both sides.

Two open portals were immediately on her right and left. A very ordinary-looking kitchen was on the right. To the left was a lounge spotted with comfortable sofas and armchairs upholstered in what looked like dark velvet. The room was softly lit and it reminded Jeseque of a music venue in Wesmork that Ferist and a few other students had taken her to in her college days.

The crew was in the lounge, awaiting the captain. They relaxed in the plush seating. All except the black robes, who stood together at the far end.

Ferist was sitting near the back. Their eyes met briefly. He gave her a tiny reassuring smile as she found a seat near the door.

Captain Abrim walked to the front. He looked about the room, making eye contact with each person individually, except for Jeseque and, she noted, the black robes.

"The moment has arrived," he proclaimed, "an historic moment, a landmark moment. We are to be the first interstellar travellers."

Jeseque raised her eyebrows. She tried to catch Ferist's eye, but he seemed enraptured.

"We embark upon a sacred mission," the captain continued, "to extend the Velkren's care to a heathen and ignorant world. You have sacrificed much to this noble cause, but your rewards will be eternal.

"And that is not the only reason to celebrate this exceptional mission," he went on, his tone changing almost imperceptibly as he glanced at the black robes. "For the first time in history, magic and engineering have been combined."

Jeseque could hardly believe her ears. She wondered what kind of looney show she'd been thrown into.

"It is thanks to these men," Abrim said, gesturing to the magicians, "that we are able to walk about the ship in comfort, even though it's in free fall. They will also provide propulsion, subjecting the ship to a constant acceleration that will again provide us with a comfortable one gravity and take us to our destination in as little as thirty years from Earda's point of view. For us, of course, less than seven years will have passed. Another landmark moment, as we will be the first to accelerate to velocities where time dilation becomes staggeringly apparent. But we won't even have to while away the half dozen plus years in boredom as most of the time we'll be asleep, thanks to the revolutionary new technology, Deep Sleep."

Jeseque frowned. She didn't like the sound of Deep Sleep.

Abrim held out his hands and smiled. "It promises to be a very relaxing trip." This was greeted by sounds of approval. "No other pioneers were ever promised such an untroubled voyage. But let's not be complacent. During our times awake it is imperative we ensure all is right with the ship.

"Let us now begin the way we wish to continue. Before the orbital will be set free, before we initiate launch, every system on board will be rechecked and verified." He clapped his hands once. "You know your duties. Go to them."

***

The systems had been checked, the orbital sent home, and the ship accelerated out of orbit. The crew got into their hibernation units and slept for a year.

At least that's what they'd been told. Jeseque wasn't buying it. She'd wondered about cosmic radiation, which would be a serious problem if they truly were in deep space. Prolonged exposure to cosmic radiation would have serious health effects on the astronauts. But according to the ship's documentation, this problem was conveniently dealt with by the shroud, some kind of field generated by the magicians that kept the ship hidden as well as protecting it from radiation.

As far as Jeseque could see, there was no evidence the shroud really existed.

Though there was no way to know for sure (Jeseque was well aware there was no test she could perform that would distinguish gravity from acceleration), it seemed much more likely that they'd been moved back to Earda while they slept. And they'd only been asleep for days, maybe as little as hours, not an entire year.

She played with her lip as she pondered the more nagging question: why? Even if she was convinced the mission was a hoax, it didn't explain why they would go to all that trouble.

Jeseque decided to read the magicians' files, to see what she could learn about them. She was surprised to find she couldn't open them. She could see their files on the system, but was denied access, even with control status. They had to belong to another group, one above control. A super group. "Now I know who's really in charge here."

Almost three hours later, Jeseque gave up trying to break into the super group. She got up from the desk, stretched her cramped limbs and massaged the small of her back where the ache was most insistent. She headed for the kitchen, craving coffee.

As in the washroom, the kitchen sparkled to life once she crossed the threshold. To the left were three aluminium tables surrounded by matching chairs. To the right, the refrigerator sat beside a large sink. Opposite the door were hot plates, an instant oven and a coffee machine. Jeseque walked across to the machine, selected a cup from the overhead cabinet and popped it under the spout. After pushing a few buttons, a stream of the finest artificial coffee steamed and hissed its way to the rim.

Jeseque stood with her back to the counter, sipping the dark beverage while contemplating the night's achievements and discoveries. She'd raised her computer status to what she had assumed was the maximum, only to find there was a level above, with much tighter security. It was now evident the magicians held the real power and that Abrim was top of the second tier only.

But were they really magicians? Though she referred to them as such, she was far from believing in magic. It could all be sleight of hand. Or maybe not. Maybe the magicians were genuine and the military had finally discovered their secrets, brought them into the realm of science.

Jeseque decided it was pointless to debate further as she didn't have enough information to work on. She pushed away from the counter with her butt and returned to her room to read up on the ship's weapons system.

***

Jeseque piled the clothes into the machine, slammed the door shut and stabbed a few buttons on the control panel. Abrim had found something for her to do after all and she was pissed off. It was, he'd declared, her duty to ensure the clothes in the hamper were washed, dried, folded and placed on the shelves. He'd got enormous pleasure from assigning such a menial task to a woman. She had so desperately wanted to create a fuss but knew well she couldn't. It made more sense to grit her teeth and get on with it.

A relay clicked and water poured into the machine for half a minute then stopped. The drum rotated, first one way, then the other, the grey clothes tumbling, the water gurgling. She watched the white soap run down the glass door. Somehow, it soothed her raging spirit. She'd always found the automated process of clothes washing very satisfying. She wasn't sure why. There was something about being able to walk away from the machine knowing it would go about the task systematically and reliably.

"At least it doesn't take long, and I can do it at night," she said as she walked out of the washroom. She noticed she was talking to herself a lot. As a loner, it was something she'd always done, but it was becoming more prevalent. She shrugged. "So what?"

Ferist used to tease her that it was the only way she could converse with someone as intelligent as herself.

Other than the degradation of having to play housemaid, everything was wonderful. She slept during the day and worked at night, encountering no one. Two nights earlier she'd scoured the computer system and its documentation for a hint of some form of transmitter but found nothing. The following night she tried again. When she sensed her frustrations growing, she decided to put her hopes of communicating with the outside world on hold. For a change, she returned to the craft's weapons system.

A new missile had been developed, one designed to be fired from orbit at targets on the planet's surface. How NALO would appreciate being made aware of this alarming threat.

Jeseque entered the kitchen and brewed a mug of coffee. Standing with her back to the coffee machine, she sipped the hot beverage. Instead of alerting NALO to the danger, perhaps she could remove it.

Suddenly deciding she didn't need the coffee, she poured it down the sink, rinsed the cup and left it on the draining board. She stepped from the kitchen and turned left. A few paces away the corridor swung right, then left as it continued down one side of the ship. The first set of double doors she encountered led to the food stores. After that came the control centre, the nuclear reactor, the hangar for a pair of orbit-to-surface vehicles and lastly a compartment into which, like the super group areas within the computer, she was unable to gain entrance. She stood and looked at the sealed door for a moment, again wondering what secrets it hid.

Shrugging, she moved on, passing the airlock on her right and following the corridor around to the left. Halfway down on the right stood the entrance to the missile bay. The bay itself was at the very end of the ship, with the launch tubes advancing up either side, according to the ship's schematics.

By the entrance was a small keypad and into this Jeseque entered her personal crew number. If she hadn't elevated herself to control, she would have been denied access. But now, as expected, the doors slid apart and the lights inside came on.

The computer had reported an arsenal of 20 missiles, each one 12 feet long and one foot in diameter. Jeseque knew little about them and cared less. From her cursory glance at the documentation, she had learned they were kinetic, their destructive potential due to tremendous velocity. Designed as orbit-to-surface missiles, speeds many times that of sound were easily achieved.

While humans had advanced in so many ways, she found it depressing to see the inordinate amount of effort they still put into throwing stones at each other.

Jeseque stepped into the bay and walked down the aisle that formed a line of symmetry. On either side of that line, ten missiles were stored vertically in metal racks, only their bulbous noses visible. With their matte beige finish they looked like eggs in a carton.

From each rack a conveyor system looped around, like a baggage belt at an airport, to terminate at a launch tube door, into which a missile would be loaded.

The launch sequence was entirely automated. As Jeseque reached the far end of the bay and turned back, she felt like an insect inside a gargantuan gun, double-barrelled. These could be the largest and fastest bullets ever fired, and if they struck a planet, they would cause catastrophic damage. It would be best to ensure they never would.

And it might also help answer the question: was she amongst the first interstellar voyagers, or were they dupes in an elaborate and mystifying deception? If the latter, then activating the launch sequence might be enough to shatter the illusion.

***

The following night, Jeseque was surprised by a timid knock on her door. She got up from the desk and placed her hand on the handle. "Who's there?"

Before the reply came, she was certain of whom it would be. "It's Ferist," came the whisper, almost like déjà vu.

Jeseque opened the door and smiled.

"I know we're supposed to pretend we don't know each other," he said, "but that's only when people are watching. Right?"

She hesitated. In the small hours of the morning, with the rest of the crew fast asleep, she'd been about to head for the missile bay. But it seemed Ferist too had been waiting to make sure he wouldn't be noticed. She watched his smile evaporate in the heat of her hesitation. "Yeah, of course," she responded, before she'd properly made up her mind. "Come in." This had better be a quick chat, she thought as his smile rekindled. She had work to do. She sat on the bed while Ferist sat by the desk.

"So, how are you getting on with Abrim and the crew?" she asked.

"Fine. They showed me about the ship and have given me a few things to do. But the ship pretty much runs itself so there's not a lot to be done. Our real work begins when we arrive at the new world."

"Is that so?" she said.

"I wish they'd let you get involved. The captain's being a bit ridiculous."

"He's a sexist prick! They all are."

Ferist laughed. "Straight to the point, as usual. But you're right."

"So what do you make of all this?"

Ferist frowned. "What?"

She rolled her eyes. "This, you clown," she exclaimed, throwing her arms wide to indicate their surroundings.

"It's a spaceship," Ferist replied, as if it should be self-apparent.

"With a perfect one gravity."

"Acceleration."

"And where are we accelerating to in such a hurry?"

"You know where we're going."

"I do?"

Ferist smiled mischievously. "I've waited so long for you to say those words."

"That's not even funny."

"I thought you said I was a clown."

"The sad type. So where are we going?"

"Oh, all right. To the new world—"

"Why?

"What do you mean, why?"

"Why are we going?" Jeseque gave Ferist an intense look.

"To make way for the Velkren."

"Really? Who says?"

"Everyone. They all say it. They're very excited."

"I bet they are. So, the Velkren. Looking for a new holiday destination, is he?"

"You shouldn't talk like that. The Velkren will safeguard this new world, the same as he does ours."

"So it's subjugation."

"Why is everything so negative with you?"

"Because that's the way things are. I have no idea what all this is about, but there's one thing I'm absolutely sure of. Whatever it is, it's not for the benefit of the ordinary people. It's for the rich and powerful. People like your father."

"All of a sudden it's my father's fault."

"He's one of them. He lives a life of luxury while his serfs make him richer each day."

"My father does the best he can for his tenants. He keeps their rents low and if anyone is finding it hard to pay, he provides them with very low interest loans."

"So not only does he get the rent out of them, but he gets extra from the very ones who are struggling the most. And they're the ones working the land. Why should they be his tenants? They should own the land."

"But it belongs to him."

"Only because he inherited it. He didn't earn it."

"So you don't think people should inherit?"

"Exactly. When someone dies, their assets should be shared amongst the people."

"But you know that will never happen. It's not in our nature. Thousands, millions of years ago, we had to be aggressive to survive. And we've never lost that trait. Like animals, we fight for ourselves. But what separates us from the animals is our compassion. Even though it's against our nature, we try to help others. And all we can hope is that those with power and wealth do the best they can for those less well off."

"Hope? I think we need to do more than hope!"

Ferist smiled. "I've missed this about you. How passionate you are."

"You can't just end the argument with that sort of patronising crap."

"I'm trying to end it before you tear me to shreds. I never stand a chance against you."

Jeseque laughed. "All right. Enough for one night. Do you want a coffee?"

"Yeah." He got up. "But you stay there. I'll get it."

Ferist left and Jeseque sat back, propping herself up with her elbows and stretching out her legs. She was actually enjoying herself. She hadn't realised how much she missed conversation. Before Ferist, she had never even noticed the void, because she'd never had someone to talk to. She hadn't known what she'd been missing.

Her smile faded. What was she doing? Why had she mentioned coffee? She should have told him she was tired and sent him back to his room. Instead, she realised, she'd been glad of the diversion, because she was afraid to perform her duty. Oh sure, she could do it the following night. But what if something happened and she missed her chance?

157

Ferist arrived back and Jeseque sat up to receive a steaming mug. "You say the rich don't care about the poor," Ferist continued as he retook his seat. "But look at your situation. You were poor, and now you're an engineer. Who paid for your education?"

"I won a scholarship," she answered, allowing herself to be drawn into the conversation once more, the chance to say goodnight slipping by.

"Exactly. Money provided by wealthy people. And they get nothing in return for it."

"Maybe they do. Maybe it makes them feel good, to think they've helped one poor soul up out of the gutter. But anyway, that's not the point. I got a decent education because I excelled. But what about those who aren't as good as me but who are more intelligent and hard-working than the rich brats in college?"

"Like me."

Jeseque smiled. "Yeah," she answered playfully, "like you."

"All right, tell me what my father should be doing."

"Zervnia's greatest asset is its wine. Right?" At his nod, she continued. "Who owns the vineyards?"

"We own most of them. Something like seventy percent. The rest is owned by a handful of families."

"But don't you see that's unfair? I'd redistribute the vineyards equally among the people."

Ferist laughed. "You couldn't do that. Everyone would own a few acres. It would be ridiculous. Most people don't know what it takes to make a vineyard work."

Jeseque sighed. "I'm not an idiot. I don't mean literally share them out. I mean the people would own shares in the vineyards. They could still be run by those who are so successfully managing them right now, but the profits would be shared with everyone."

Ferist shook his head. "The owners wouldn't like that."

"Well of course they wouldn't. But that's a poor reason for not doing it."

Jeseque put her mug on the floor and lay back on the bed, relaxing completely as they talked some more. She yawned and stretched, arching her back. Ferist's eyes opened wide as they fixed themselves on her breasts. Jeseque collapsed on the bed, laughing. "You look like you're about to lick your lips."

Ferist looked away. "I'm sorry."

"It's all right."

He turned back to her and smiled. She wondered why he was always so happy. "I thought you didn't want anything to do with me any more," she said, "the way you were behaving."

"Don't be ridiculous, Jeseque. I was just playing the part. Major Tavenar said it was vital they think we don't know each other."

"I have a feeling that was simply because it made it easier for him to get us aboard. It probably doesn't matter now."

"Yeah," he said. "Maybe." He joined her on the bed and kissed her. "I'm sorry. I don't like pretending we're strangers."

"It's OK. You stick with the crew. Abrim wants me to remain invisible and I prefer being nocturnal anyway."

***

Jeseque peeked out of her cabin. Both the lounge and the kitchen were in darkness. By ship time, it was a couple of hours past midnight, a time when she normally felt confident about wandering the corridors undisturbed. But this night she was tense. A little earlier, when Ferist had come knocking for the second night in a row, she'd pretended to be asleep. She was still annoyed at herself for feeling a tad guilty.

Though she was perfectly alone, Jeseque kept looking over her shoulder on the way to the missile bay. It brought back unwelcome memories of walking along the dark corridor to her apartment, a frightened little girl expecting a hand on her shoulder at every step. More than once the hand had been real, and she'd had to face her unforgiving mother who saw nothing but a useless brat who couldn't do a simple thing like go and get a pack of cigarettes.

With a conscious effort Jeseque banished such enervating memories. She reached the missile bay, glanced over her shoulder one last time, and typed in her number. The doors slid open and she quickly stepped inside, closing them behind her. She took a couple of deep breaths, willing her heart to slow down. Though she knew it was very unlikely, she kept expecting the doors to slide open again.

Each missile had a self-destruct mechanism built in, just in case a strike needed to be aborted after the missile had been launched. Jeseque considered this extremely important. Officially they were in deep space, but she was afraid they might still be in orbit. She didn't want to be the one to indiscriminately fire 20 missiles at Earda and perhaps wipe out humanity.

Back in her cabin, she had set up a program to expel and destroy the entire arsenal. She would love to have been able to stay in the cabin and execute the program from there, but her presence in the bay was necessary. She walked to the computer console, eyeing the big red button next to it.

She hesitated. What if the self-destruct mechanism didn't work? Not for the first time, she considered aborting the mission, but she was afraid she would end up ruing that decision. If they were in orbit, then the missiles might eventually be used against NALO. This was her chance to prevent that.

Jeseque ran the program. The computer requested confirmation. She responded in the affirmative. As if it was genuinely surprised, the computer asked her was she sure she wanted to launch all the missiles. "Yes!" she said as she stabbed a few keys. The red button glowed and Jeseque lifted her fist, ready to slam it down. Then she paused as another scary scenario developed in her mind.

If they really were in space, then launching the missiles would be harmless. But what if they weren't? What if they were on Earda, perhaps in a warehouse outside Wesmork? Launching the missiles might kill her, the crew and many more innocent bystanders.

She stood with her lips tight, her eyes entranced by the glowing red button. She tried to think logically. If it was a hoax, then surely the missiles would not actually contain rockets. They would be duds. Launching them wouldn't actually do anything.

With this thought foremost in her mind, she lifted her fist again. Gritting her teeth, she tried to ignore a voice in her head that claimed the missiles would have to be real if they were to convince the engineers. Before that voice became too loud, she slammed down her fist.

There was a click and the left rack's gate opened. Metal hands reached in and grasped the first missile. The hands retracted, then lowered the end of the missile into a circular slot in the conveyor belt. The belt jumped to life, looping around the rack to present the missile to the open launch tube door. More mechanical fingers turned the missile on its side and slid it into the tube, out of sight.

Jeseque held her breath. She pictured the bay doors opening and a stranger running in with his arms flailing, screaming stop before she killed them all. She watched the tube door close. For a second or two, nothing happened. Then there was a rumble. The missile was on its way. Jeseque's mind formed two pictures at once. One was darkness scattered with tiny points of light and one bright light receding into the distance. The other showed that same bright light rapidly approaching a brick wall. She actually hunched her shoulders, awaiting the explosion.

It didn't happen, and her mind banished the second picture. She let out a long breath as the conveyor belt on the right came to life.

As she ran another program on the console, one that would open a virtual window to the outside, she decided they truly were in space. Surely the subterfuge would not have made provisions for her unexpected actions.

The program ran and the window appeared, showing nothing but stars. There was no sign of Earda, but that didn't prove they weren't in orbit, and she was desperate to see evidence of the missiles self-destructing.

As the second missile was launched, she felt the ship shudder slightly. The flare of the rocket appeared on the screen almost immediately. The missile receded rapidly, then exploded. There was no sign of the first missile. She was confident it had exploded too.

Now she could relax and enjoy the missile parade—left, right, left, right...She was suddenly glad that the red button had forced her to be there. Watching those rockets disappear one after another was very satisfying. She was sure NALO would approve.

Jeseque would have preferred to stay, to watch all 20 missiles self-destruct. She was concerned some might fail. But, she reasoned, there was nothing she could do about that now and she was a little worried the noise and the shaking might wake someone.

She returned quickly to her cabin and opened the same virtual window again. She listened to the rumble of another missile as it was fired into space. On her side of the ship, the gymnasium wrapped around the cabins, extending down the back to meet the kitchen. On the other side, the lounge met the washroom. She hoped these buffers, between the launch tubes and the crew, would muffle the noise enough to leave them sleeping.

A missile was being launched, from alternate tubes, once a minute, approximately. In 20 minutes, the gun was empty, and there was no way to reload. Jeseque thought about going down to the bay, just for the satisfaction of seeing those empty egg cartons. Instead, she hid her actions by resetting the missile quantity in the database to 20 and deleting all references to her actions from the logs. Before removing the control status from her own account, she created two control accounts, for later use, one much harder to find than the other.

Even though it would be hours yet before the crew awoke, she got into bed. She tried to sleep, but excitement and apprehension kept her awake.

Chapter 10

The snail slithered along the ground, leaving behind it an acidic trail that slowly seeped into the porous rock. Ponderously, but with great determination, it approached a fork in the tunnel, which it could just make out in the pale light emanating from the cave walls. Which way to go, left or right? It didn't really matter, as its intention was to cover as much of the labyrinth as possible, depositing its latent secretion along the way. Both tunnels led to areas the snail had not yet visited.

It chose left. As it moved along another nondescript passage, it pondered its decision. Why not right? Was it a purely random decision, because it made no difference either way? Or was randomness intrinsic to the nature of the universe itself? Was the snail's decision to enter the caves in the first place just as arbitrary, despite the fact it was a decision that had not been arrived at lightly?

Hours passed. It approached another intersection. Again, it didn't matter which one it chose, but for the sake of balance it went right.

A day later, it regretted the choice. As it approached the next junction, it sensed a physical alteration in the maze of tunnels. Suddenly, instead of leading to virgin territory, the path led to an area the snail had traversed perhaps 15 years earlier.

The snail stopped. For nearly 40 years it had crawled about the endless and featureless tunnels, quietly suffusing the rock with its dormant agents. It was making progress, but there was still a long way to go before an adequate percentage had been infected. And these setbacks, due to the dynamic nature of the labyrinth, were not helping.

And yet what was the point in becoming despondent? The snail had known from the outset it wasn't going to be easy. It trudged on, bolstering its spirits with memories of happier and more interesting times. It had the ability to relive those days in perfect clarity, but it refrained from doing so in case such mental activity would betray it to the caves. Instead, it made do with low-fidelity recall, the type creatures were limited to.

***

The snail felt relief. For far too long it had gone about in circles, desperately trying to reach untravelled territories. Most of the time when it was thrown off course it was able to get back into untouched tunnels relatively quickly. But on that particular occasion almost a year earlier, subsequent shifts of the paths had led the snail deep into infected areas. Many times, while slithering along rock it had slithered along decades earlier, it had considered giving up. The task was simply impossible, at least for a lone snail.

But at last, it made it. It inched across rock that was exactly the same as the smooth grey substance that had slid beneath it for over 300 days, except for one glorious difference. One delightful absence. For the first time in 7,482 hours, the snail resumed its secretion.

It was a few hours later when the snail first noticed the sound. It began as a slight hiss, but it quickly grew to a rumble, and then a roar. For a creature grown used to events unfolding over days and months and years, it was an abrupt, almost instantaneous change. Before it could react, the water was upon it. The torrent easily ripped the snail from the rock and threw it back through the caves. The snail tumbled about in the water, helpless. Seconds later it was spat from the mountain, its years of toil amounting to nothing.

Rocks tumbled and crashed as the mountain shook with fury and fear.

***

"Very fanciful, Arnelius," I laughed. "But I can't picture you as a snail. You're much too hasty."

"There's no better way to describe it. Can you imagine putting in all that laborious effort? Forty years of my life!"

"Forty years is nothing."

"Don't be so flippant!" Arnelius snapped. "Would you do it?"

"Of course not. I don't know what possessed you. Are you mad?"

"It's all your fault. You're the one who told them."

"I didn't tell them. They wouldn't communicate with an unnatural like me."

"So how did they find out?"

"You know how stories spread. Destlar is rather fascinating."

"Fascinating! It means nothing to you, the pain he causes."

"And why should it? When a wolf tears a lamb to pieces, does it bother you? Why don't you entwine yourself within the mind of the wolf and try to change his nature?"

I still couldn't understand why it mattered so much, but I felt bad for destroying his plans. "I'm sorry, Arnelius. I didn't think they'd get involved. I've never known the Necrophobes to act before. It's against their religion. But of course they've never been in this position before. They probably think what you were doing was sacrilege."

News of Destlar and his extremely brief and terrified sojourn amongst the Grid Riders, during his dramatic encounter with Prunsios the Prefect, had eventually reached the Necrophobes, thanks mainly to me, as I'd been telling the story to any who'd listen for years. It threw them into a frenzy. Usually, they only get to worship the Perpetuators (their ludicrous appellation for entities like Destlar who unwittingly join the grid) after their ascension. But here they could honour one before his birth. Arnelius's efforts to tame Destlar by embedding himself inside the lunatic's mind must have horrified them. Nevertheless, I was amazed they became involved.

"It is their central tenet," Arnelius agreed, "that one should never act, only observe. But it seems one of them, Listur, was unable to resist. He's been threatened with excommunication, apparently."

"So he's unlikely to get involved again," I said.

"I don't care. I'm not about to start from scratch."

Chapter 11

Blindfolded, the young man was helped from the car. A coat was placed upon his shoulders and he quickly drew it together as the stinging wind cut through him. At least the blindfold protected his ears. A strong grip on his right shoulder guided him, his shoes crunching snow. It was a welcome sound, a familiar sensation, a childhood memory.

Up three steps, through a door, then another and into warm air in which the smell of chicken stew mingled with the scent of burning candle. The grip was released, he heard the door close behind him, then the outer door closing, then silence. He stood still, waiting. There was movement in another room, the clank of a lid on a pot, the rattle of crockery. Then footfalls.

"Lieutenant Olsker," said a gentle voice. "I'm terribly sorry. Please remove the blindfold. A necessary inconvenience, but your escort should not have left you like that."

Olsker pulled the black cloth up over his head. He was standing in a small room, a wooden table between him and a diminutive figure holding a plate of dark heavy bread with a thick crust. The man set the plate in the middle of the table and gestured to a chair. "Please, sit down. You must be hungry. The soup is ready. Make yourself comfortable while I dish out a couple of bowls."

Olsker removed the coat from his shoulders and hung it on the back of the chair, then sat down. The table was bare but for the plate of bread. About the table were three other chairs. The timber floor was worn and scratched, but clean. To his left there were two old armchairs either side of a fireplace. The armchairs looked comfortable. A small coal fire took the chill out of the air.

Beyond the fireplace was the door to the kitchen, from which drifted the enticing smell that was making his stomach twist in anticipation. To his right, heavy brown curtains held at bay the coming night. The room was illuminated by one naked bulb hanging from the centre of the ceiling.

The aroma of burning wax had all but dissipated. He wondered if he had interrupted something. A ritual, perhaps? He looked about for candles but found none. Perhaps he had imagined the smell.

The man emerged from the kitchen, carrying two steaming bowls. With a round face and a bald pate, he looked like an old farmer. Olsker had expected something different, someone exuding strength and intelligence. But he felt comfortable in the presence of this ordinary man in his modest abode.

The man placed a bowl in front of Olsker and handed him a spoon, then sat down and tucked into his own, his head close to the bowl. With his free hand he grabbed a slice of bread and, peeping out from under his heavy eyebrows, gestured to Olsker with a nod. "Don't be shy."

Olsker took a large mouthful of the thick broth filled with lumps of chicken, carrots and potatoes. Following his host's example, he dipped bread into the bowl, letting it soak for a moment, then fought a little with the hard crust as he took a bite. It was wholesome and filling, as was the stew, the simple food he'd grown up with, non-pretentious, cheap and effective. He enjoyed every spoonful.

The man pushed the empty bowl away and sat back, satisfied. Olsker a moment later did likewise. "Again, I apologise for the manner in which you were escorted here. You have of course earned our trust, but it is a necessary precaution."

"I understand, sir."

"You have done very well, Lieutenant. Others have failed where you have succeeded. And now we've reached a point where a decision must be made."

"The decision is made, sir. I'm ready."

"Yes, you are. From what I hear, you are determined, resolute. However, I want to remind you of the risks." The older man raised his hand, arresting the lieutenant's response. "Even if you succeed in this undertaking, there is very little chance of you surviving. If you go through with this, you'll most likely be dead in two weeks."

No one had ever put it to Olsker so bluntly and the words caused him to pause, which of course was their purpose. But the lieutenant forced the negativity from his mind and decided to be annoyed instead. He had hoped the intention of this meeting was to encourage him, to congratulate him on his bravery. He was determined to proceed. But of course he was afraid, and reminding him of the danger did nothing but feed his fear. It just meant he had to try harder to suppress it.

"I understand and appreciate your concern, sir. But I've made up my mind. I've worked hard for this moment and I won't let it pass me by."

"Then all I can do is wish you good luck." Knowing the interview was closing, they both stood up. "Go now. Spend some time with your family."

Olsker was met at the door and again blindfolded. As he was taken to the waiting car, he wondered what the point of the meeting had been.

***

Hervan Willkob pulled the curtains aside and watched the young man being helped into the car. In a few hours, he would be home, at the house where he had been born. Willkob had been advised not to meet the lieutenant, but he'd wanted to see the boy's face, to commit it to memory. He knew there was a good chance he'd be haunted by that face, but he didn't see why he should be spared the pain. Even then, it would hardly be just penance for sacrificing a fellow human. And what about the others who would die? Would they be denied the chance to torment him, just because they remained anonymous?

Willkob sighed. Was he wrong to send this boy to his death, even if it was for the greater good? Was he wrong to ask him to kill many innocent people? He knew that over the next two weeks leading up to the Northern Solstice, he would consider calling the whole thing off many times. "May Lurg damn them forever for putting me in this position."

As the car went out of sight around a bend in the road, the ex-priest of the Order of Lurg opened the curtains wider, then went to the kitchen to fetch the candles. He placed the pair in the middle of the table and lit them with a match. Melted wax ran down the sides of the white cylinders to solidify at the bottom, adding to the mounds that kept the candles upright on the small plates.

He pulled out a chair and knelt before it, elbows on the seat, knees cracking as they took his weight on the hard timber floor. He tried to clear his mind, to seek guidance, but it was difficult. As it often did, his mind's eye returned to that fateful moment in the apartment building in Gernaturov, when he'd witnessed the murder of a precious child. Murdered by a man hundreds of miles away, in the safety of a luxurious palace. A man who pretended to be a guardian of the people.

His chest tightened and tears formed, the memory's effect undiminished over the decades. Willkob forced his inner eye elsewhere. He recalled the day he quietly left his post in Gernaturov, not long after meeting the Prelate in Wesmork. His early years as a teacher in the small town outside of which he now lived. Holding class in the little stone building with its single room, in the centre of which a black stove squatted below a pipe that connected with the chimney in the hipped roof. The only request Willkob had made was to have the interior painted in the spectrum; the right side of the wall opposite the entrance was painted red, the left side violet, with the other five colours processing in order around the room. Those in the know within NALO connected this request with Willkob's devotion to the

God of Light. Everyone else thought he was simply decorating the school in a manner pleasing to children.

Though it was never talked about, the townspeople knew the quiet teacher was a NALO agent. Some even suspected he was quite important. But no one dreamed he was in fact its leader.

Even now, the bittersweet memory of sitting by the fire with his predecessor left a lump in his throat.

***

The meeting of NALO's High Command ended. There had been a brief discussion over whether to proceed with the planned robbery of a bank. Some felt the job was being rushed. Others felt it was worth the risk, if the intelligence they'd received was accurate. "The vault is full," one of the enthusiasts had reiterated, "because the convoy is stuck, thanks to the early snow. But it will surely make it through by next week and we'll have missed the chance. It's easier to rob a bank than that heavily armed convoy."

It was decided to go ahead with the raid and the men and women rose from the table and made for the exit. Willkob, recalling his first outing with NALO years earlier, was putting on his hat and gloves when the leader called to him. "Come sit by the fire."

Willkob was surprised. He said farewell to his comrades, then removed his hat, gloves and coat and laid them on the bare table. He walked across the thin carpet to the armchair by the fire. The leader slowly lowered herself into the opposite chair. The timber creaked as it took her weight. "Will you throw another log on there before you sit down, Hervan?"

"Yes, ma'am." Willkob reached over to the bucket by the fire and grabbed a short piece of a stout branch. He threw it into the smouldering embers, then sat down. He looked about the austere cabin. The curtains were light, the carpet threadbare, the furniture old and worn. "You should be living in greater comfort than this," Willkob said.

"And what would be the use? Would it make my muscles feel any better, or younger?"

Willkob looked at the old woman's hands as they lay upon the armrests. The rheumatism had twisted them into claws. "It might," he replied as he looked up and allowed himself to be trapped by a pair of sparkling blue eyes. Willkob couldn't help but smile. Each time he met the leader, she seemed more worn and disfigured. But those eyes always radiated happiness, contentedness.

Her jet-black hair was pulled back into a ponytail. There wasn't a touch of grey. Whenever she was asked about this marvel, she claimed it was because she didn't wash her hair as often as others. She would laugh as she said it, like it was the first time she told the joke.

"I will soon retire, Hervan."

"No!"

"Yes. Of course. I can't go on forever and I want to spend more time with my grandchildren." She smiled as she shook her head. "They're getting big far too quickly."

"But we need you."

"I'll still be here. But I won't lead. You will. Don't look so surprised. You know you're the one for the job."

"But Dirc..."

"Yes, he thinks he should replace me. And a few more are considering their chances. But they all expect you to be their biggest threat, and they're right. I can't see anything preventing you winning, once I endorse you. But I need to know you're willing."

Willkob looked at the log in the hearth and the few adventurous flames that were licking its sides. Though he was confident in his abilities, he was frightened. Six years earlier, when he had been elevated to the High Command, he had been put in charge of education. And he had done a lot of good. More children were in school. The schools had better resources. He had directed his agents in Wesmork, teaching them how to appeal to the guilty conscience of the rich and powerful. Donations of books and supplies had increased dramatically.

Sick children used to regularly fail to turn up at his own school, all for the want of medicines that families in the South took for granted. And so his agents began another appeal, and Willkob set up mobile clinics that visited schools.

He was proud of his efforts. On the High Command, one could do so much. But the leader had the ultimate responsibility. Not just for education, or health, or food, but for everything and everyone. It was a daunting task. And yet he believed he would do better than any of the other likely candidates.

And of course it might allow him to pursue his primary goal, one he had neglected for years, due to a complete lack of support. In fact, this might be an opportunity to do something about that.

"I will accept," he answered at last, "if you agree to support my efforts to assassinate the Emperor."

The leader laughed. "Nice try."

Willkob was hurt. "I'm not joking."

"Hervan," she pleaded, "I thought you had put that nonsense behind you. You haven't mentioned it in years."

"Because no one takes me seriously. And I can't understand why. Is it not in our manifesto?"

"Yes, it is. And I would love to remove it. Because it's only talk, but damaging talk. It makes us appear more sinister, more frightening to the people in the South. We would gain more sympathy if our ultimate goal was not the murder of their spiritual leader."

"But that is our goal!"

"It is not. Anyway, to try would be suicide."

"I disagree. Of course there would be retaliation. But we could withstand that, if we were properly prepared. And Alyna would then come forth, the rightful heir."

"Luckran would wipe us out in a matter of days, then take Alyna to Wesmork, to be his puppet."

"If he could so easily wipe us out, then why hasn't he done so already?"

"Come on, Hervan. Don't pretend to be so naive. He hasn't wiped us out because he doesn't need to. We say it's because his troops are afraid to come into the mountains, but that's just propaganda."

The old woman sat forward. "If I am to endorse you, I need to know you will not put us all at risk, Hervan. Luckran enjoys the status quo. We're his bogeyman. He can justify all sorts of draconian measures simply by pointing to the savages in the North. But should he even suspect the leader of NALO is plotting the Emperor's assassination, then he'll wipe us out and find someone else to scare his citizens."

By now the log was surrounded by dancing flames. Sap bubbled and hissed as it seeped from the end and dripped onto the ashes below. Willkob pictured the sap as a multitude of tiny creatures desperately trying to escape the heat, leaving their beloved home to be destroyed by the relentless fire. Would that happen to his people if he dared to attack Destlar?

He silently watched the flames dance. The log settled some more into the consuming flames. "You're right," he said at last. "It's not worth the risk."

***

But Willkob had been unable to forget completely his principal desire. It lay dormant, until it was awakened by a chance reading of a report submitted years earlier by a novice agent. The information within the report—detailed schematics of the Imperial Protector fighter jet's electronic systems—was of little use. But it gave NALO's leader an idea. More than two decades after the report was written, Willkob's plan was about to go into action.

Lieutenant Hurfle Olsker was of the Kervilian tribe, a small group of people who'd been forced from their fertile valley to the south-east three generations earlier. They had a strong representation in NALO, their sons and daughters encouraged from early years to fight. Olsker (which was not his birthname) was no different, and by the time he was 15 he was joining raids into the lands that used to be home.

Willkob's scouts, charged with finding a courageous, talented and intelligent young man, had heard of the Kervilian who was showing himself to be fearless but prudent, an unusual combination in the young. Since it was imperative that he remain anonymous, Willkob had made his proposition to the family by proxy. Would they be willing to send their son to a couple in Wesmork, where he would attempt to infiltrate the Imperial defence forces? It was not surprising that they jumped at the opportunity, even though it would mean they would have little contact with their only son. To fight Destlar's machine was highest on their list of honours.

The Olskers from Wesmork, long-time NALO agents, agreed to take in the teenager as their son. Expertly forged documentation gave him his new name, but their feelings for the boy with the curly black hair developed into a love that could not have been more genuine than if it had been their blood in his veins. They were devoted surrogate parents, encouraging but expectant. For the camera, they stood smiling either side of their son in his pilot's uniform on his graduation day.

His real parents didn't seem to wonder what help to NALO a lone fighter pilot could be. They were simply too proud of their son to be distracted by such minutiae. Unlike the surrogate parents, they were unaware that their son was about to embark on a most dangerous mission.

Hervan pictured them hugging him goodbye as they stood outside their house in the snow. He wondered if the Kervilian honour system would have been strong enough to hold back their pleas and protestations, had they known how unlikely it was that they would ever see him again.

***

"Captain, why have I been relieved of duty?" Olsker asked, standing before his commanding officer's desk. "I worked hard for this."

"Orders from above, Lieutenant. I will admit, I don't like it any more than you do."

"I can guess who'll be flying in my place. Some of us get places on merit, others by having Daddy on the Assembly," Olsker sneered.

"Olsker, be careful. Daddy on the Assembly can do more than have you temporarily grounded."

Olsker considered arguing, but decided it was pointless. With gritted teeth, he saluted the captain, then marched quickly from the office, muttering expletives on his way and bumping into the base doctor just outside the door.

***

Luckran stood in the palace roof garden with the tower to his left, the sun disappearing behind it. The Solstice ceremonies were well under way in Lurg's church five miles to the north. In years past, the Velkren would at this stage be on the altar, sitting on the marble throne, majestically silent, secretly bored, while the congregation gazed at him in awe. But Destlar's fear of the public had intensified. The more his security forces bragged about the technological marvels ensuring the security of the church, the more he worried about imaginative and ingenious devices designed to overcome them.

So a compromise with the Church had been reached. Twice a year, on the evening of the solstice as the sun was setting, the

Velkren would step out of his tower and into the roof garden. He would bow his head in concert with a particularly solemn moment in the religious rites being performed in the church to the north, then return inside. Many people were disappointed that he remained in the palace. His absence was even less palatable to the people south of the equator, because the images of the Velkren with the setting sun at his back were exclusively northern. When he appeared for the last rays of the Southern Solstice, the Imperial gardens were already in darkness.

One of Luckran's assistants approached. "Everything is in order, My Lord." Consulting his electronic notebook, he continued. "I received a message from a Dr Fertin, claiming he has information you might be interested in. I only bring it up because of his persistence. He has called several times."

Luckran looked directly at the skinny young man for the first time, who received the stare like a slap. "You should have come to me immediately! Give me the message!"

The assistant's self-assurance evaporated. He fumbled with his notebook's buttons, feeling the seconds it took to locate the message stretch into hours. Under the First Advisor's glare, his palms started to sweat. "There's been some suspicious activity at the Air Force base," he read at last.

"The Air Force base, on the day we have jets circling the palace. You didn't think this worthy of my attention?"

"I'm sorry, My Lord. I thought if he was genuine, he'd use his code."

"Leave!" Luckran snapped. The young man scampered away like he'd been prodded with an electric rod.

Of course he was right. Fertin should have used his code. Luckran produced a phone from within his robes, entered a code, then made a call on the secure line that opened. Every one of his agents had been equipped with a similar phone. When answering a secure call, the recipient first had to enter his numeric code.

"Codename?" Luckran barked at the unsure voice that answered. When he received the expected answer and this secondary security check was complete, he continued. "Why didn't you use that name when you left your message?"

"I thought I wasn't supposed to say my codename to anyone but you," came the perplexed reply.

Luckran sighed, marvelling at how difficult it was for some people to follow simple procedures. "What is this suspicious activity?"

"I overheard one of the pilots this morning. He was very angry at being dropped from the patrol. Later on, I found his replacement in the infirmary, with a violently sick stomach, which means the other pilot, Olsker, is back on duty."

"What do you know about this Olsker?"

"Hails from a very loyal and religious family. Parents attend the Church of Fertility daily. Olsker himself is highly regarded at the base, a fine pilot."

"Then why was he dropped?"

"It seems to have been done to honour a favour. His replacement, the pilot now sick in bed, is the son of an Assembly member."

Luckran hung up, then made another secure call, this time to the base commander, General Sebasdeen. To his amazement, there was no answer. Cursing, he stabbed the off button, then looked out across the darkening city to the sea beyond. He was torn, wondering whether he should stay close to Destlar, or go to the base and have this pilot called back. He hated to leave the palace today, of all days. And perhaps there was nothing to these shenanigans at the base other than a young man's desire to fly on the Solstice, to be part of the fun and celebrations.

Yet he instinctively felt it was more. If someone was planning an attack, this would be the ideal time, when everyone knew for sure the Emperor would be on the roof. Luckran cursed again. The generals were all for the patrol, but Luckran had never liked the idea. He couldn't see what the jets and their pilots could achieve, except make the Air Force feel useful on the big day. Now he saw how the patrol heightened the risk rather than reduced it. Heavily armed planes flying close to the palace with Destlar in view. He couldn't understand why he hadn't seen it that way before.

Luckran tried to reach the general again, but still there was no reply. Anxiously he regarded the tower, off to his left. In about 20 minutes Destlar would make his brief appearance. He had just about enough time to take a helicopter to the base and back. Cursing for a third time, he made for the elevator.

***

Luckran stormed into the general's office. "Why don't you answer your phone? What's wrong with you?"

Sebasdeen jumped to his feet. "I'm sorry, My Lord. We're having trouble with the phones today."

"And you didn't think to come up with an alternative? I have to leave the Emperor and fly out here to speak with you." He waved away the general's apology and attempted explanations. "You have a pilot named Olsker in the air. Order him back immediately. I assume you're in contact with your own pilots."

"Yes, My Lord. I'll go down to the radio room myself."

Luckran followed him along the corridor and into a small room where a uniformed man sat before a microphone. The order was sent. "He's not responding," the radio operator said.

"Try again," Sebasdeen ordered.

"Shoot him down," Luckran countermanded. His words were met with amazed stares. "Now!" he shouted. As the radio operator relayed the order, Luckran stepped out of the room and made another call, this time to Rubyan. His disbelief mounted with each ring of the phone. He was about to hang up and return to the palace when his old friend's whispered voice reached his ears.

"Rendal!" Luckran barked. "Where are you?"

"In the church," Rubyan answered quietly. "This isn't a good time, Oulezandur."

The church? Rubyan and his newfound faith! "Well I'm sorry to interrupt your time of worship," he said in a voice filled with sarcasm. "Get outside, quickly. I may need your help."

***

An urgent beeping sound filled Olsker's helmet and lights flashed on the cockpit display, announcing the rapid approach of several missiles. "Shit!" He didn't have time to wonder how he'd been found out. He jerked the joystick to the left in the first of many rapid and debilitating accelerations that took him streaking and swerving across the cloudless sky. He knew he was doomed, with at least half a dozen missiles closing in. But another few seconds and his erratic course would bring him close enough to the monstrosity upon the hill. Gritting his teeth, he dived towards the palace and, five seconds before his death, he fired.

Chapter 12

Rubyan wandered about aimlessly as everyone else left the church. It was almost midnight, and the acolytes in their white robes gently ushered the last few stragglers to the main door, then locked it. They all recognised the tall dark man with the privileges bestowed upon him by the Prelate. They knew one of them would be told to come back later to let him out.

Rubyan regarded the ceiling fresco as he strolled up the aisle. Wind and Fertility were directly above him. The depiction showed the former, standing to the left, blowing seeds from the outstretched hands of the latter. Rubyan circled the stone basin and continued to the top, kneeling at the pew closest to the white throne.

If Luckran could have seen him, he would have shaken a sorrowful head. Though his friend's belief that he was the Velkren's chosen magician suited the First Advisor, he was nevertheless surprised and saddened by Rubyan's conversion from atheist to believer, a process so gradual no one else seemed to have noticed. It was ironic that he should become more like his wife, whose beliefs he used to mock.

Luckran had always been puzzled by Rubyan's choice of companion. The man Luckran first met was inquisitive, logical, taking nothing on faith. A talented magician who knew his unusual abilities would one day be explained by science. A man determined to lead science in that quest. His wife, on the other hand, had been a pious woman, attending daily the Church of Kerl, God of Death. Until she took ill with a tumour in her throat 15 years earlier. Within weeks, she was on her way to the God she worshipped.

Rubyan would have been surprised to know of Luckran's disdain for his beliefs. There was never any hint of disaffection when they sat together, swirling brandies. Rubyan fully expected his companion, fellow long-lifer, to accept the story of the Gods and the Velkren and their part in it. He would have been shocked if he was somehow taken back decades to see his younger self speak of the Velkren as nothing more than emperor and magician. Granted, an astonishingly powerful magician, but one whose abilities allowed him to hoodwink the plebs into worshipping his divinity.

Rubyan turned in his seat to look down the church. For a moment, his eyes were pulled upwards to the image of Kerl in his red robes. Quickly he looked away, the shadow of guilt passing over his soul. He was 103 years old and as fit as he had been 50 years earlier. His wife too had lived a good long life. And yet it felt wrong somehow that she should die while he lived. The fact that, unlike himself, she was not essential should have been justification and yet it wasn't. If he were true to himself, he would have admitted it was the secrets that plagued him. He'd never told her of his special relationship with the Velkren and how death was now refused him. If he at all remembered the arguments they'd had over the afterlife, where he'd smugly reasoned its human-derived existence was due to a primitive fear of death, he would say it was just his way of playing with her.

And then there was shame over the women. To her last day, his wife had been unaware of his nights of fun with a succession of beautiful females. She used to complain that he spent too many hours hard at work for the First Advisor. He reasoned it was a natural weakness. That young women should be such beautiful creatures was hardly his fault. Animal instinct coerced him into having Luckran replace the girl in the luxury apartment every so often, whenever he grew tired of the current model and felt the need for something fresh.

But these were thoughts to which he gave little time, evicting them from his mind almost as soon as they formed. He certainly didn't give himself a chance to wonder what became of the replaced girls.

His eyes settled on the Velkren's image at the back of the church, upon his throne at Lurg's feet. The divine protector. And he, Rendal Rubyan, was the Velkren's protector. It might seem strange that the Velkren required such protection, but the ways of the Gods were mysterious. Perhaps the Emperor's potency lay not in his magical abilities alone, which were inarguably immense, but also in his shrewd mind, in his ability to surround himself with talented individuals. One only had to look at his choice of First Advisor for proof of that.

When Luckran had called earlier, Rubyan had considered ignoring him, such was the poor timing, with the Solstice ceremonies reaching a crescendo. But the pair of old friends met often at the Governors' Rooms for long and enjoyable chats. They regarded the phone as an inadequate substitute for face-to-face company. Rubyan had therefore decided it was unlikely Luckran was calling him to ask him how his day was going. Reluctantly, he'd answered.

***

Rubyan forced his way through the crowd at the back of the church, where it was standing room only. He tried to ignore the angry stares from those who no doubt considered his departure an outrage. Ten of thousands would have given practically anything for his ticket.

At last, he made it outside, to the top of the semicircular steps. He quickly retreated into the shadows, away from the eyes of the thousands of worshippers standing outside the church.

He brought the phone to his ear. "I made it outside. For the love of the Gods, Oulezandur, what do you want?"

"Listen to me, you old fool! There could be missiles closing in on the palace at this very moment."

"Missiles?"

"Yes, fighter jet missiles! Search for them. Destroy them!"

Rubyan had never heard Luckran sound so anxious. "I don't know if I can."

"Yes, you can. Stop talking to me and get on with it."

"OK. I'll try."

He dropped the phone to his side, took a deep breath and closed his eyes. He let his mind expand high and wide through the air. There were many distractions, especially the media helicopters about the church, but he focused his senses upon the rapidly moving objects. Once he felt the numerous missiles in the air, it was easy to ignore everything else.

He grabbed at the two that were travelling along parallel paths, towards the palace and away from the other missiles moving along erratic trajectories.

And then they were gone, and he gasped. He'd never tried to take hold of something moving at such speed. But a second later he caught one of them again, and this time held on. He took a tiny piece of matter and converted it to energy, enough to destroy the missile. How exactly he'd done it was like all magic: beyond the ability of even a scientific magician to explain.

For a moment, when seeking the second missile, he was distracted by the others in the sky. But he managed to remain focused upon the one heading for the palace upon the hill, and a moment later it too stabbed the darkening sky with a flash of light.

Rubyan exhaled deeply, leaned against the wall and raised the phone to his ear. "I don't think I have the energy for the others," he said.

"Don't worry about them," Luckran reassured him. "They're left over from the destruction of the traitor's jet."

Rubyan staggered back inside the church's foyer. A young man jumped up from a bench by the wall, concern for the old man evident on his face. Rubyan collapsed on the seat. He was too exhausted to comprehend how close the second missile had been to the tower, outside of which stood the Velkren, when it exploded.

***

An acolyte let Rubyan out of the church. As he walked towards the waiting car, the magician looked up into the sky. Though it was a clear night, the city lights drowned out the stars. But up there, somewhere, a ship was decelerating towards a planet uncannily like Earda. A planet he might soon visit as he facilitated the Velkren's extension of His divine care to an ignorant people.

Chapter 13

Jeseque climbed out of the Deep Sleep unit and stood in shorts and short-sleeved top. With her eyes closed she held on to the smooth rounded plastic of the raised lid with one hand, waiting for the first few dizzy moments to pass. Once she felt stable, she let go of the lid and opened her eyes. Absently curling her toes on the cold tiles, she looked about the chamber with its two rows of units that always reminded her of coffins. With all the lids open, it looked like a legion of the dead was slowly and unwillingly staggering back into life. Some grunted, some groaned. A few even farted.

Ferist was standing across from her, rubbing his eyes and yawning widely, his pudgy stomach poking between his top and shorts, belly button like a bewildered pupil. She laughed quietly. And when she caught his eye, she threw him a wink.

He smiled back, then looked about quickly, hoping no one had noticed.

Jeseque shook her head. What a nervous little boy he was. "Later," she mouthed to him as she made for the exit.

She walked through the double doors, past the gymnasium and the washroom and along the corridor to the kitchen. Though she craved a shower, she was resigned to waiting until night, when everyone else was asleep. There was one advantage to skipping the group scrubbing: she had the kitchen to herself. After a plateful of sausage, rice and vegetables, smothered in some kind of tacky sweet sauce that she found strangely palatable, she sat in front of her computer terminal, wondering if someone would finally notice the missiles were gone, now that they'd supposedly arrived at their destination. The morning after she'd fired them into space, she lay in bed, listening to the others moving about, expecting a rap on her door at any moment. Though she had covered her tracks well, she knew she would be the prime suspect.

But the day wore on, unexpectedly quiet. She'd logged into the computer, using one of her hidden control accounts. Scanning through the messages sent to and from the captain, she found only one reference to the missile system, which stated all was in order. Obviously, they were taking the computer's word and no one was actually bothering to have a look inside the bay itself. She wasn't impressed with the way the ship was being run, but it was in keeping with her opinions of Abrim.

And so it had continued, day after day, and on through the following resets. (Ferist had told her that 'reset' was the word everyone was using to describe their periods awake. She had to admit it was suitable. The ship ran itself and the crew had little to do during the time it took, supposedly, for their bodies to become ready for another spell in Deep Sleep. And the few duties they had weren't performed very diligently, it seemed.)

But now at last, during their final time out of Deep Sleep, something finally happened. Jeseque heard a commotion outside her room, voices raised in excitement, though she couldn't make out what was being said. Then there was a light tap on her door.

So here it was, at last. She logged off the computer and opened the door. She was a little surprised to find Ferist.

"A disaster!" he said, wide-eyed. "The mission's a failure."

"What do you mean?"

He stepped into the room and she closed the door.

"They're as advanced as us." The words rushed from his mouth. "There's no way we can go down. We're not even safe up here."

Jeseque pushed Ferist gently towards the bed and made him sit. "Calm down. Tell it slowly."

Ferist took a deep breath. "We're in orbit, but the planet below is not the primitive one we expected. And they probably know we're here. Did you notice the magicians were already gone from their bunks when we came out of hibernation?" Jeseque shook her head. "Neither did I. The computer woke them first, after it had completed the manoeuvres about the star and then into orbit about the planet. We were in free fall then, and they had to activate their gravity spell. And the computer informed them the shroud had failed. Which means we might have been seen from the planet. And the inhabitants are not what we expected." His words were speeding up again. "They're as sophisticated as us. There's hundreds of artificial satellites, and a lot of radio waves. What a disaster. We're stuck up here, hoping to remain hidden, now that the magicians have raised the shroud again. Can you imagine what will happen if they find us?"

Jeseque sat down beside him. "What was Abrim's response?"

"He has us trying to decode the radio signals to see if there's any mention of us. Not an easy task if you're in a hurry."

"And there's no system in the computer for analysing and deciphering these signals."

"No one expected these people to have even discovered electricity yet."

Jeseque rolled her eyes. "We can communicate across dozens of light years, back to Earda, but we can't listen to the planet below us."

"Yes, well that's completely different technology."

"Can we really believe we are transmitting data faster than the speed of light?"

Ferist shrugged. "The magicians. How can we know what they're capable of?"

"Magicians!" Jeseque snapped. "It's all magic. Gravity, propulsion, communications, the shroud. Don't you think that's weird? Basically, Imperial Engineering built a house in the sky and the magicians did the rest. Why do they need engineers at all?"

"We should be very happy to have them. They might be able to protect us."

Jeseque shook her head. "You're not at all suspicious?"

"Of what?"

She couldn't believe it. During the past few resets, while they snuggled together in bed, she had expressed her doubts about the mission. But it seemed her words had not registered with Ferist at all. She was about to try again but was interrupted by a pounding on the door.

Ferist looked at her wide-eyed, then shot under the bed.

"What the hell?" Jeseque asked.

"Pretend I'm not here," he hissed.

***

Abrim marched up to Debrone's cabin and thumped the door with his fist. The door opened and the witch stood before him.

"Captain?" she said.

"Second Lieutenant Debrone, you are hereby charged with wilful disarmament of this ship and I am therefore placing you under arrest." He stared at the girl, but her face was unreadable. "Don't bother feigning ignorance," he continued, despite the annoying fact she wasn't reacting one way or another. "The magicians have proof. They found your fingerprints all over the missile bay."

The magicians, unnerved by their arrival at a destination that was unexpectedly dangerous and by the system malfunction that had left them without the shroud just when they were approaching the planet, were enraged at finding the ship completely lacking in firepower. They wanted Debrone eliminated immediately.

But the captain had refused. "Gentlemen," he said, "we obey the law on this ship. Second Lieutenant Debrone will be confined to her cabin until the time is right for her to face trial."

Now, standing in the girl's doorway, he was intrigued to find he admired her somewhat. Perhaps it was because her actions upset the mystic meddlers so much. But his admiration quickly died when he considered the predicament they found themselves in.

"I knew from the beginning you were bad news. I told Tavenar, but he wouldn't listen. So now the magicians are furious and want you thrown through the airlock. But I won't allow it. When things calm down, you will face trial. In the meantime, you'll stay here."

He grabbed the handle and slammed the door shut.

***

Ferist came out from under the bed. He regarded Jeseque sadly. "Why did you do it?" he asked quietly.

She frowned. "You immediately side with Abrim? You're not going to hear my side?"

"I've known all along. I've been covering for you."

"What?"

"I was the one who reported on the missiles during each reset."

Jeseque sat down slowly by the desk. Ferist sat on the bed.

"You knew?" she said.

"Yeah. I saw you go down to the bay that night. And I checked afterwards and saw the missiles were gone."

"And you didn't say anything."

He shrugged. "I didn't want to get you in trouble."

"You could be in trouble now. They'll figure out you were covering for me."

Ferist shook his head. "Why would they assume that? They might just think I'm stupid. Or they might even forget it was me who checked the missiles. It wasn't considered a very important task and I always sent the report using another crewman's account, when he wasn't watching."

Jeseque was impressed. "Very sneaky," she said.

"You're not the only one who can be sneaky. You still haven't told me why you did it."

"I'm wondering why you didn't tell me you knew."

"I wanted to, but I could never bring myself to do it. I suppose I was afraid of the conversation. I wanted to avoid it."

"And now?"

"Now I'm wondering why you've thrown your life away." He stood up. "I'd better leave. They'll come to lock you in shortly." He left quickly.

Jeseque was angry. Throwing her life away? That's how he saw it? She refused to see it that way.

***

Sometime later, when Jeseque's anger at Ferist had abated, to be replaced by surprise at his deviousness, she heard a drill outside her cabin. Opening the door, she discovered a large man on his knees. His bald head, golden brown, reflected the ceiling lights. When he looked up at her she saw he wore a tight beard. Jeseque wondered what kind of man shaves his head but not his chin.

He sighed, placing the electric drill on the carpet. "It's hard to drill a hole in a door with you opening it."

Used to being ignored by the crew, Jeseque was surprised by his everyday reaction, like he was a repairman in an apartment building and she was an awkward tenant getting in the way. She looked down and saw a latch from one of the washroom's toilet cubicles lying on the floor. "So you're locking me in," she remarked, matching his casual air. She stepped into the corridor and pulled the door closed.

"That's right. Captain's orders. It seems I've been assigned to you." Again he sighed. "Here you have a systems engineer with seventeen years of experience. He travels billions of miles to another star system so that he can play the part of babysitter. Certainly not what I expected."

Jeseque shrugged. "Sorry?"

With a shrug, he set the drill bit to the door. "I suppose it's not what you had in mind either," he said as he drilled two small holes. "But you've only yourself to blame." He went on to drill two more holes, in the door jamb, then picked up a screwdriver and the latch. "Why'd you do it?" he asked.

"Because I don't think we should be armed, especially with offensive weapons."

"Is that so? To be honest, I don't see why it's such a big deal. I doubt if the missiles would ever have been used anyway."

"Really?"

"Yeah. We'll just hide behind the shroud while they bring the Velkren to us. He'll put this planet in order, and he won't need missiles to do it."

"You really think it's that simple?"

He nodded. "Especially since they have no magicians below."

Jeseque sighed inwardly. When it came to magic and the Velkren, this guy was as bad as Ferist.

"You really believe in these black robes?" Annoyed by his fumbled attempts to secure the latch, Jeseque held it for him so that he could easily insert the screws.

"They're an odd bunch. But what else would you expect from magicians? And to be fair, they got us this far."

"Have you seen them actually perform magic?"

He looked up at her. "Why do you think you're not floating about the place?"

Holding the slot as he attached it to the jamb, she was half inclined to argue that just because you don't know how something's done, that doesn't mean it's magic. "That should keep me at bay," she said instead.

He got to his feet with a grunt. He was taller than she expected. "Oh, the captain's not stopping at that. You're a bit of a fox, the way you created that control account. It wasn't till we went looking, wondering how you'd managed to get inside the missile bay, that we found it. Very clever. How'd you do it?"

Jeseque shrugged. "It was ridiculously easy. If you examine the system, you should be able to figure it out."

"Really? I might just do that. But first I need to rig up a sensor and place it between the hinges, just in case you somehow manage to get the door opened. Once I'm done, if it's opened by anyone but me, an alarm will go off in the captain's cabin."

"That's me neutralised."

"I certainly hope so. Here," he said, proffering a phone. "I didn't think we'd need these until we were down on the surface. Use it to contact me whenever you want to get out. You know, for the kitchen and the washroom. I promise I won't peek when you're in the shower." He laughed and gave her a comradely thump on the shoulder. Jeseque was again surprised by his demeanour. She guessed Abrim had chosen the one least likely to complain about such a menial task.

She again found herself wondering what kind of people volunteer for a mission like this. Religious zealots, she supposed, content with whatever the Gods throw at them.

"And now," he said, "I need to remove your computer terminal, since it's not safe to leave you alone with one. You might have us all sucked out into space."

"That's what'll happen to me, if the magicians get their way," she said as a test, wondering if it were true.

His smile faded. "If it wasn't for the captain, you'd be out there already."

"You're serious? They're that crazy?"

"I wouldn't say they're crazy, but the captain's all that's standing between you and them."

Jeseque looked at the floor. "Sounds like I owe him my life." She glanced at the engineer. "Will you tell him I appreciate it, even though I doubt he'll care?"

"I might, if I get him at a quiet moment. But you're right; he won't want to hear it."

He stepped into the cabin and held up the phone. "I'll respond to your calls as soon as I can, but I don't want you disturbing my sleep, so I'll come by each night before I go to bed."

"Fine."

He got down under the desk and unplugged the terminal's power and data lines. "And in a little while, after I install the sensor, I'll drop off a media player with books and films. The captain doesn't want you going crazy, stuck in this tiny room all alone."

"Very thoughtful."

"And water and snack packs."

"It's like a hotel."

A moment later he had the terminal tucked under his arm. "Seldin's the name," he said as he stepped through the door.

"Jeseque," she returned.

"I know that." He looked down at her and for the third time he sighed. "You got yourself into a lot of trouble, young Jeseque, for nothing. The captain can hold off these magicians. But I wouldn't like to be you when the Velkren arrives."

Jeseque stood staring at the closed door. The bolt slid into place. Though she was confident the story about Destlar coming aboard was nonsense, this did not prevent her shuddering at the thought.

***

"Prisoner, to her cell," Seldin said in mock seriousness as he opened Jeseque's cabin door and gestured inside. Jeseque rolled her eyes. She was still surprised by the engineer's playfulness, and she wondered how his mood would change if Abrim suddenly came into view. In the kitchen, with just the two of them, he'd even chatted to her while she had her evening meal.

After the initial excitement of having arrived at their destination, Seldin was happy to see ship life return to a relaxed routine. Abrim and the magicians were apparently awaiting developments at home. Seldin had known all along it was panic over nothing.

"Lights out," he continued as he closed the door and locked it.

Jeseque sat on the bed, forlorn. Her second night of captivity; she'd just had a shower and a meal and now could either read or watch a film, neither of which she found appealing right then. It was maddening to be stuck in the cabin, not knowing what was going on.

Something moved under her bed. Jeseque jumped off the mattress with a scream.

"Ssh!" came a voice, followed by a head.

"Ferist!" she hissed. "You scared the life out of me."

"Sorry," Ferist said as he got to his feet. "I sneaked in while you were in the shower. I was hoping Seldin would leave the alarm disabled."

Jeseque smiled, her heart slowly decreasing to a normal beat. "Another flaw. This lot aren't the best at security."

Ferist didn't return her smile. He seemed very rigid, cold. "I've been trying to figure out why you would do something so stupid, but I can't."

"Really?" she answered, her voice filled with sarcasm. "You're having trouble figuring something out? I don't believe it."

"That's it, Jeseque. Avoid the issue."

"I don't have to do anything with the *issue* with you. You're not going to put me on trial. It'll be bad enough to have to face Abrim and his wizards."

"You jeopardised the mission."

"Oh bullshit! What is the mission? To pulverise the planet below?" She took a deep breath and sat down by the desk. "Ferist, what do you think's going on here?"

"Don't try to change the subject."

"You believe we've arrived at a new world and the Velkren plans to come here, to place the natives under his protection. It's utter nonsense."

"Of course you know exactly what's going on," he shot back.

"The whole thing's a conspiracy, Ferist. There is no new world. We're still in orbit about Earda."

"Rubbish!"

"You and the others are believing exactly what he wants you to believe."

"Why would the Velkren—?"

"Not the Emperor. Luckran! He wants to destroy the Velkren. He has become so corrupted by power that he believes he should be on the throne."

Ferist sat down on the bed. Jeseque remained silent, giving the lie time to take hold.

"That's..." Ferist mumbled. "No, I don't see how that could be true."

While alone in her cabin, she had come up with a story she hoped might entice Ferist to help her, if she ever got the chance to use it on him. She was still amazed that he'd known about the missiles all along and never said a word. It helped her believe he was on her side, despite how happy he seemed to be with Abrim and the crew.

And now here he was. Each reset, they had spent many hours together and Jeseque had used the time in an effort to convert him. In some ways, she had made progress. He was becoming quite altruistic, at least in principle. However, he remained stubbornly faithful to the Church and the Velkren. She'd decided to use that, rather than fight it.

"The Velkren recruited me," she began, eyeing him carefully, wondering if there was any chance of him accepting such a ridiculously sensational story. "I was supposed to find out whatever I could about Luckran's activities, and report directly to His Majesty."

The fact that Ferist didn't scoff, or burst out laughing, encouraged her to continue. He was looking at her with interest.

"But Luckran had me removed from the project. You remember? You thought it was your father who had me bumped for you."

"Yes," Ferist said. Jeseque was delighted to see that bit sink in. She smiled to herself. It was little details like that that lent substance to the lie. "It wasn't my father?" he asked.

"No. It was Luckran. But then the Emperor acted, through Major Tavenar, and here I am, aboard ship."

"And Luckran doesn't know?"

"I'm not sure. There's so much I don't know, because we're cut off."

"And that's why you extracted the information from me, about the ship. You somehow knew what Tavenar's response would be?"

Jeseque was surprised by his acuity. How could he be so clever in some instances and so gullible in many more? "I didn't know what would happen, but the Velkren must have."

"But you were using me. I always wondered why someone like you would be with someone like me. I'd assumed it was the money."

"Ferist. It's not like that. Well, it was at first. But not any more."

"I don't know," he said. "The Velkren's agent? It sounds outlandish."

"More outlandish than two inexperienced astronauts aboard the first interstellar spaceship?"

Ferist frowned, then shook his head. "I can't believe it," he said, but she could see he wanted to. Maybe he found the notion exciting, to be the lover of a secret agent. Was he picturing himself in a spy novel?

"You think we're in orbit about a new world," she said. "I'm telling you it's Earda down there. Think about it. Doesn't it make sense? Luckran wanted this secret weapons platform, so that he could fire missiles at the palace. You see why the magicians are so angry? I managed to spoil the entire plan, for now. But they will replace the missiles. That's why it's so important I somehow warn the Velkren. Let him know we're up here."

Ferist remained quiet.

"You're not sure," Jeseque said. "You still think we've travelled to another star. All right, this is what you're going to do."

***

"I was just getting comfy in my bed," Seldin complained as he escorted Jeseque back from the washrooms.

"Sorry."

"What did you drink so much water for?"

"I was thirsty."

"You were thirsty. Here," he said as he opened the door.

"Goodnight, jailer."

"Goodnight, prisoner."

With the sound of the bolt sliding into place, Jeseque took a step to the bed and looked under. Straightening up, she laughed at herself. "What did I expect?" she asked the empty room. "That he'd get confused and forget to leave?"

All she could do now was wait. She opened the media player and searched for articles about magic. She wasn't surprised that the number of scientific papers on the subject was zero. There was a lot of talk about the Emperor, the Velkren, as the source of all magic. Of course it was difficult to explain the man's lifespan. Though Jeseque was sure the Palace exaggerated Destlar's age, she realised he had to be at least a couple of centuries old. But what of it? He was nothing more than an outlier, an anomaly, a freak. His sidekick, Luckran, was another. Jeseque was sure there were more, keeping quiet, anxious to avoid attracting the attention of the two bullies in Wesmork.

Closing the player, she drummed the desk. Time dragged. She got up from the desk and lay down on the bed, staring at the ceiling.

She had almost dozed off when she heard the rustle of paper at the door. She sat up. A sheet with writing slid under. She recognised Ferist's scrawl.

It's not Earda. Looks completely different. Ice caps are far too small.

Jeseque sighed, then scribbled a reply.

Of course it's different. They have to fool us into thinking we've travelled. You're supposed to be finding out how they're messing with the stream. Find the raw data.

A moment later, the paper was back.

I tried. It seems real.

Go back. They have to be modifying the images.

I really don't think they are.

Jeseque's shoulders slumped. She knew Ferist didn't want to try because he thought it was pointless. He was losing faith in her. But it was also true that he wouldn't figure out how the stream was being modified, not if he sat there for a month. Ferist was no programmer.

Jeseque snapped her fingers. "A month," she whispered. She quickly wrote another message, then waited. Five minutes went by, and still no response. "What's taking him so long?" she complained to no one. Eventually, his message arrived beneath the door.

You were right. Not full, but almost. Sorry for doubting you.

Jeseque smiled. They'd forgotten about the moon. So much for being the first interstellar travellers.

Chapter 14

The rock, 200 miles in diameter, would have missed the planet by a long way, if it hadn't been purposely nudged into a collision course. Perhaps the terrified inhabitants, who knew the deadly impact was imminent, would have had room for anger as well as fear and despair, had they known this was no chance event, had they known they were about to be murdered.

The asteroid smashes into the ocean, ripping the skin from the planet and throwing it beyond the atmosphere and into space. A towering tsunami races out in all directions, moving at many times the speed of sound.

The planet is betrayed by its own gravity, as enormous chunks of rock are pulled back through the burning atmosphere to bombard the surface. The remaining rock is vaporised. Hotter than the surface of the nearby star, a ball of orange vapour rises out of the crater. From a distance, it looks like the planet is giving birth to a new star. The circle of fire spreads across the surface, as if the newborn star were gathering the mother planet in a loving but smothering embrace.

The sadist travels before it, unnoticed. He basks in the mental spikes of a trillion terrified creatures as they are consumed by white-hot vapour.

The oceans boil. The vapour reaches the coast and tears the continent from the mantle like a plaster from a wound. The polar caps instantly evaporate. High mountains, forever covered in snow, are stripped naked. Forests burn even before the vapour reaches them.

The vapour expands across the far side of the globe, and the perspective flips: now the circle is that of the untouched land, rapidly diminishing as the super-hot air and rock rush in. Finally, the green circle shrinks to a point and vanishes. All life goes with it.

The sadist moves on, hunger abated but only temporarily.

***

Another planet. The dominant species is intelligent and peace-loving. Its adult population suddenly and collectively suffers from a very specific mental aberration. The comforting and guiding knowledge that their children will inherit their place in the world is twisted into a horrifying neurosis. They believe these children are monsters, emerged from the depths of the ocean, intent upon destruction and usurpation.

Infanticide spreads across the globe like a voracious predator. The children cry in terror and bewilderment as their adoring parents turn on them, attacking them with knives. They plead and struggle as they are wrestled to the ground. The knives are brought down swiftly and repeatedly, the attackers' eyes alive with hatred, disgust and manic purpose. The last cries escape before the little throats are filled with blood.

The unnatural mental breakdown, like a parasite that resides in the adults but feeds off the young, was fashioned by a demented Grid Rider. Upon its departure, the adults regain their faculties and true sight is restored. Realisation and horror plunge them into the abyss of insanity. The parasite is gone, but it leaves in its wake nothing but husks.

***

A planet's atmosphere and oceans are sucked into space. Another is sent into a spiral orbit, burning up as it falls into the sun, while yet another is dragged away from its star and placed in orbit about a gas giant. Too far from the sun, it becomes a ball of ice.

***

A civilisation that has lasted millennia crumbles within days as its artificial and biological memories fail completely. Another race succumbs to extreme cases of agoraphobia and social anxiety. The once noisy cities become quiet as graveyards as the residents lock themselves in dark and lonely rooms. Many take to isolation units and slowly go insane.

**

"Oh, enough of this nonsense!" I complained. "Why would he do such things?"

"Why not?" Arnelius asked. "What makes you think he won't? Remember, Luckran has kept him in check for over a hundred years. Who knows what atrocities he's prevented?"

"But Destlar will be different when he enters the grid. The picture you draw is implausible. No Grid Rider has ever behaved in such a manner."

"You think all Riders are mentally sound? What about the Necrophobes?"

"I will admit, they're an odd bunch. But they don't go around throwing rocks at planets or driving whole societies crazy."

"They're irrational," Arnelius argued. "They think the Perpetuators will save them. When the universe is dying, these unusual entities who inexplicably found their way into the grid will somehow pull the same trick again and elevate them and their devotees to a new level of existence."

"The Necrophobes don't just think it," I clarified, "they're absolutely convinced. Without a shred of evidence. Of course they're in raptures over Destlar. His entering the grid will be the single most important moment in their history. Never before have they witnessed a Perpetuator's birth. Which is why they're very nervous about you. Especially Listur, from what I hear. Aren't you afraid he'll close the portal?"

"Apparently he's on his last warning, but that might not be enough to hold him back. There was a temporal glitch in the portal and now the ship is in orbit about a much more advanced world than I'd planned."

"What caused the glitch?"

"I don't know. But I fear it may have been Listur and his 'investigations'."

"So you're not convinced the threat of excommunication is enough to keep manners on him?"

"No, I'm not. And don't you see what that means? He's desperate to stop me, but he's afraid to, partly because he can't figure out what I'm up to, but mostly—and this is the crux—mostly because he might not be invited to the party in the new universe. That is not rational behaviour."

"And you think that justifies your opinion of Destlar. You think that if they're crazy, then he might be too. But isn't there's a big difference between harmless belief and planet-killing?"

"That's not the point. You seem to think Destlar will somehow be enlightened when he enters the grid. But Listur and the Necrophobes throw doubt on that.

"And there's more. For a long time, I've questioned my motivations: altruism or vengeance. But recently I realised it doesn't matter. If it's the welfare of innocent creatures that concerns me, then fine. Can't argue with that. But if I'm out for revenge, or I simply wish to punish Destlar, then that would indicate I brought some of the dark side of my psyche with me when I entered the grid. If that's the case, then it's not only possible, but probable, that Destlar will do the same."

I considered Arnelius's reasoning and tried to find a hole in his argument, but I couldn't. And yet I remained unconvinced.

"You of all people should be able to see what I'm getting at," Arnelius said. "You think everything I'm doing is extremely weird behaviour for a Grid Rider. Perhaps humans aren't meant to join the grid."

"Now that's the best argument you've made so far. Still, you're not a raving lunatic. You're just a bit nutty like the Necrophobes. But unlike that shower of snobs, you're willing to talk to me."

"It's always a pleasure."

"Thank you. So somehow or other, you intend to prevent the manic Destlar from joining us," I probed. Listur wasn't the only one who couldn't figure out what Arnelius was up to.

"Maybe."

"And the fact that no one else thinks this is necessary doesn't bother you?"

"Why should it?"

"Why indeed? I may have figured out how you're going to do it."

"Is that right?" Arnelius replied sarcastically.

"At first I thought you just wanted to get him off Earda, away from the people you obviously care for. I didn't think there was any way to keep him out of the grid. With physical death, he'll probably make it. And you can't keep his body, his flesh and bones, safe forever. But then I realised there is no forever. And that's when it dawned on me, though I really hope I'm wrong. Because if I'm right, then it's an even crazier scheme than before, when you tried to infect his brain."

I waited to see if Arnelius would respond, but he kept quiet. So I went on with my conjecture. "You want him off Earda because before long it will be a ball of ice, and even Destlar would not survive that, physically. His body would die and he would suddenly be amongst us, wreaking havoc across the cosmos, as you say. So you opened up a portal to a more hospitable planet, and you made sure Luckran and Rubyan found it. Soon they'll transfer him to the new world, as they so imaginatively call it.

"And then you'll do it again, when that planet is about to die. And again and again, until the end of time. And you will remain forever vigilant, protecting his delicate body, the prison for his demented mind. Could that be it? I said you were nutty like the Necrophobes. Could you be even more bonkers than them?"

I didn't expect an answer, one way or the other. In that at least, Arnelius didn't surprise me.

Chapter 15

Luckran and Rubyan were at their usual spot, either side of the fire in the lounge of the Governors' Rooms, brandies at hand. Although technically summer had arrived, the weather was still cold and the building's central heating was not yet shut off. Even though there was no need for an open fire, Luckran liked it, and it burned as long as the oil did in the furnace below.

"I don't understand it," Rubyan said. "Last time I looked, not more than six months ago, the planet had changed very little. I had a look this morning, to confirm the news from the ship, and I see it's as advanced as us. How can that be?"

How smug he sounded, casually speaking of taking a look at a planet 30 light-years away. Had he been asked to explain the means by which he achieved such a wondrous feat, he'd have waffled his way to an uncomfortable silence, avoiding the word that had become an embarrassment to him: magic. How stupefied he'd have been had he known the planet was in fact on the other side of the universe and he was seeing it through Arnelius's portal. And now the sudden change in the indigenous civilisation had him flummoxed. He was like a man looking at a television screen for the very first time and thinking it was a window. No wonder he was bowled over when the picture changed.

"Somehow, you must have been seeing events from ages past?" Luckran replied.

"Yes. But why am I seeing it for real now? Maybe the supralight link with the ship has somehow put me in synch." Rubyan shook his head, unhappy with his own conjecture. "Well, whatever the reasons," he said forcefully, slapping the arm of his chair, "we must inform the Emperor."

"I've already done so," Luckran lied. "He wants you to transfer to the ship." Luckran was saddened to see Rubyan swell with pride. He pined for the old days, when he could talk openly to his friend about the project's primary purpose: get Destlar off Earda. Now, the magician was in awe of the Emperor, believed in the Velkren and saw himself as one of his indispensable instruments. There was nothing Luckran could do but play to that. He hadn't spoken to Destlar about the new world for quite some time. The Emperor had no interest in the new world, at least not yet. As for Rubyan, Destlar didn't even know he existed.

"So he wants me to go to the ship?"

"Yes. He is anxious to extend the care and vigilance of the Velkren to the new domain. For the moment, the ship will remain hidden behind the shroud. Rendal, are you listening?"

Rubyan returned from a dream where he welcomed the Velkren to the new world. "Sorry. So, remain behind the shroud. You don't think we should try to communicate with the natives? Negotiate?"

"Not yet. Not before we get those missiles replaced. Then, if it came to it, we could launch one or two at some sparsely populated area, just to show who's boss."

"We can MatScan the missile parts, and the crew can assemble them there."

"Good. And of course there's you. A couple of demonstrations and you would appear godlike. You will assume command of both the project and the ship."

"What about the traitor?"

Luckran thumped the leather armrest. "Tavenar, the fool. What a mess he made. As soon as you get a chance, send her and Kryslor back here. I'll deal with them."

***

Destlar entered the dungeon and sat on the leather couch. "Be ready to wake the mother and child in two hours' time," he commanded the doctors.

"Yes, Your Majesty," they replied in unison, bowing together like a well-rehearsed double act.

While the doctors retreated into the back rooms, Destlar made himself comfortable. He closed his eyes and let his mind expand, seeking the mother and finding her in the first room to his left. He entered her, traversing her body at a microscopic level, seeking out and destroying damaged cells, rejuvenating healthy cells, thereby reversing the ageing process. It was a technique he'd discovered when he became excessively worried about his own degenerating tissue. Killing off those malignant cells that caused so much harm was especially satisfying, even in a body other than his own. It left him drained but thoroughly satisfied.

He performed the treatment upon himself and his trusty First Advisor whenever he felt like it. For the mother and child, it was every few months; whenever he felt like playing with them.

The procedure took close to an hour to complete. He felt no desire to rush it. It kept the mother at almost the same age, physically, as she had been on the day he'd first raped her, 30 years earlier.

He rested a while before subjecting the boy to a similar treatment, one that wasn't quite as satisfying as it didn't take as long and there were fewer diseased cells that needed to be destroyed.

The doctors reappeared. They woke the mother and child and escorted them from two separate rooms. As usual, the mother was put in the chair on Destlar's left, the child on his right. She regarded her son longingly while he shuffled his bum back along the cushion, his feet dangling over the edge. She could clearly recall every one of the many times they'd been brought before their tormentor. Already her tears were flowing.

Since Destlar erased the boy's memory after each performance, the child had no idea what to expect. He frowned, wondering why his mother was crying. He looked about, searching for his father, not realising the magician who had once shot a bolt of lightning at a fighter jet had been dead for decades.

"Please," the mother cried, "don't do this. Just me this time. Leave my son alone."

The boy didn't know why his mother was crying, but it scared him. "Mommy," he said, as he too started to cry. She got up and ran to her son, picking him up and hugging him close.

"Sit down!" Destlar shouted. She ignored him, until something pushed them apart. She tried frantically to hold on to the wailing boy, but she was picked up and thrown back into the seat while the boy was laid gently on the floor before her.

The doctors returned, leading a fat naked man. The mother started to scream when she saw him. She leaped at him, attacking the rolls of fat with her tiny fists. But again, she was slammed back into her seat.

The fat man regarded the boy hungrily.

***

Destlar entered his living room, suffused in a warmth he often felt upon returning from the dungeon. He sat on the couch with a glass of wine and switched on the television to watch the news. "The fourth night," shouted a reporter, taking shelter under the porch of a deserted café, "and the storm is as fierce as ever!" He was in the mountains south of Wesmork. Behind him trees bent in the gale, their branches' erratic movements exaggerated by a shop's neon sign that had been ripped from its mounting and was being whipped about on the end of its electrical cable.

"This little town," the reporter continued, clasping his hood tightly about his head, "is in the eye of the storm and has been the hardest to reach. The townspeople are being loaded into army transports and taken down the mountain." The camera shook, the reporter ducked involuntarily as the night was brilliantly lit by a deafening, crackling bolt of blue-white light.

@

Chapter 15

Meteorologists were confused by the storm that formed rapidly out of placid conditions and had raged for four days without moving, apart from spinning about the town below.

The camera panned and zoomed in on the last few locals being helped into the back of a truck. An old man in a dark robe threw back his hood and looked directly into the lens.

Destlar jumped up, his wine glass dropping to the floor. Ignoring the crimson seeping into the blue carpet, he stared at the screen, into the brown eyes that, even in the low light, sparkled. The wrinkled face, framed by bushy grey hair and beard, seemed to be aware of him. The trace of a smile said hello.

Destlar ran across the room and pulled the rope. Moments later, his valet found him pacing between the windows. Spotting the spilled wine, he went to pick up the glass. "Never mind that," Destlar shouted. "Find Luckran. Now!"

"Yes, Your Majesty," bowed the valet, quickly retreating from the room. When he arrived back a few minutes later with a maid to clean up the mess and with the news that the First Advisor would arrive within the hour, the Emperor had calmed much.

"Tell him not to bother. I will see him tomorrow." Destlar was a little embarrassed by his ridiculous reaction to an old man who happened to remind him of an adversary centuries dead. Yet his stomach was tied in a knot. "Bring me a girl. Petite."

"Yes, Your Majesty."

***

In the early hours of the morning, Destlar lay on his back in his gigantic bed, snoring. Before he went to sleep, the valet had had another mess cleaned off the carpet, this time a teenage corpse. The climax of His Majesty's encounter with the girl had been strangulation with the belt from his bathrobe, after which he'd tossed her lifeless naked body to the floor, rung for the valet and got into the shower.

211

A crashing sound startled him from a dreamless sleep. He sat up in the darkness, confused, attempting to identify the sound that was already disappearing below the waves of his consciousness. To his left, between the edges of the east window curtains, he could see a flickering light. He got out of bed and pulled back the curtains. At the far end of his roof garden, trees were on fire, branches waving and flames dancing in an intensifying wind.

Night flashed brighter than day, the tower shook and a sizzling clap caused him to reflexively cover his ears. Instinctively, he knew this was no common storm, that the bolts were far from ordinary lightning. As another struck, directly above his head, he knew with terrifying conviction that the colossal torrent of energy would slice through the tower and his skull, if he did nothing to stop it. In a tiny fraction of a second, he raised a shield above the tower. The jagged white light struck the invisible barrier and dissipated harmlessly down its sides.

For more than an hour, Destlar fought for his life. At first, raising the shield to meet each attack was easy. But after the tenth strike, he began to feel the strain. Initially, he held his arms aloft, as if they had something to do with holding the shield in place. Half an hour into the battle, he was lying flat on the bed, all his efforts put into raising the life-saving barrier.

As soon as the latest stream of electrons was exhausted, he dropped the shield and exhaled forcefully. He closed his eyes, waiting for the next attack. It didn't come. He crawled to the edge of the mattress and pulled the rope. Moments later, the valet entered. "Where's Luckran?" Destlar croaked.

Five minutes went by before Luckran entered the living room to see a pale Destlar stagger from his bedroom and collapse on the couch. Luckran was amazed by the grey circles about the tired eyes.

"Where were you?"

Luckran looked puzzled. "There was a fire on the roof. I was overseeing the efforts to tackle it. I am happy to report it has been extinguished with minimal damage."

Destlar sat forward and stared at the blank television screen. "I thought he was dead," he mumbled. His tiny black eyes betrayed his bewilderment and fear. "Why now, after so many years?"

"Your Majesty?"

Destlar looked at his First Advisor. "Arnelius is back."

"Arnelius? Surely not."

The magician sighed and collapsed back onto the cushions. "You recognise the name?"

Luckran nodded. "A warlock whom Your Majesty defeated, seven hundred years ago."

"Not as thoroughly as I thought. I saw him on television earlier tonight, in the middle of that strange storm in the mountains. Now I know he created it, probably as some kind of test. Then he launched his attack here. You think that was just lightning?"

"With respect," Luckran said, sidestepping the question, "is Your Majesty sure? Could he really have survived this long?"

"Why not? I have. I don't know why he's waited till now to attack." He ran his hands through his dark hair. "So strong. So, so strong. I was just about able to hold him back, Luckran." For the first time ever, Luckran felt pity for the tyrant. "What if he strikes again?" the Velkren whimpered.

"Your Majesty believes he will?"

Destlar gave the tiniest nod.

"Then I think it would be wise to leave the palace. If he doesn't know Your Majesty's whereabouts, how can he attack?"

With great reluctance, Destlar agreed.

Chapter 16

Willkob was surprised to hear a knock on his front door during such a ferocious blizzard. He walked into the vestibule and opened the door. A large man stood outside, his black robe and wispy grey hair whipping about in the biting wind. Willkob, shivering in sympathy, held the door wide. "Come in. Come in," he said.

"Thank you," the stranger replied as he stepped inside. His robe and shoes were clean and dry.

Willkob held his arm out, inviting his unexpected guest into the living room. He noticed the man's broad shoulders and hair were free of snow, as if he hadn't just walked through a snowstorm. Willkob glanced outside, expecting to see a vehicle. There was none. "How did you get here?"

The man turned to him with a smile. "I dropped out of the sky."

Not wishing to be impolite, Willkob decided to probe no further. Perhaps the man was too embarrassed to admit he'd got lost. But why had he been out walking on such an awful day? And he wasn't dressed properly either. Could the robes be a clue? Was he a magician who had overestimated his own prowess to the same degree that he had underestimated the severity of the northern climate?

"You must be cold. Let me get you some soup."

"I appreciate the offer, but no, thank you. Shall we sit, Hervan?"

Willkob raised an eyebrow. "You know me?"

"Of course." The stranger pulled out a chair and settled down, both elbows on the table.

Willkob took a chair opposite, perplexed but unafraid. Though he was NALO's leader, he didn't believe he was in danger. If the police somehow discovered the position he held in the so-called terrorist organisation, the most they would do is arrest him. And they wouldn't send an old man dressed like a magician to do it. "I'm afraid I don't know you. Are you a magician?"

"My name is Arnelius. And I used to think I was a magician, before I discovered it's not magic, just mystery. To man, that is. Of course Luckran has worked hard to make sure it stays that way."

"Ah, the First Advisor. You represent him?"

"In a way."

"I've dealt with his agents many times over the years, but this is the first time he's sent one to my house. He could have picked a better day."

"I'm not his agent. We're more like partners."

"Partners?"

"Our goal is the removal of Destlar from this world."

Willkob laughed. "You might want to pay more attention to your partner, because he's done nothing but protect the same Destlar for more than a century. He's the chief reason the defiler is still upon the throne."

"I agree. He's done a magnificent job in keeping the man safe. That was his top priority. But he's also kept things running pretty smoothly. No wars. No one starving."

"Oh yes, a wonderful job," Willkob answered, his voice full of sarcasm. "No wars, but plenty of suffering. No one starving, but many hungry. The police keep the rich safe but harass and abuse the poor. And the Velkren," he continued with venom, "sits in his tower and picks and chooses those he will torture and murder."

Willkob dropped his head, disappointed he had allowed anger to get the better of him. There was no point in ranting and raving about Luckran and Destlar. Like illness and death, they were a part of life, and nothing would change that. Like the harsh winters and the slowly encroaching ice, they shaped his and everyone's existence. They were obstacles and difficulties that one had to struggle with throughout the first existence so that the second, the eternal, would be all the more rewarding.

"I know," Arnelius said softly. "Destlar is a very sick man. And though I don't expect you to believe me, let me tell you Luckran has prevented him from doing so much more. Thousands would have died, if Luckran had not been the First Advisor. There would have been terrible carnage. Magicians would have risen against Destlar, and would have fought valiantly, only to be destroyed by immense power. Massive energies would have been released, evaporating the ice in some areas and scorching the ground beneath, while the resulting rains would have flooded others."

"You paint a horrific picture, and I think you are perhaps exaggerating Luckran's importance. But I accept the crux of your argument. Though I've never met the First Advisor, I've had enough dealings with him to understand that, unlike Destlar, he's not an evil man. He's doing what he believes is right, accepting inequality as the price for stability."

Is this what he'd been reduced to, accepting the status quo? Was he afraid of adding more martyrs to his dreams?

But this strange man with the kind eyes had spoken of killing Destlar. Perhaps Luckran finally realised he didn't need the Emperor. Could it be possible? "You said you want to kill Destlar."

"Well, those weren't my exact words, but basically, yes."

"And you think I can help you. Well, I don't—"

"Oh no, you can be of no help," Arnelius interrupted. "I didn't come here for your help. I came to offer you a job. The top job."

"And what top job would that be?"

"First Advisor, of course."

Willkob laughed again. "I don't know what you expect to gain from such nonsense talk." He was beginning to wonder if the man was some kind of nutcase.

"I don't expect you to believe me. I only came here to plant the idea in your head. Luckran will want to speak with you too, at a later date, when he's not so busy."

"Ready to retire, is he?"

"Indeed he is."

"I see. Well, I look forward to finally meeting him. I'd better have the place decorated before receiving such an important guest."

"You'll be his guest, at the palace."

"To take up my new position. And who will I be advising?"

"Alyna, of course."

"Alyna?" Willkob said, trying to sound puzzled.

"Now Hervan, are you really going to pretend you know nothing of Alyna? I'm one of the few who's aware of her existence. Even Destlar doesn't know he has a daughter. Sheltered by NALO since she was little more than a child, she will readily accept you as her First Advisor."

Willkob shook his head. "Do you really expect me to believe Luckran, or anyone else, would allow Alyna to sit on the throne?"

"Luckran's counting on it. There is proof of her lineage. He is very pleased she exists, for without her there would be a fight for the throne. Who knows how that would turn out. Civil war, most likely."

"And the Assembly will accept an unknown woman and a terrorist?"

"They will accept the true heir and a priest of the Order of Lurg."

Willkob stood up. "I don't believe a word of this."

"Please, sit down and let me finish. Then I'll leave. The storm doesn't bother me."

Willkob hesitated.

"Please," Arnelius reiterated. "Just a few more minutes."

Willkob sat down slowly. "For the sake of being polite, I'll let you finish."

"Thank you. The Palace will announce the Velkren's imminent departure from this world, his work complete. The Velkren will present his daughter, naming her his successor. The Assembly will be taken by surprise, as they expect the Emperor to live forever. But, since Alyna really is his daughter, they will be happy enough to accept her as a figurehead, since that's the way they view her father. With Luckran remaining as First Advisor, they will see it as business as usual."

"Ah, now it makes sense," Willkob said with an ironic smile. "Luckran will be the one with the power, and Alyna will be his puppet. My task is to persuade Alyna to accept."

"Luckran will step aside when the time is right. Believe me, he can't wait to. And he sees you as his ideal replacement. You've cared well for the people of the North for these many years, always with compassion and understanding. But you've never looked upon the South as your enemy. Only Destlar, whom you tried to kill once."

Willkob winced as Olsker's boyish features appeared to his mind's eye. "How do you know about that?"

"I just know," Arnelius replied. "And I also know you regret it. But you didn't shy away from that tough decision, nor have you allowed yourself to forget." He leaned forward. "Alyna will need you, will rely on you to bridge the gap between North and South."

"If what you say is true, why did Luckran not come and present his case in person?"

"Right now, he's too busy preparing for Destlar's departure." Arnelius sat back and smiled. "You're wondering am I mad or is this some kind of trick. I'll leave you to ponder. But once you hear the official announcement of the Velkren's departure, get packing." He stood up.

"What about Alyna? Do you expect me to give her the good news?"

"That's something else for you to think about."

Arnelius left Willkob at the table and walked out into the snow.

Chapter 17

Rubyan made his way down a quiet corridor in the basement of the Imperial villa in the Swutland mountains. He walked up to a steel door and entered his code. The door clicked. He pulled down the steel handle, pushed the door open and entered a small windowless room. Ceiling lights came on, reflecting off the white walls and floor, off the Deep Sleep unit with its open lid in the centre of the room. The door clicked closed behind him. He walked over to a computer terminal against the wall. As he sat down, it came to life. He checked that everything was in order. The Deep Sleep and MatScan processes were operational, kept alive by the nuclear generator in a lower basement. So was the shield that he'd spent years creating, but it was suspended, awaiting the Velkren.

Rubyan initiated a transfer. Behind him, the Deep Sleep unit beeped. A moment later, acknowledgement arrived from the twin unit aboard the distant spaceship. He smiled, still amazed he had developed this supra-light communication. He stood up, removed his clothes, folded them and placed them on the desk. Conscious of the fact that only he and Luckran had access to the MatScan chamber, he chuckled as he pictured the First Advisor removing his clothes from the room, underwear and all.

Rubyan turned around and climbed naked into the unit. Sensing his presence, it beeped again. All he had to do now was close the lid and the MatScan transfer would begin. But he hesitated, scared. He wasn't afraid of MatScan, or of entering Deep Sleep. He had full confidence in the systems he'd designed and built. No, what scared him was leaving Earda. He was afraid of putting 30 light-years between himself and the Velkren. Would the anti-ageing spell work over such an enormous distance? "Have faith, Rendal," he said as he reached for the lid. Quickly, before he could change his mind, he pulled it closed.

The sequence began. He was put to sleep, his body scanned, torn asunder in the process. The gathered information was fired along the supra-light channel to the distant receiver.

***

Rubyan became aware of a rapid clicking sound. At first, he could see nothing. Then the lights appeared, as if the idea of sight brought them into being. Tiny balls of light, each one appearing with a click and shooting off into the distance along the same slightly curved path. Their origin was hidden from view, but he sensed it getting closer as time slipped by.

And though the terminus was also out of sight, he could feel each ball slot into its correct position with unerring accuracy. It was very satisfying.

Until the birthing of the lights eventually drew close to his centre of being and he became anxious, afraid of the inevitable leap.

And then abruptly, the perspective switched. He was at the other end, the tiny yellow balls flying towards him and slotting into place. He felt his whole being ripple in pleasure and relief.

The last ball reached its new home and then there was nothing but darkness, and silence.

***

Later, Rubyan would have no recollection of his strange experience during the transfer, except in his dreams.

***

Rubyan woke in a strange bed in a small room with no windows. He looked to his right. A bearded man sitting at a desk smiled at him.

221

"Welcome aboard, Dr Rubyan," the man said as he stood up, his robes settling about him. "It is good to see you again."

"I'm on the ship!" Rubyan gasped. The man—the magician—nodded.

He'd made it. He'd travelled to another solar system in a matter of minutes.

But elation was instantly replaced by fear. He held his breath and searched for the spell. He couldn't find it. He started to panic, his heart pumping. He was almost ready to ask them to send him back when he found it. He relaxed. It was there, working. He could just about feel it. The Velkren's quickening hand was reaching across interstellar space, invigorating His Majesty's loyal and indispensable subject.

"How long have I been asleep?" he asked.

"A couple of hours," the magician replied. "It is normal to be tired and sleepy when coming out of Deep Sleep, especially the first time." Then he smiled and shook his head. "Listen to me, explaining Deep Sleep to the man who invented it."

***

Ferist and Jeseque lay together in Jeseque's cabin. "It's great fun, having to hide under your bed every night," Ferist said. "It's like we're having an affair and Seldin's your husband."

"A husband who locks me in my room every night." Jeseque smiled, enjoying his playfulness. "What a pair of clowns I'm stuck between." She propped herself on her elbow and looked down at Ferist, her smile fading. "But it's time to get serious. Tomorrow night, stay in your cabin and look through the logs again."

"We tried that already," Ferist complained. "I found nothing."

"Yeah, but maybe some of the logs are being hidden from you," Jeseque said, though she thought it unlikely. Why would any of the logs be hidden from an engineer? "I have a control account I want you to use."

"I thought they deleted it."

"I have another one. It becomes active at two in the morning and remains active for three hours."

"What do you mean?"

"A program is scheduled to run at two. It creates a control account, which you can then log into. Everyone's asleep then, so hopefully no one will notice. Another program deactivates it and scrubs it from the logs."

"You wrote these programs?"

"Yeah. They're hidden in the waste system folders. No one will find them."

Ferist shook his head, smiling. "Fantastic. I never would have thought of that. And even if I had, I don't think I'd be able to write them."

"Yes, well you can save the congratulations for later. There's no guarantee you'll find anything more interesting with the control account. But we have to try. We can't lie about here doing nothing."

"I'm insulted you call it nothing."

Jeseque thumped him. "Idiot!" she smiled. "Can you try to stay focused?"

"Yes, ma'am."

"Eventually, this new guy is going to find the time to send us to Luckran, and that'll end our hopes of alerting the Velkren."

"You're right, of course. But I'm still not sure what I'm supposed to be looking for."

"I don't know. Something might jump out at you." Jeseque wasn't too hopeful, and from the look on Ferist's face, she could see he was about as confident. "What do you think of this Dr Rubyan?" she asked as she got off the bed and sat by the desk.

Ferist sat up, his back to the wall. "He's the new boss. There's no doubt about that."

"Definitely." Rubyan had informed Jeseque, brusquely and with a hint of scorn, that she would be returned to Earda at the earliest convenience to be dealt with by the First Advisor. Since then, two uneventful days had passed, so it seemed that getting her off the ship was not a priority. "He looks ancient," she said.

"Yeah. But full of energy."

Another long-lifer, Jeseque thought. They're all getting together now. What is this, the start of a new race?

"And you don't believe in this MatScan they're talking about?" Ferist said. "You think he came up in an orbital and was sneaked aboard."

"Of course. It's nonsense. The magicians are boasting about this incredible technology just to hide the fact we're in orbit about Earda. You and I know we haven't gone anywhere, unless there's another planet out there with a moon identical to ours."

"And you don't believe we've been on this ship for decades?"

"No. More like months."

"You really think so?"

"Of course."

"I hope you're right." Ferist stared at the wall, his inner eye somewhere else. After a moment's silence, he spoke quietly. "I was thrilled to be part of this mission, travelling to another solar system. What an honour. But what a price to pay." He turned to her. "If I didn't have you, I don't think I could have coped."

Jeseque was confused. "What do you mean?"

Ferist frowned. "My parents, of course. I thought I'd never see them again."

Jeseque was shocked. Having no father and a loveless mother, it had never occurred to her that Ferist might have been grieving.

She was appalled. She always knew her upbringing had warped her, made her different. But not until that moment had she realised how deformed she was. Had a life without love resulted in her inability to even imagine it in others? Like

Jeseque, Ferist's relationship with his parents was far from perfect. She'd assumed it too was without feeling. But it wasn't. Though flawed, there must be real love there. She wondered what it was like.

For Ferist, she belatedly realised, it was as if his parents had died suddenly. He had been quietly dealing with a terrible loss. The others on the ship had known for a long time what they were getting into. They had made their choice, knowing, or believing, they would be away from Earda for decades, perhaps forever. But Ferist had been given no choice. When he had said goodnight to his parents that evening in the villa, he had had no idea that it would be for the last time.

"I thought," Ferist continued, "I would return to a younger brother who would be decades older and ruling in my place. And my parents would be...you know..."

The few times Ferist had mentioned his brother, Jeseque had complained about his father's status allowing him to freely have a second child while for ordinary people this was forbidden. Others were punished with a life sentence in the mines, or had their second child taken away, perhaps even murdered. Now she felt bad that she had not listened to him, that she had been so uncaring. "What's it like, to have a brother?"

"I don't really know him that well. Even for my father, a second child is not something you want to show off. Cloron was sent away to school, so I had very few dealings with him. He's six years younger than me. But I enjoyed the odd moments we spent together. He seemed quite nice. I think, when we get back, I'll make a better effort to get to know him."

Jeseque returned to the bed and took Ferist in her arms. He snuggled his head on her neck and shoulder. For a time, they sat together in silence, listening to each other's contented breathing. Then Ferist turned to Jeseque with a big smile. "Thanks to you, I no longer grieve. I looked up at the moon and I knew everything was all right."

Jeseque groaned. "That is so corny."

**

Destlar collapsed amongst the pillows, his consciousness sinking further, blissfully accepting precious sleep. Then suddenly, in every part of his being, he sensed the impending bolt. His eyes snapped open and a pitiful moan escaped his thin blue lips. For the umpteenth time he raised the shield. A torrent of electrons crashed against it and crackled down its sides. For one horrible moment, he felt the shield weaken and was sure it would fail. But somehow it held.

Arnelius had found him again, despite Luckran's assurance that he wouldn't. For more than two hours Destlar had deflected attack after attack. At times the strikes came in quick succession. Then there would be a lull. Minutes would pass, but just as Destlar would begin to hope it was over, it would start again.

This time, however, it was over. Destlar was in a deep sleep before he had a moment to wish for no more.

Luckran walked into the room. He regarded the unconscious form sprawled on the mattress. "This is torture," he whispered. "We're no better than him."

"Regrettable," Arnelius answered, the words forming inside Luckran's head. "But necessary."

"We can't be sure of that. He might not find his way into the grid. And even if he does, he may not be the monster we envisage."

"You doubt?"

Luckran sighed. "Of course I do. Isn't that natural?"

"After all I've shown you?"

"You've shown me conjecture."

"All right, then. What about the girl he strangled only a few nights ago, just so he could luxuriate in her neural spikes? Or the mother who has had to watch her child being systematically raped for thirty years? Have you forgotten them already?"

"No, I haven't forgotten them! How could I? I allow it to happen. Of course you're right, we must proceed. Otherwise, they will have suffered for nothing."

***

Destlar woke in a strange bed, in a strange room. To his right, sunlight streamed through a wide window, reflecting off matte walls, a sloping timber ceiling and a multitude of dancing dust motes between. Everything was white: the walls, the ceiling, the pillows and blankets, the bell rope to his left. He reached over and pulled it.

A moment later, Luckran entered. "Where am I?" Destlar asked softly.

Luckran bowed. "Forgive me if I erred, but I felt it wise to move Your Majesty to the Imperial residence at the MatScan terminal. It is most secure."

This was now the third time Destlar had been relocated since Arnelius had launched his first attack. Initially he had moved to a secret site within Wesmork. For the first time in his life, the Emperor had donned an ordinary suit of clothes, grey jacket and trousers, common amongst members of the Assembly, then boarded a helicopter, wearing a hat and dark glasses. Even the pilot had no idea who it was he was carrying. Arnelius had waited six nights, just to let Destlar begin to feel safe. Then he attacked. The following morning, they were off again, this time to a chalet a thousand miles from His Majesty's capital city. Again, Arnelius waited, this time for three days. He then fought Destlar to total exhaustion, and while the man was unconscious, Luckran moved him to the remote villa in the Swutland mountains. They had him where they wanted him.

"How is Your Majesty feeling?" the First Advisor enquired.

"Tired." The rings about his eyes were getting darker, and his face was drawn, even paler than usual. Most nights he found it hard to sleep, tossing and turning for hours, wondering if Arnelius would catch up with him again. With sunrise, he'd finally drop off, as his antagonist seemed to prefer nocturnal assaults. But his sleep was disturbed by a recurring dream where he fell through ice and was trapped in a terribly cold river that swept him forever onwards. Each time, when he was about to run out of air, he would jump awake.

"Perhaps some breakfast, Your Majesty?"

"Just coffee."

"I'll have it brought up."

"Tell me about this MatScan. Is it safe?"

"Perfectly, Your Majesty."

"You recommend it?"

"Yes, Your Majesty, if the situation becomes dire. But perhaps he will fail to locate Your Majesty this time."

"No," Destlar whispered, lying back on the pillows and staring at the ceiling. "He has already found me. I can feel him."

***

Luckran left the room, put the order in with the kitchen, then entered his own room and sat at his desk. "He's almost ready," he said quietly.

"I see that," Arnelius replied.

"He thinks he can sense your presence."

"Rubyan's shield. Even though it's not active, its latent energy is confusing him. But that's good. It'll keep him on edge."

"You need to be careful." The searing bolts of light were pushing the man close to the edge, but it was imperative they did not push him over, lest he fall and, like a chick from a nest, learn to fly.

"I am being careful. One more attack should have the invincible Emperor running for the exit. You'd better get on to Rubyan and have him extend the shield."

"You really think we need it?"

"Yes. The Necrophobes are gathering, Listur amongst them."

"Rubyan won't like this. He'll want more time."

"Convince him there is none. I don't want to wait any longer. The time glitch has left the ship in orbit about a dangerous planet."

"We considered that eventuality. Hence the shroud."

"I still don't like it. I wish we had developed the alternative terminal here on Earda, like we'd planned."

"That would have required bringing Rendal fully within our confidence," Luckran said. "Unfortunately, he went in the other direction. Anyway, the local terminal would only have been used as a last resort. Destlar might have spotted the ruse. It is so difficult to judge his abilities."

"You're right. And of course there's no point in wishing. Get on to Rubyan and let's get this over with "

"You think you're desperate to get this over with? Ha!"

***

Rubyan's shield, primed and ready at the MatScan terminal, was a staggeringly impressive piece of work. The First Advisor had charged the magician with developing a spell that would protect the Emperor from any threat imaginable. Rendal Rubyan must have had an unbounded imagination, for what he produced would even keep Listur at bay. I wondered how the magician could have designed such an effective barrier if he didn't even know the Grid Riders existed. My theory was that Arnelius helped him, subliminally. But when I suggested this to Arnelius, he denied it. Maybe he didn't trust me to remain quiet. He was afraid Listur would find out.

***

Luckran turned to the computer on his desk and typed in a code that was known only to himself and Rubyan. A few moments after initiating a connection, a groggy face appeared on the screen before him. Rubyan was dressed in a grey short-sleeved top. "Oulezandur," he said, his voice cracked with sleep.

"I'm sorry for waking you," Luckran answered. "But this is important. The Emperor will be visiting you quite soon. You'd better get ready."

Rubyan's eyes grew wide. "We haven't even begun to prepare for that yet. We're working on restocking the missile system."

"No time for that. His Majesty has made his decision. He said thirty years is long enough to wait."

"Please, Oulezandur. Persuade him to wait."

"I've already tried, several times. But when he gets like this, nothing will change his mind. So you'd better get to work extending the shield."

Rubyan shook his head. "I can't believe the moment has arrived."

"You've done well, Rendal. Your whole life has been leading up to this. It's what you were born to do."

"Thank you, Oulezandur. It's been an amazing journey." He frowned. "But you're sure we're not rushing things?"

"No. Everything is set."

***

Rubyan and his acolytes assembled the following morning in the MatScan chamber. One side of the room was taken up by a standard MatScan terminal. Its purpose was to receive goods. Currently, it was being used to restock the arsenal. On the other side of the room sat the specially modified Deep Sleep unit that kept live subjects in suspended animation during transfer.

Dressed in black robes, the magicians sat in a semicircle, with Rubyan at the centre, similarly attired. When, five days earlier, he'd found himself in a small bed in the tiny cabin assigned to him by Captain Abrim, he'd also discovered he was naked beneath the blankets. The bearded magician, Irou, had handed him a robe, then stepped outside to allow him some privacy. Donning the robe, Rubyan had smiled at the thought of Irou and the other magicians lifting his naked self from the Deep Sleep unit. It seemed he had nothing more to hide.

Finding the robe unexpectedly comfortable, Rubyan had decided to continue with the new wardrobe and now his regular clothes lay unused in his cabin.

Rubyan regarded his eager group, each one a gifted magician. They sat with their hands resting lightly in their laps, regarding their mentor with awe. He found the attention as pleasing now as it had been 30 years earlier. He was pleased to be leading these remarkable men once again.

"Gentlemen, it seems we are to be honoured with His Majesty's presence much sooner than expected." The magicians exchanged surprised glances, then turned as one to look at the empty hibernation unit to their right, as if they expected the Velkren to emerge from it that very moment.

Rubyan followed their gaze. He'd built that unit decades earlier. The same unit that had later built him. Naturally, he'd pondered the philosophical questions: Was he still Rubyan, or just a copy? If there truly was an afterlife, was the real Rubyan there now, reunited with his wife? Would he, the copy, join them sometime in the future? And would they fight over her? The absurdity made him laugh inside. Though he'd found the Gods, he was still a pragmatic man who felt there was little to be gained from trying to answer the unanswerable. As far as he was concerned, he was Dr Rendal Rubyan, magician to the Velkren.

"The missiles will have to be left for now." Most of his time on the ship had been spent planning and then implementing the restocking of the arsenal. Before he made the world below aware of their presence, with some powerful mystic demonstration that he hadn't yet settled upon, he wanted the missiles as back-up. And while the goods terminal could receive reasonably bulky items, the missiles were large and had to be sent in pieces and reassembled by the engineers. It was time-consuming, but already they had three missiles in place. However, all that would now stop.

"We don't know when the Emperor intends to arrive, but it is likely to be very soon," he said. "We need to extend the transmission shield to enclose the receiver."

"Is the shield anything like the shroud, doctor?" Irou asked. If Rubyan's memory served him correctly, Irou had been chiefly responsible for the development of the shroud. While the man had a right to be proud of his achievement, Rubyan couldn't help feeling the shroud would not have failed if he himself had taken charge. But with so much work to do back then, he'd been forced to delegate.

"No. The shroud hides us only. The shield, once activated, will leave us invulnerable. Nothing will be able to get through. You'll see how different it is, once we begin.

"Now, this will be a challenge, because once we begin, we cannot stop the weave until it is complete. We will therefore work in shifts, four at a time while the other two rest.

"We need to be able to relax while working, and we cannot afford interruptions. Therefore, each of us will retire to his cabin. I suggest stretching out on the bed, but you should go with whatever makes you most comfortable. But remember, you will be working for hours without a break.

"So, let's start by drawing up a schedule. For the first hour, all six of us will work together so that I can familiarise you with the spell and the task before you. Agreed?"

"Yes, doctor," the magicians chorused. As always, they were eager to learn.

***

After Seldin locked Jeseque in for the night, Ferist came out from under the bed, dragging a computer console and its cables with him.

Jeseque frowned. "What the hell?"

Ferist stood up. "Well, since you can't get to my cabin to access the computer, I thought I'd bring the computer to you."

Jeseque looked at him with wide eyes. "That's brilliant! Why didn't I think of that?"

Ferist shrugged. "Even a genius can't think of everything."

"You're the genius. Come on, let's plug it in."

Ferist lifted the console onto the desk while Jeseque got in under it to plug in the cables. "How's Seldin treating you?" he asked.

Jeseque stopped what she was doing to look up at him. "What the hell are you talking about?"

"I just wonder if he's getting as bitchy as the others. They're bored. By now they expected to be down on the surface."

"That's what they believe?"

"Yeah. They were told there would be a population of only a few hundred million, so it would be easy to find an isolated place to set down."

Jeseque scootched out from under the desk and sat in front of the console. "I can't believe none of them have figured it out," she said as she pressed the power button. "Just look at the moon."

"Actually, speaking of the moon..."

"What about it?"

"A couple of them were talking about how amazing it is to see a moon so like ours. It seems they were expecting it."

"What do you mean, so like ours? It's the moon."

"Actually, it's not."

"You said it was."

"I thought it was. But if you look closely, the craters are very different."

"What about the size?"

"Same size. And it's the same distance from the planet."

"Oh for the love of Lurg! Don't you see? They're disguising it, the same as Earda. What are the odds of this so-called new world having a moon the same size as ours, the same distance away?"

"Not good."

"Exactly. Religious nuts. They can't stop and think for themselves. They'd believe the world was flat if they hadn't gone into orbit." Jeseque sighed.

"Anyway," she said when the console was ready, "let's have a look at these logs."

***

"I knew it!" Jeseque exclaimed, waking Ferist from slumber.

Lying on the bed, he propped himself up on his elbow and looked over at his girlfriend. "Knew what?"

"It's not magic."

"You found something?" Ferist got off the bed and crossed to the desk to look over her shoulder. "I knew you would."

"You see that code?" she asked, pointing at a line of text on the screen. "I remember seeing that before, on the electrical schematics. Most of the schematics were standard. I could see the circuits that power the lights, the water heaters, and so on. But then there were some sections that were designated with cryptic codes only, codes like this. I guessed those circuits provide power for artificial gravity and the shroud. You see? It's not magic. Who ever heard of magic needing electricity?"

Ferist frowned. "Are you sure that's what those circuits are for?"

"I am now." She pointed to the log. "Look at that entry. This circuit failed shortly before we came out of hibernation this last time."

Ferist nodded. "Right. It was Seldin who fixed it. When we were all finished in the washroom, after coming out of hibernation, we met him already relaxing in the lounge, like he'd been awake for hours. He told us the magicians woke him up first so that he could repair a break in one of the circuits. They were very anxious."

Jeseque pointed to another line, further down the page. "And there's the evidence of his handiwork. The circuit comes back online."

"But artificial gravity and the shroud. How are they doing this? We don't have the technology."

"Obviously we do, but it's being kept secret. What is it with the engineers on this ship? Why aren't they more inquisitive?"

"They believe in magic. A lot of people do, even engineers. I was one of them, until you enlightened me."

Jeseque was pleased to hear him say it, only for him to then go and ruin the moment.

"They don't realise magic belongs to the Velkren alone."

Jeseque sighed. "Well anyway. To think that's all I'd have to do to make the ship visible: kill that circuit."

Ferist smiled. "You mean all I have to do."

Jeseque spun around to look at him. "No," she said, "I can't ask you to do that."

"You're not asking, I'm offering." Jeseque shook her head. Ferist ignored her. "If we hesitate," he pressed on, "we might be too late. Remember, they have three missiles on board, so your earlier action is almost undone. If they intend to strike the palace, they might do so at any time. Where's the sense in waiting?"

Jeseque felt pity for the poor fool. It wasn't long ago that he was a dutiful member of the crew, delighted with any little praise he got from the captain. Now he was ready to betray. She wondered if he simply craved approval.

"This is my mission," she said. "Not yours."

What mission? a little voice asked. Whose orders was she following? She'd never received any encouragement from NALO. She'd risked jail, maybe even her life, to forward classified information on the IP fighter jets. Those efforts had never even been acknowledged, let alone approved. Would they approve of her actions now? Would they even care? Was she again putting her life in danger, and now perhaps Ferist's life too, for nothing?

"Think about it, Ferist. The ship was visible while under construction. Making it visible again probably won't achieve anything."

"Yeah, you're right. That alone might not do the trick. But it's a start."

"Listen to me, please," Jeseque said. "I'm already in trouble. There's no point in you getting yourself mixed up in this."

"Darling, save your breath. The Velkren, in his mysterious ways, got you aboard this ship. Perhaps he meant for me to be here too, to help you." He grabbed his shirt from the floor and pulled it on. "Now, give Seldin a call, tell him you're having bladder trouble."

"No, Ferist. I'm only guessing that's the shroud's circuit. I could be completely wrong. It might be something critical."

"You're not wrong and you know it."

"There's not enough time. You'll need my control account to open the circuit panels."

Ferist glanced at the time on the console. "It'll be active for another half an hour. Plenty of time."

"But you need to study the schematic."

Ferist laughed. "I may not be the programmer you are, but I can read a schematic. Now come on, call Seldin."

He crouched down, ready to get under the bed. Jeseque stood up and grabbed him by the shoulders, pulling him upright. "No, Ferist. Let's leave it. Let's keep out of trouble."

"You're already in trouble. And where you go, I go." He tilted his head and narrowed his eyes. "Jeseque Debrone losing her nerve at the vital moment. Whatever would the Velkren say?"

"Ferist, sit for a second." He sat on the bed, but only to pull on his shoes. "I don't think you realise the seriousness of what you're about to do," she pleaded. "The magicians will go crazy. Abrim might not be able to stop them killing us both, especially now with this Rubyan aboard. You don't have to do this just to impress me."

"Jeseque, I love you and I would do anything for you. But that's not why I'm doing this. Don't you see what's happening? Despite everything, despite Luckran, the Velkren managed to get us aboard this ship. He knew we'd get this opportunity. We must act!"

Deluded idiot, Jeseque thought. She wanted to tell him that there was no Velkren, no gods and Destlar was a fraud, a despot who had half the world fooled and the other half terrorised. But she said nothing. She had been using his naivety, and again she felt the stab of guilt. For a fleeting moment, she considered telling him the truth, all of it, but fear and shame kept her quiet.

Ferist got under the bed. "Call him."

***

"What kind of a treacherous crew have you assembled, Captain!" Kelso the magician yelled. Abrim had summoned him and fellow magician Irou from their sleep as soon as he'd received the computer alert. In preparation for the Emperor's arrival, the other magicians, including Dr Rubyan, were busy weaving a powerful spell that apparently would leave the ship impervious to attack. Abrim wished it had been completed already.

The three men stood in the control centre, watching a recording of Kryslor punching in an access code on the keypad next to the electrical control panels. A crewman sitting at a computer console looked furtively at the furious magician.

Abrim wondered if he should have seen this coming. Kryslor and Debrone had been added to the crew at the same time. If she was a traitor, should he have deduced that Kryslor was too? But there had been nothing to suggest the engineer was anything but faithful. And he had been a member of the ancillary staff. Why should the captain suspect someone assigned to him by Major Tavenar of the Imperial Engineering Corps?

As for Debrone, he hadn't been surprised by her actions, considering it typical behaviour for a shunned female.

But it turned out they were in league and there was a bigger conspiracy here. He wondered if the two had secretly known each other all along.

"You're not in control of your own ship," Kelso continued.

"Well that's quite obvious, isn't it," Abrim shot back. "It's you and your boss, the great doctor, who are in charge. You want the power? Then accept the responsibility."

"Gentlemen," Irou said calmly, before his colleague could reply. "Let's not argue. We've all made mistakes. We should have wasted no time in returning Kryslor and Debrone to Earda, but we considered restocking the arsenal a higher priority. It's obvious now we got that wrong, but let's move on. Captain, how long will it take to fix the circuit?"

"Ten, fifteen minutes should do it. And I suggest we also move into a higher orbit, for added security."

Irou nodded. "Good idea."

"Captain," interrupted the crewman at the console. "A missile! Rising from the surface, heading this way." He turned away from the screen to face Abrim, his eyes wide. "Just under five minutes to impact."

***

Rubyan was stretched out on his bed, above the blankets. Even though they were in their own cabins, he could sense the presence of the other three magicians as together they continued the weave. In his mind, the shield was like the copper mesh used to protect data transmission lines from interference. It stretched all the way from the terminal on Earda through unfathomable subspace to surround the ship. When his shift was over, he'd hand the threads he was working on to his replacement, wondering what metaphors that man would use to allow his mind to focus upon the repetitive task.

Abrim stood in the doorway to the little cabin while the two magicians tentatively approached their master. Rubyan would have appeared sound asleep, if it wasn't for his hands. Abrim found it difficult to look at the long digits that jumped and twitched and tapped together in a macabre dance. He was relieved when the magicians shook the doctor's shoulder and the fingers stopped moving.

For a moment nothing else happened. They shook him again. Abrim noticed they did so in unison, as if they needed each other's support.

Rubyan ignored the interruption for as long as he could. He tried to concentrate, to remain in the weave, but eventually he had to let go. He carefully handed over the strands he was manipulating to the other weavers. It was a delicate manoeuvre and it put pressure on the magicians, but they were up to the task. Despite his anger and frustration, he was proud of his protégés.

Rubyan's eyes shot open. "What the hell are you doing?" he shouted. "Have you gone crazy?"

"I'm sorry, doctor," explained Irou. "We wouldn't have done so if the situation wasn't dire. In just over a minute, unless you can do something about it, the ship will be smashed to pieces by an incoming missile."

"What? How?"

"The shroud has failed."

Rubyan sat up. "Again!" he said, staring at Irou.

Irou didn't flinch. "Explanations later, doctor," he said. "Right now, we desperately need you."

Rubyan closed his eyes.

***

There wasn't a sound but for the buzz of the corridor lights and the throb of a blood vessel behind Abrim's left ear. He tightened his fists, his nails digging into the palms of his hands. He found he was holding his breath and tightening his bowels. He almost laughed at the pointless but instinctive reaction of the human in a moment of crisis. He forced himself to relax, knowing there was nothing he could do now but hope the faith these men put in their master was justified. However, a moment later he found he'd stopped breathing again.

The magicians stood stock-still, brows furrowed as they stared at their comrade. Perhaps they were trying to see what he was doing. Perhaps they could see what he was doing but were powerless to help. Or maybe their faith was being tested and found wanting. Whatever caused the expressions of concern, Abrim certainly gained no reassurance from them.

He was afraid to look at his watch. He felt time must surely be up. With hunched shoulders and twisted face, he anticipated the jarring impact, the explosion. He wondered if he'd have time to notice he was dying.

Rubyan opened his eyes. "It's done," he stated.

"You destroyed it?" asked Kelso.

"Yes."

The two magicians embraced, letting forth short yelps of delight and relief. They then turned to their saviour to congratulate him, faces beaming reverence.

Abrim looked at his watch and was amazed to find that only 20 seconds had passed since Rubyan had closed his eyes. His legs felt weak, but he was determined not to show it. "Truly amazing, Dr Rubyan."

"Why did the shroud fail?" Rubyan snapped.

"I'm afraid we were sabotaged. I'll let your colleagues fill you in." Abrim hurried off in the direction of the control centre.

***

Rubyan listened as the two magicians explained the situation.

"Where's Kryslor now?"

"Confined to his cabin, just like the girl."

Rubyan shook his head, wishing he had taken the time to send them back to Earda. "The other three will have to continue with the shield for the moment. I want you two to activate the shroud as soon as the circuit is repaired."

"Yes, sir," they said together, then turned to go.

***

"Oulezandur," Rubyan said, sitting at the console in his cabin. "We came very close to never speaking again, unless as guests of Kerl." He went on to explain what had happened.

Luckran gasped. "Damn it, Rendal, what's going on? What happened to the shroud?"

"It was disabled. Kryslor."

"That idiot! How did he get out?"

Rubyan frowned. "Get out?"

"Surely you had him locked up. He and Debrone were put on the ship together. Don't you remember? They've known each other for years. They're in league!"

"Nobody told me that."

Luckran was about to yell that he'd told Rubyan. But he wasn't sure that he had. There was just so much going on and he was tired. Tired beyond belief.

"You should have sent the two of them back," he said with a sigh, "like I told you to."

"I know. We were just so busy with the missiles and then the shield."

"Well, it could be worse. At least you were there to save the day. No harm done. I'm sorry for getting angry."

"No problem," Rubyan said, recalling how he had been about to go after Irou about the shroud, until he learned the man was completely innocent.

"Send them back now," Luckran said. "I don't want them there while Destlar is transferring across."

Rubyan rubbed his forehead. He looked tired too. "I'm nervous, Oulezandur. Something's not right. I think we should pause."

"Rendal, we've been over this. The Emperor is unwilling to wait. Anyway, you're just feeling a bit jittery, which is to be expected after such a close call."

"No, that's not it. I was going to call you anyway because I've had this nagging doubt for days. And if anything, the attack should encourage me to move forward, quickly. Bring His Majesty here so that he can take control of this heathen world."

"Exactly. And the shroud won't fail again so you're perfectly safe."

"I know, but still, I'm anxious. I can't shake the feeling we've somehow missed something. It's been bothering me for a while."

"Of course you're anxious. You've spent sixty, seventy years on this project and now you're almost there. It's natural to be worried, right at the end. But stick it out just another day or two. Then you'll be able to relax. You will have done your duty and the Emperor will reward you."

"I suppose you're right."

"Of course I'm right. Stay calm, Rendal. We're almost there."

Chapter 18

Seldin unlocked the door and pushed it open. "You crazy bastards!" he said to Jeseque. She was sitting on the bed, expecting some kind of reaction from Abrim and his crew. However, the angry look on what was normally a jovial face shocked her. "That idiot Kryslor nearly got us all killed."

"What do you mean?"

"Don't play innocent. You put him up to it. We know you did."

"But it was just the shroud, wasn't it?"

"Just the shroud," Seldin repeated with a shake of his head. "What do you think the shroud's for? As soon as he dropped it, they fired a missile at us. What kind of xenophobic lunatics are they down there? Nice way to welcome your first interstellar guests."

"I don't understand."

"They tried to destroy us! If it wasn't for Dr Rubyan we'd all be dead." He stepped into the room and reached out. Jeseque flinched, thinking he was going to hit her. But instead he grabbed her roughly by the upper arm and pulled her to her feet. "Come on!"

"What about Ferist? Where is he?"

"You first, I've been told." He shoved her out the door.

"Where are you taking me?"

"To Dr Rubyan." Seldin shoved her down the corridor ahead of him. "I wouldn't be surprised if he throws you out the airlock. I can tell you, no one will try to stop him."

Jeseque felt her stomach tighten as she considered what might be the last few moments of her life, being ushered along a windowless corridor by a man who suddenly hated her. She gritted her teeth and shook her head, as if to physically expel her thoughts of impending doom. She forced her mind to contemplate the shocking development instead. A missile? Could it be true? And if so, who fired it? Certainly not NALO. She wasn't sure if even the Imperial forces possessed such capability.

With unnecessary pushing, Seldin marched Jeseque past the empty kitchen and lounge, around the corner to the right and then back to the left. "Wait here," he said. Jeseque wasn't surprised to see they had stopped outside the one door that had always remained closed to her. Despite her fear, she was curious to see what lay inside.

The door slid open to reveal the ancient magician in his dark robes. "Leave her with me."

Seldin pushed her across the portal. The door slid closed behind her. The magician turned his back on her, walked across the small room and sat down at a console. Jeseque regarded the Deep Sleep unit to her left, surprised to find one there. To her right she saw what seemed to be a long flat container with a roll-back top. She took a step closer. Inside were two rows of electronic components. At a cursory glance she was unable to discern their function. They looked like they were on display.

Her musings were interrupted by the magician, who was still facing away from her. "Take off your clothes," he said in a casual tone.

Jeseque wasn't sure she had heard him right. "What?"

"Take off your clothes."

"Why?"

"I don't have time for your questions. Just do it!"

"No!"

The magician sighed. He turned around and fixed her with a steady gaze.

Jeseque yelped when a sharp pain erupted in her left cheek, then faded to a light sting. It felt just like a slap. A soundless slap. She stared at the magician with wide eyes, far more shocked than hurt. How had he done that? She looked down at the floor, wondering if she was standing on a conducting pad, but all she saw was the same blue-grey carpet that was fitted throughout the ship.

"I can inflict a lot more pain than that," the magician said calmly, "if you do not cooperate. Take off your clothes!"

Jeseque looked up at the ceiling. Maybe she'd been struck by a tiny dart.

Her mouth erupted in pain. Every tooth in her head ached. She clasped her hands to her chin, groaning. Tiny knives stabbed her gums.

"I warned you." As soon as he spoke, the pain ceased. Jeseque massaged her jaws and stared at him. He had her full attention now, her curiosity stifled. "Believe me," he continued in the same calm voice, "you do not want me to go to the next level."

Jeseque stood still for a moment. Then she slowly dropped her shorts and top to the floor and stood with her arms folded.

"All of it," ordered the magician.

She hesitated for just a moment, then dropped her underwear on top of the rest. She was about to try covering herself as best she could, then decided it was pointless. She joined her hands behind her back, lifted her head and looked across at the magician defiantly.

He smiled at her. She couldn't decide whether he was admiring her courage or her body. Wondering if she was about to be raped, her bravery diminished as quickly as her fear grew. She wondered if she might even be shared out to the crew. Seldin's snarling face appeared in her head and she was surprised to find how sad it made her feel. She had really liked him.

But the magician redirected her mind by pointing to the Deep Sleep unit and telling her to get in.

Jeseque frowned. "What?"

"Is it impossible for you to simply do as you're told?" He sighed again. "Girls should do as they're told."

Jeseque opened her mouth to reply, some caustic remark forming in her brain, but she bit it back. "I'll do as you ask," she said instead, "if you let me see Ferist first."

Pain stabbed through her teeth and gums again. She cried out and the pain ceased, like he was flicking a switch.

"You are in no position to bargain. Get into the unit now or I will make the pain last until you do. I have very little patience left."

Without another word, Jeseque walked to the unit and climbed in. She was surprised to find the interior was not soft and comfortable like the other hibernation units, but was smooth plastic, hard and cold against her skin. She wondered why she was being put to sleep there. Why not in the hibernation centre? And why was she naked?

The magician appeared above her. When he reached out, she flinched, but he was only closing the lid.

The darkness had never bothered her before, but now she recalled how the units always reminded her of elaborate coffins. Suddenly it all became clear. This was not a Deep Sleep unit, but some new form of execution. Her breathing became shallow and rapid and she reached for the lid. However, her rising panic was smothered by the Deep Sleep process.

***

Jeseque looked up as the door opened and a naked man was pushed inside. "Ferist!" she cried as the door was quickly closed and locked from the outside. She jumped up from the bed, ran over to him and threw her arms about him. She kissed his cheeks, then hugged him tighter.

He looked down at her, dazed. "Jeseque?"

"Yes, it's me." She guided him towards the bed and helped him sit. "Ferist? Are you awake?" At last, his eyes focused, and he smiled. She kissed him again.

"What happened?" he asked.

"Rubyan. He forced you into the Deep Sleep unit too?"

Ferist's brow wrinkled as he tried to remember. "Yes. That's right. I was...but what happened? Where are we?"

"I don't know." She hugged him again. "Oh Ferist, I was so scared. I thought I was going to die in that coffin."

Ferist shuddered. "Me too."

"Then the next thing I know I'm being helped along an unfamiliar corridor by some woman. She put me in this room. I've been sitting here for I don't know how long. I was so worried about you. I've seen no one but that woman. She came back with these clothes."

Ferist looked at what she was wearing. A short black skirt and a white blouse. "Looks like a maid's outfit," he said. He then looked about the tiny room, with its bare white walls and a single bed with a cabinet next to it. "No window. Just like our cabins."

Jeseque smiled. "We still can't see outside and I'm still locked in my room."

"This time I'm locked in with you." He smiled back. "So things have improved."

Suddenly she was crying. "This is all my fault."

"No it's not. You couldn't have known what would happen. Anyway, we survived."

"But not for long," she replied through her sobs. "Luckran will have no mercy."

"But you're the Velkren's agent. He won't allow that to happen."

The Velkren's agent. What a joke! She wasn't even NALO's agent. It was time to admit that it wasn't just Ferist she'd been deceiving for years.

***

Back in military school, Ferist had once managed to drag Jeseque to the dark campus bar. She ended up in a corner with an older student, the beer before her going flat. She was drunk. She had no idea when Ferist had left as she'd pointedly ignored him.

The older student listened to her bitch and slur about the Emperor, the Palace, Luckran. He agreed with her, encouraged her, told her he could get her into NALO. He wrote something on a scrap of paper. "Use this," he said, "but not from your own computer. Use a public booth. Tell them about yourself. Don't expect an answer right away. It could be a while before they get in touch."

After that one night, he kept his distance. To be on the safe side, he'd explained. He'd never tried to get her into bed, which had lent him some credibility. But that was as close as she'd ever got to NALO.

A few months later she received a code for an electronic drop box. She was encouraged to deposit any information she considered useful in the box.

She was in. So she believed, or wanted to believe. But deep down she'd always known she was communicating with no one.

It was time to face the fact that Jeseque Debrone was a mythomaniac.

***

The door opened, a set of clothes was thrown inside onto the floor, then the door closed again. They didn't even catch a glimpse of the supplier.

"Friendly place," Ferist said as he walked over to the small bundle. He picked up a pair of white trousers, stepped into them, then pulled a short-sleeved white shirt over his head.

Jeseque laughed lightly. "You're the cook and I'm the waitress." Then she started crying again. Ferist sat beside her on the bed and gathered her in his arms. "Am I a bad person, Ferist?"

"No. Why would you say that?"

"I seem to cause nothing but misery. I nearly killed us all. Not just me and you but the entire crew. And look at the trouble you're in now, just because you became involved with me."

"I'm the one who brought down the shroud, remember."

"But it was my idea. I'm the worst thing that ever happened to you."

"Utter rubbish! You're the exact opposite."

She wiped her eyes with her sleeve. "When I was a little girl, about eight, I had a friend. We used to play together, until I ruined everything. I destroyed her life. Her parents should have kept me away from their daughter, like the others did. But they were too kind and they didn't believe I should be punished for my mother's sins."

***

Jeseque's favourite place in the whole world was Acoony's apartment. Her friend's parents always seemed to be in good humour. It didn't matter if they were running short of milk or bread, or if the rent was overdue. "Fretting about it isn't going to make the money appear," Acoony's father would say. "Remember, girls: care, but don't worry." It was a favourite phrase of his.

Most days Acoony took Jeseque home with her after school. For the first few hours they would have the place to themselves as Acoony's mother and father both worked.

One fateful evening, when her friend was in the toilet, Jeseque decided to have a peek at the parents' bedroom. She was intrigued by the large statue standing on a table just to the right of the window. It was made of smooth shiny stone, a golden-haired woman in a long white robe and with a ring of flowers in her hair. The statue rested on a white lace cloth, with red candles in small glass holders arranged about it. Three red cushions sat on the floor before the table, obviously for kneeling upon.

Jeseque walked over to the statue. Its head was tilted to one side and it looked upon her with a tiny smile. The large blue eyes caught Jeseque's and suddenly she stopped. Though she knew the statue was only stone, she couldn't help but feel there was life in those kind eyes. It was so different from the representations of the Gods she saw in the Church of Oshkar, the God of Water, to which her mother took her every week. There the statues' faces were severe, the eyes were cold, the postures imperious. Magnificent paintings had sinners cowering before enormous punishing waves and drowning in retributive floods. They evoked notions of discipline and punishment, whereas the white lady made Jeseque think of comfort and warmth and understanding. Jeseque imagined the lady knew her, knew her secret thoughts, her hopes and her fears.

"You're not supposed to be in here."

Jeseque spun around. Acoony was standing at the door, her face a mixture of anger and fear.

"I was only looking."

"But you're not supposed to be in here," Acoony reiterated sharply.

"All right," Jeseque answered petulantly. "What's the problem? I didn't touch anything." She left the room and Acoony quickly shut the door. They went back to the kitchen table and resumed their drawing. The unusual silence was heavy, and it made Jeseque uncomfortable and a little ashamed. She wanted to say something, but couldn't think of anything natural, unforced. And the longer she remained silent, the worse it got, because no matter what came out of her mouth, Acoony would know she was only trying to make them both forget what had happened, which would only make it even harder to forget.

Jeseque tried to concentrate on her picture. It was supposed to be a snow-covered hill with a house at the bottom and trees at the top, but it wasn't much like the image she had in her head. She sighed, then looked over at Acoony, sitting around the corner of the table. They had agreed to draw the same thing, but Acoony's looked so different. Jeseque turned her head to one side to get a better view. She wondered how Acoony did it. She noticed the tree trunks weren't brown. They were different shades of blue. But everyone knew a tree trunk was brown. Yet it looked right. Jeseque watched Acoony work. She was using a blue crayon to colour in different parts of the hill, seemingly at random. A little patch here, another over there. Jeseque frowned. She was colouring the snow blue. Well, not all of it. Most of the snow was represented by the white paper. The little blue patches were shadows caused by hillocks and bumps and tracks in the snow. But shadows are grey, not blue.

In fact, the entire picture was made up of different shades of blue and it looked...it looked beautiful.

Whereas Jeseque's page was pasted with large gaudy patches of plastic colour. The hill was a big blob of white crayon on white paper. She stared at the page, then continued to colour in the sky. Very hard, and with gritted teeth, she rubbed the blue crayon across the top of the page.

Acoony looked up. "I need that," she said.

"I'm using it."

"But I only need it for a second."

"Wait!" Jeseque snapped. She continued pasting the page with blue.

"You're going to use it all."

"No I'm not."

"Yes you are. You're wasting it. And it looks horrible."

"Does not." Jeseque felt the tears welling up.

"Does. You're hopeless."

Jeseque threw the crayon. Though she didn't mean to, she hit Acoony in the face, close to her left eye. Acoony yelped, then jumped up, grabbed Jeseque's picture and scrunched it into a ball. Jeseque retaliated likewise.

"Bitch!" Acoony screamed. "Just like your mother! We all hate her. We hate you!"

Jeseque made for the door, crying. Moments later she was inside her own apartment. She ran to her room and dived on the bed, face down.

"What's the matter with you?" her mother asked from the bedroom door.

Through her sobs, Jeseque told the story of the drawings and the crayon.

"You need to learn how to fight better than that, girl."

Jeseque spun around, her eyes flashing. "They have a statue hidden up there."

"What kind of statue?"

"It's not one of the Gods. It's a woman."

"A woman. What does she look like?"

"She's..."

"What? She's what?"

"Nice."

"Flowers in her hair?"

"Yeah."

Her mother regarded her in silence for a moment, then walked away. Jeseque heard her lift the phone and dial. With her mother's muffled voice in the background, Jeseque pictured the lady with the blue eyes. There was sadness in those eyes.

The following morning, as Jeseque was getting ready to leave for school, she heard a commotion outside. She looked out the window and was surprised to see two police cars with flashing lights. Several policemen were dragging a big man to one of the cars. They were finding it hard to hold on to the man as he kicked and flailed. Jeseque's heart thumped as she recognised Acoony's father. Another policeman came into view, carrying the statue. He stood before Acoony's father and held the statue aloft. Jeseque imagined the gentle woman crying. The policeman then slammed the statue down on the concrete footpath.

She shattered into a million pieces.

Jeseque jumped when her mother spoke behind her. "Heathens. All three of them. And yet they're only taking the father."

Jeseque turned with wide eyes and a pale face. She looked up at her mother and noticed something she would never forget, no matter how hard she tried. Her mother was smiling, a smile of triumph and malice.

Jeseque ran. Down the stairs and out of the building. She hadn't taken the time to put on her coat and she shivered in the freezing wind. But she hardly noticed the cold. Acoony was outside too, screaming and crying and scrabbling at the policemen. Her father was yelling to be let go. He got one arm free and threw a punch at one of his abductors, catching the man on the side of the head. The response was immediate and vicious. Neighbours stood by, horrified as their friend was forced to the ground then kicked repeatedly in the face and the stomach and the groin. In moments he was unconscious. Jeseque thought he might be dead.

The policemen dragged the inert body across the snow and lifted it onto the back seat of one of the police cars. Then they were gone with sirens blaring, as if they'd just captured a most dangerous criminal.

Acoony turned to look at Jeseque. The hatred emanating from her eyes was too much for Jeseque to bear. Again she ran, unprepared, through the harsh and unforgiving conditions.

***

Ferist rocked Jeseque in his arms as they sat together on the bed, the intensity of her anguish frightening. She cried loud and long, her cheeks wet with tears. After a time, the torrent began to subside and eventually she was able to speak once more, though with a cracked voice through a raw throat.

"I didn't know that was going to happen. I thought they'd just take the statue away. But her father was never seen again. I don't know if the flunkeys killed him there and then, or if he was taken away to the mines. I don't know if anyone ever found out. Acoony never spoke to me again, and neither did anyone else. People didn't like or trust my mother before that day, but from then on it was worse. Much worse. We were hated. Being ostracised made it difficult for my mother to report on people, but she adapted. She just made stuff up, which worked just as well."

"It wasn't your fault," Ferist consoled, kissing her forehead.

"Yes it was. I was angry. And jealous. Acoony was better-looking than me and more talented and had wonderful parents. And the statue. The damn statue. It was only a lump of stone, but I was enthralled by it. I've never understood why. And because of that I ruined a happy family."

"You were only a child. And it was your mother who made the phone call." Ferist hugged her tight. "You must not blame yourself. You were only a child," he reiterated.

Jeseque breathed deeply. "I never told anyone. Not anyone."

Chapter 19

Rubyan woke gradually, his dream blending with reality. He was lying in bed, but he was alone. For a moment, he'd thought the First Advisor was in the cabin with him.

In the dream, Luckran had been there, by his bedside. A hospital bed. He was back in the same room, the one he'd woken in after his terrifying encounter with the Velkren. But this time he was much older. So old. He was dying.

Luckran stood beside him, holding his hand. He looked exactly the same as he always had. "You performed your duty," Oulezandur said. "You did what you were born to do. And now the Emperor rewards you. Sleep, my friend."

Rubyan sat up and ran his hands through his hair. His heart thumped as he understood at last. The closer he got to the time of the Velkren's arrival, the more frightened he became. He finally realised it was because afterwards, he'd be obsolete. The Velkren would have no further use for him.

It was so obvious. The Velkren kept his First Advisor ageless, whereas he only kept his magician alive. Why? Because His Majesty didn't intend on keeping him around forever. He, Rendal Rubyan, had one task. Finish it and he was done.

It was Luckran's fault. The man was obsessed with his damn scheme to bring the Velkren to this objectionable planet. He seemed to live for nothing else and he expected the same of his so-called friend, except that he, Lord Oulezandur Luckran, would survive the delivery date.

Rubyan sometimes wondered if it was all for Luckran's sake and not the Emperor's. Was he the one desperate to get off Earda? Was he simply using the Emperor? There were times when he behaved in a disrespectful manner towards His Majesty. Rubyan remembered that well, but he'd tried to ignore it.

"And he's always been so determined to prevent me from meeting the Velkren," Rubyan whispered to the empty cabin. He got out of bed and paced the tiny room. He pictured his father looking down on him, disappointed, but relieved to see his son finally wake up. "I should have been working with the Velkren all this time. I could've honoured my promise to you. I could have discovered the true nature of magic and then...and then we could do so much. We could do anything." He paused. "We could fix the climate!"

He stopped and stared at the blank bulkhead. "That's what we should be doing. Fix our own planet instead of putting all our efforts into a pointless journey to another one."

He sat heavily on the bed. "What are we doing here?"

***

Somewhat reluctantly, Destlar entered the small room. Luckran followed him, then closed the door firmly, making sure it was locked. The Emperor looked about, his eyes betraying his unease. The unremitting gaze that induced fear in proud, audacious men, the penetrating orbs that cut to the core like lasers through wood, were gone. In their place, two black holes darted about, like mice trying to escape a trap.

Luckran walked over to the Deep Sleep unit. "This is what we use for transferring people, rather than goods." He spoke in a prosaic tone as he tried to make the whole thing sound routine. Destlar walked over and placed his hand lightly on the lid, his mouth a thin line. "Due to its design," Luckran continued, "one must enter the unit naked as that makes the transfer more efficient." Luckran turned around and walked over to the computer terminal. "And the process is controlled from here. Once activated, this entire area is enclosed in a nucleo-binding field that shields the transfer from interference," he explained, making sure to sound very scientific. "Would Your Majesty care for a demonstration?"

Destlar nodded. Luckran touched the green circle in the middle of the screen and Rubyan's suspended shield dropped into place. Destlar's eyes opened wide. "He's gone," he said in a whisper.

"Your Majesty?"

"Arnelius. I can't feel him."

"That's the shield. Nothing can get through." Luckran allowed himself to enjoy the irony. Rubyan's shield was so good Destlar could not sense the fields that were generating it. It was amusing to see this man, so terrified of any magic other than his own, oblivious to the fact that he was now immersed in one of the world's finest magical feats. In fact, inside the shield, Destlar was more at ease than he had been for days.

Destlar took all technology for granted. The inner workings of the computer terminal before him were mysterious but uninteresting. And the shield was no different; he enjoyed its effects without caring how they were achieved.

In a sense, he was right; the shield was no more magic than the computer. But Rubyan was manipulating fields that every other scientist and engineer was completely unaware of. If Destlar was on the other side of the activated shield, he would have immediately recognised it as magic. Even suspended, he sensed it, but mistakenly attributed it to Arnelius.

The Emperor sighed. He turned around and looked at the Deep Sleep unit. He was conflicted, caught between fear of the known and fear of the unknown. He turned to the door, making it clear he desired to leave. Luckran's finger hovered over a red square on the bottom corner of the screen.

The moment had come.

***

High above the Imperial residence in the remote regions of the Swutland mountains, Arnelius floated. In every direction to the horizon jagged snow-covered peaks and sheer grey cliffs rose, like the misshapen teeth of a gargantuan monster. Fixing his attention upon the tiny rectangle that was the villa, Arnelius waited.

Beneath the villa, an opaque prism popped into existence, enclosing the MatScan chamber and the nuclear generator that powered both the terminal and the exotic barrier itself. The barrier stretched through the higher dimensions to the ship on the other side of the universe. It was strange to behold, delightful, as if a section of the universe had been surgically removed.

A few moments later, the barrier was gone. The flesh was replaced, the universe was whole again. Seeing this as his cue, Arnelius cleaved the air with a colossal burst of energy, the awesome display reflecting magnificently off the mountains, deepening the contrast between snow and rock.

***

Destlar sensed the bolt. He threw his hands over his head and cried out. Above the villa, lightning crashed against an invisible dome erected instantly by the beleaguered magician. Though as instinctive as his impotent physical reactions, the dome performed its purpose, absorbing the titanic energy. But only just.

"Your Majesty?" Luckran said in a calm voice.

Destlar fell to his knees. "Turn it on!"

"Your Majesty?" Luckran reiterated.

"Turn it on!" the Emperor screamed. The clear sky was lanced once more with a jagged stream of light. Destlar responded, whimpering. His dome held.

Luckran touched the green circle. The shield dropped into place, cutting off the attack. Destlar collapsed on his back, breathing heavily. "Leave it on," he whispered.

"Yes, Your Majesty."

"Safe," he mumbled. "Safe in here."

"Your Majesty cannot remain in here forever. Eventually, the air will run out."

"I'm not going back out there."

"Perhaps, Your Majesty, the time has come."

Destlar lifted himself on one elbow. He looked up at his First Advisor, then at the Deep Sleep unit above him. Luckran wondered if Arnelius had frightened him enough.

The Emperor looked back at Luckran, his expression one of resignation and fear. He nodded. Luckran turned to the computer screen. As he reached for it, a chime sounded. Luckran's eyes opened wide. Someone was coming through, from the other side. He couldn't believe it. After all those years of painstaking preparation, and just when Destlar had agreed to submit himself to MatScan, the system was unavailable.

"Rendal!" he hissed between clenched teeth. "Your Majesty," he continued in as normal a voice as he could muster, "I am sorry to have to report there will be a slight delay. A routine test of the system has just begun. One of the ship's engineers is coming through as we speak."

Destlar got to his feet and regarded the closed lid uneasily. "He's in there now?"

"Part of him." Luckran wondered why Destlar chose not to look through the lid, which would have been a simple feat for such a gifted magician. The Emperor was not squeamish. The body's internal organs were a savoury delight for him. But perhaps they only interested him when the subject was in pain. Or perhaps he was too scared, knowing he would shortly be in a similar state himself. "The process will take about fifteen minutes. Your Majesty may then proceed."

Welcoming the reprieve, Destlar grunted his approval. He began to pace, crossing from the door to the computer terminal in a few steps. Luckran watched the screen. A long rectangle slowly filled with green, indicating the transfer progress. It seemed to take an eternity. Destlar began to mumble about escape and new beginnings and an absence of magicians. "But it can't be safe," he whispered. "Fired through the air like a television signal. No good. No good. Pictures get distorted. Interference. Come out all mixed up."

"The shield, Your Majesty," Luckran interrupted. He spoke a lot more calmly than he felt. Again he cursed Rubyan. He and Arnelius had briefly discussed the magician's unexpected anxiety and its inconvenient timing, but neither of them could figure out what was causing it or what to do about it. The only solution Arnelius came up with was a timely heart attack.

"Why not?" he'd argued. "Now that he's extended the shield, we don't need him any more."

"Have you no heart?" Luckran had asked.

"Oh codswallop! I'm doing all this to save trillions. What's one old man who's lived way longer than he ever should have anyway. And I would make sure it was painless. He'd go in his sleep."

"No," Luckran had pleaded. "Please don't. He won't be a problem."

How wrong he'd been. Luckran now wished he'd listened to his old comrade.

But, he figured, regrets are pointless. He would quickly get rid of Rubyan. Which would mean suspending the shield, but only for a moment. And he considered that a boon, in fact, as Destlar was beginning to waver. Another stab from Arnelius should put him back on track.

"The signal is completely cocooned inside the shield," Luckran continued. "There can be no interference."

Destlar shook his head, mumbling incoherently.

Finally, the rectangle filled, the terminal chimed. The transfer was complete. The Deep Sleep unit unlocked itself with a clunk. Luckran opened the lid. Destlar peered in at an old man lying naked within. "As Your Majesty can see," Luckran said, "the system works perfectly."

Under different circumstances, Luckran would have given Rubyan time to wake up properly. But he was anxious to get him out the door before he became fully conscious and started babbling to the Emperor. "The system leaves one sleepy, for a time. Please allow me one moment, Your Majesty, to escort this man from the room." He guided Rubyan out of the unit and across to the door. He then skipped back to the computer screen, his habitual hunch forgotten, and touched the red square, suspending the shield. As he leaped back to the door, Arnelius struck. Destlar cried out.

Rubyan snapped awake. He looked up, his eyes focusing not on the ceiling but on something distant, as if there wasn't an entire building above his head. He could see through the timber and stone, to the clear sky above as it exploded like a thousand suns. He saw death race towards him. But before he had time to react, the blinding torrent was met by a stout obstacle. Lightning crackled down the sides of an energy field. He marvelled at its potency and the speed at which it had been generated. But the torrent continued, and the field began to weaken.

Rubyan closed his eyes and concentrated, adding strength to the field. He sensed the Emperor's presence, observed his mind working feverishly to sustain the barrier. For one glorious moment, he felt immensely proud to be working in tandem with the Velkren. But then suddenly he was alone, desperately trying to keep the field in place.

"Wizard!" Destlar screamed. "Magician!"

Luckran's mouth fell open. Destlar rushed at Rubyan. Luckran stepped in his way. Later, he could not understand why. Rubyan was too focused on trying to keep the massive energies at bay to notice what was happening. He was like a man who unexpectedly finds himself holding aloft a large rock all by himself. He struggled for a moment, then let go. His shoulders hunched as he anticipated the end. But instead, the rock disappeared. The torrent ceased. He just about had time to sigh in relief before he was hit with something else.

Destlar's arms shot out towards Luckran and Rubyan and they were lifted off their feet and sent tumbling towards the closed door, limbs flailing like swimmers caught by a freak wave. The door exploded outward and the two men, one naked, the other robed in green, were thrown into the hall to land among its wreckage.

Luckran spun around. Getting to his feet, he saw Destlar run to the console and reach for the green circle. Luckran ran for the door but was too late. He stopped when the room instantly disappeared and he found himself closing upon his own reflection.

Luckran stood looking at himself in the perfect mirror that was the shield. The wall and doorway had disappeared behind it. "Thanks, Rendal," Luckran said, addressing the magician's reflection. "I'm supposed to be in there."

Propped on one elbow, Rendal made no reply. Everything had happened so quickly and he was still reeling.

Luckran regarded the shield. It looked just like a full-length mirror, floor to ceiling and about ten feet wide, the width of the MatScan chamber. A casual observer would not find it strange, other than to wonder at finding such a large mirror in a narrow dimly lit corridor. Luckran touched it lightly. It did not feel like glass. It was smooth, but not cold. Nor was it warm.

"Why aren't you inside?" Arnelius asked incredulously.

That's the moment Luckran did something completely unexpected. Rubyan's jaw dropped and his eyes opened wide when his friend popped out of existence. He was astonished.

***

'Astonished' is far too small a word to describe my reaction upon discovering Luckran there beside me, in the grid. If I had been human, I think I would have had to sit down, maybe have a stiff drink. My mind reeled. Another human joining the Grid Riders? Could this race be on the cusp of transcendence? Were Luckran and Destlar the forerunners? No, it didn't make sense. Evolution had a lot more work to do before this species would, en masse, enter the grid. In fact, they probably never would. Luckran had to be an instinctive jumper, just like Destlar. But what were the odds of a single planet producing two such enigmatic beings? Then again, the universe is enormous, so even extremely unlikely events happen somewhere.

All this ran through my mind in a tiny fraction of a second. I pondered the fact that Luckran had spent more than a century trying to prevent Destlar from doing what he had just done. Given a moment more, perhaps I would have arrived at the correct conclusion. Then again, perhaps not.

Very often, when the reasons for some stupefying event are explained, the event loses some of its wonderment. It might even become mundane. In this case, the opposite was true.

"Meet Arnelius the ninth," Arnelius said, formally introducing Luckran.

For a moment, I didn't know what he meant. Then it hit me. "No, no, no!" I said. "It can't be."

"But it is," Arnelius replied. "It never occurred to you there might be many versions of me? That I would copy myself into the grid several times while Destlar kept me imprisoned?"

"I'm the only one foolish enough to get involved with you!" Luckran interjected.

Had I been human, I'm certain I would have passed out. Luckran one of us! A Grid Rider! All along! Impossible!

Picture a man with a pet tortoise that lived with him for years. Then one day, the tortoise shows himself for what he really is: a man. For decades everyone thought it was a slow and simple creature with a hard shell and tough green skin. But it was a man. All along, it was a man, pretending to be a tortoise. And no one ever suspected, not even once. It's difficult to imagine the shock. The mind won't accept something so ridiculous.

That's something of how I felt. The physical creature I had known as Luckran had only been a puppet. But the puppeteer had been completely hidden. Not once did I notice the strings. To be able to hide one's true nature for so long, it is the single most awesome act I have ever witnessed. How wonderful to have been there.

And imagine, countless Arneliuses! Of course they're not identical. Neural pathways are forever changing and so each version of himself he set sail upon the grid was slightly different from the previous one. Something must have gone wrong in the creation of the two versions I know. As they themselves admitted, none of the others saw the need to get involved with Destlar.

The one who became Luckran must be seriously warped. I still can't believe he did it. He was like a man with perfect eyesight stumbling about with his eyes closed for 200 years!

***

The blue and green sphere, painted with swirling white, rotated slowly below the cylindrical mirror. With the spaceship hidden inside, the shield extended through subspace to join with its counterpart about the MatScan chamber on Earda, at the far end of the universe.

Arnelius and Luckran argued.

"How could you end up on the wrong side?" Arnelius complained.

"Rubyan's timing was awful. I had to drop the shield to get him out of there. Then you hit Destlar too hard and Rubyan tried to help, which sent Destlar crazy. Before I could react, he threw us out. Now he's hiding behind your damn shield."

"Why didn't you just drop the physical? You could have been inside before he activated the shield."

"I spent two hundred years pretending to be human. Can you imagine what it's like trying to convince a paranoid lunatic that you're just an ordinary man? I had myself conditioned. I suppressed my natural reflexes."

"That's a poor excuse. Now look where we are."

"It's your fault. I never wanted the damn shield. I was afraid something like this would happen."

"You think it wasn't needed? Look at Listur, desperately trying to get through to his idol."

"Only because he's never been cut off from him before."

"If there were no shield he would have interfered."

"I don't accept that. It was years before he finally did something about you inside Destlar's head. And he did nothing about the portal or your recent attacks. It's only now because he can't see Destlar that he's going crazy. He's forgotten about the others and the excommunication threat."

"He did mess with the portal. He caused the time glitch."

"You don't know that for sure."

"I'm pretty sure. And I also believe that if he could have seen what we were about to do, he might have decided the safest thing to do was kill Destlar, physically. The shield was absolutely necessary, but you were supposed to be on the inside!"

"Oh what's the point in arguing?" Luckran said, resigned. "I think you're wrong. You think I'm wrong. And we'll never know who's right." They remained silent for a moment, no doubt pondering their wasted efforts.

"What do you think he's doing in there?" Arnelius finally asked.

"Pacing. Mumbling."

"You don't think he'll go for it?"

"It makes no difference now."

"Are you sure there's no way through that shield?" I asked. "Surely Rubyan isn't that good."

"Can you get past it?" Arnelius asked tetchily.

I threw myself at the barrier, enjoying the way I bounced off, the way it halted locomotion. I wasn't used to finding my way blocked. I've been everywhere, even to the centre of stars, but here was a region of space I simply could not reach. It was wonderfully novel.

"Maybe," Arnelius continued to Luckran, "there's some way to prevent him taking the shield down again."

"I won't imprison him forever," Luckran replied. "That really would be torture."

"I don't mean forever. Just long enough to think of something."

"Like what? Let's face it, we failed."

"So we try again," Arnelius declared.

"If we do, we swap roles."

I spotted a blemish. The reflection was distorted, like there was a tiny bubble on the surface. "There's a flaw," I said.

"What?" they both said together.

"See there? A little force applied to that spot, and maybe you could get through."

"No," Arnelius said, "the shield's perfect."

"Maybe not," Luckran replied as we moved towards the kink. "Rubyan told me he was interrupted while extending the shield, to deal with the missile. That might have caused it."

Arnelius noticed Listur following us.

As we wormed our way through the tiny gap, I realised then what Rubyan had done. The nodes were packed so tightly together it made it difficult for us, nothing but complicated arrangements of nodes ourselves, to move between them. "Rubyan couldn't have done this himself," I said. "Arnelius, you must have shown him."

"Oh be quiet," Arnelius replied sharply. "Go ahead. I'm going to tighten up these nodes. Hopefully I can keep Listur back."

"How did you do it?" I continued unabashed.

"We didn't," Luckran answered.

"Even now, making my way through, I still can't figure out how it was done. There's no way this is Rubyan's work."

Luckran disagreed. "It is his work. All of it."

Eventually we made it through. Luckran entered the Deep Sleep unit aboard the spaceship. "I don't believe it," he said as he gazed upon Destlar's naked body. Almost all of it had already been transferred from Earda. "He went for it."

"Are we too late?" Arnelius asked.

"Just in time," Luckran replied. "No head yet."

Luckran shot along the shielded path through subspace to the transmitter on Earda. I followed. "Don't disturb him," he warned me. "Don't ruin it all again."

***

Destlar looks out upon the plane, a blue carpet that stretches into the distance in all directions. He can see no walls, no roof, just carpet. Squares. Two slightly different shades of blue. He looks at the square he's standing on...or should be standing on. His body isn't there. It was there but now it's gone, beyond the horizon. He feels uneasy.

And something else. A presence. Reassuring. *Come. This is the way.*

A ripple in the distance, fast approaching. Squares falling away, into the abyss. He somehow knows the squares beyond the horizon fell some time ago. And now the falling squares are closer and closer. He is alarmed. He recoils, pulls away.

Don't fight it. Salvation awaits on the other side.

He spins about. There is nowhere to go. Squares disappear on all sides. Terror mounts as they all tumble and he is left above.

***

"Quickly!" Arnelius shouted. "Listur's making progress. He's frantic."

"I must wait," Luckran shot back. "You know I must wait!"

***

Destlar is terrified. He does not want to die. But he cannot remain where he is. He has a vague sense of another plane, up high, too far to leap.

He looks down and sees the squares land perfectly, not one out of place. The carpet is reformed far below.

Waiting for you.

He is calmer now. Still frightened, but ready.

He falls.

***

"Now!" Luckran shouts. "Kill the receiver."

Chapter 20

"Very clever," I said to Arnelius and Luckran as, unbeknownst to the people on board, they placed the ship back in orbit about Earda. "Sidestep his survival instincts by disintegrating his mind with the promise of rebuilding it. Then renege on the promise. I'm impressed. But why go to all that trouble to find a sister planet? All you needed was MatScan."

"And Deep Sleep," Arnelius said as he closed the portal. "And they were the two most challenging systems to develop. Moving humans through space is simple in comparison."

"The sister world was crucial," Luckran said, "if we hoped to deceive Destlar. If the MatScan terminal was elsewhere on Earda, or even on the moon, there's a good chance he would have noticed and then all our efforts would have been wasted."

"And it also helped confuse Listur and the Necrophobes," Arnelius added. "They thought all I was trying to do was remove Destlar from my beloved home."

"The Necrophobes," I said. "It will take them aeons to get over this. But at least poor Listur avoided excommunication."

***

"I said I'd be back," Arnelius announced as soon as Willkob opened the door. "And this time I brought my partner."

Willkob stared at the hunched figure in the green robes, standing next to the tall man in black.

"Hervan Willkob, at last we meet," the First Advisor said. "May we come in?"

"Yes," Willkob replied absently. He continued to stare at Lord Luckran, until the man raised an eyebrow. "Yes," Willkob repeated, standing aside. "Of course, come in."

The visitors walked through the inner door and made themselves comfortable either side of the table. Willkob closed the outer door slowly. For a moment he considered contacting the High Command. The two men seemed to be alone. What an opportunity.

No, they couldn't be alone. Luckran had to have brought security with him and they were, for the moment, keeping out of sight.

He closed the inner door and sat at the head of the table with Luckran on his right.

"So, have you decided?" Arnelius asked.

Willkob turned away from Luckran. "I had decided you were crazy."

"Now you know I'm not."

"It's a genuine offer," Luckran added. "The job is yours. You only have to say yes."

"What about Alyna?"

Arnelius smiled. "You haven't spoken to her."

"Of course not."

"No matter. With you aboard, she will accept."

"But I'm not aboard. And Alyna's not a fool." He looked at Luckran again. "She will never be your puppet."

"Of course she won't. I'm retiring."

"So I've been told. When the time is right?"

"Yes. When the time is right."

Arnelius sat forward and placed his hands on the table. He stared at Willkob. "Listen, Hervan. This is not a trick. Alyna will be Empress and you will be her First Advisor. Think of what you could do, the two of you together."

"With this man in between," Willkob countered, nodding at Luckran.

"I will remain," Luckran agreed, "for a while. To advise, and to ensure you are both secure."

Willkob looked askance. Arnelius sighed. "Are you willing to risk losing such a magnificent prize, just because you're afraid of being used?"

Willkob laughed. "A trivial concern, to be Lord Luckran's slave." But the stranger was right. He was tempted. Over the weeks since Arnelius's first visit, Willkob had tried to dismiss the dark-robed man and his unlikely offer. It was nothing but a fool's nonsense. And yet part of him had hoped, dreamed. So often he'd come close to contacting Alyna, to ask her advice. But every time, he'd balked as he imagined her derisive laughs.

But now the First Advisor was at the table, and the offer stood. However, that didn't mean it was any more genuine. There was something going on here that he simply couldn't figure out. "What if I refuse?"

"We'll be disappointed," Luckran answered. "And we will be forced to approach Alyna without you."

"So Alyna will sit on the throne, no matter my decision?"

"Yes. She is the true heir."

"But we want you," Arnelius added. "She will need you. This old man," he continued, pointing at Luckran, "won't be around much longer."

"NALO would think I'd betrayed them. And they'd be right."

"Nonsense," Luckran declared. "NALO has always hoped Alyna would somehow ascend to the throne. Now the chance has come. They will expect you to go with her. Arnelius is right, she will need you. Who else could she trust?"

"But I don't trust you, either of you."

"And you're wondering," Luckran surmised, "what we're really up to. It might be safer to say no. But then you'll forever wonder if you've missed a glorious opportunity. And when the Assembly starts fighting to see who takes my position—because believe me, I am leaving—and Alyna's left in the tower to play the part of obedient Empress with no true power, then you will regret. By then, it will be too late."

Arnelius chimed in. "We're offering you and Alyna everything. Isn't it worth the risk?"

Willkob sighed. "If I were to accept, how would it be done? No one expects Destlar to vacate the throne. No one in Wesmork knows he has an heir. And as for me..."

"It will be quite simple," Arnelius explained. "The Emperor will announce his time on Earda has come to an end. He will anoint Alyna, his only offspring, as his successor. A pious woman, the story will go, who until now has led a life of seclusion, of prayer and reverence. The devout will accept her without question. The rest, including the Assembly, will believe she's nothing but a figurehead. They already see Luckran here as the true power behind the throne. So they'll think it's business as usual. You'll be there with Alyna from the start. You and Luckran will be her advisors, truly. But you'll be kept from the public eye, for a time."

"Gradually," Luckran concluded, "I will bring you into the light. Then, when the time is right, I will quietly depart."

Willkob shook his head, unconvinced. "A simple handover of power. Just like that?"

Luckran smiled. "Just like that."

***

Destlar's dungeon doctors were taken to the basement where they would await their fate. Luckran helped the mother to the armchair, then returned for her son. Dazed, they sat opposite each other, with the First Advisor in the chair usually occupied by the monster.

While he waited for them to awaken fully, Luckran moved within the mother's mind, erasing 30 years of terror.

The boy's eyes opened fully. "Mammy," he cried as he ran to her. She gathered him into her arms, smiling with tears in her eyes. She hugged him and kissed him.

Presently, she turned to Luckran. "You're the First Advisor," she stated. When he nodded, she became frightened. "We're in the palace?"

"Yes, but you have nothing to fear. You have been here for many years, but your memories of that time will remain clouded, for your own sake. Now, you are free to go."

"And my husband?"

Luckran looked upon her sadly. "That much I think you do remember."

She nodded. "Yes, I do. What will become of us?"

"I assure you, both of you will spend the rest of your days in peace and tranquillity. I owe you that much."

***

Jeseque relaxed in a sumptuous leather seat. Ferist sat opposite, staring out the window at the clouds below. Apart from the steward and the pilots, there was no one else aboard the private jet.

Jeseque was amazed and frustrated but mostly relieved. While she and Ferist travelled from the Swutland mountains to Hightower, she'd spent the time trying to convince herself and Ferist that they would at least get their chance before a judge, all the while picturing Ferist against a wall, rifles aimed at his chest.

Neither happened. At Hightower, they were met by a major who presented them with their discharge papers. They signed and were free to go. But not before the major delivered the sad news of Ferist's treasonous father's execution.

Jeseque could make no sense of it. She still found it hard to accept she'd been wrong. Three decades had passed, even though she and the rest of the crew had aged only months. She couldn't figure out what it had all been about. It seemed pointless. And yet there had to be a point. She supposed it somehow made perfect sense to Lord Luckran. She wondered if it had anything to do with the sensational news that Destlar was moving on and had appointed his newfound daughter as his successor. But where could Destlar be going? She certainly didn't believe this nonsense about him returning to the heavens. Perhaps he'd simply decided to rule from some hidden location, with his daughter facing the flak and the possible assassination attempts. She doubted if it would make any difference. After all, Luckran was the true power.

Jeseque was beyond caring. There was no point in pretending any more. She wasn't making a difference. She had never made a difference. Her efforts to save the little boy on the train were a perfect representation of her futile existence.

The world was a mess, but being miserable about it didn't change that. She needed to learn how to be happy in the moment. And here was a start. She'd found a friend. More than a friend. She looked at him. He was still staring out the window. "I'm sorry, Ferist. I was so sure."

He turned to look at her. His chubby face somehow looked drawn. His eyes were tired. She knew he'd slept little. Yet he smiled, and she felt sure he was going to be all right, given time. "It's not your fault. And you were half right. We never went anywhere, just slept for a long time. And even if you'd been spot on, my father would still be dead." He shook his head, unable to believe.

"Luckran must have found out about his dealings with Tavenar." As soon as the words were out of her mouth, she wished she could somehow rewind.

"So it was my fault."

"No!" Jeseque answered firmly. "Absolutely not!"

"But if I hadn't been so incompetent, he wouldn't have had to always fix things for me."

"Look, Ferist. I spent years punishing myself for something I did when I was a child. You helped me see that. So I'm not going to let you do the same, not when you're completely innocent."

There was silence for a while, except for the soothing drone of the jet engines. Ferist returned to looking out the window. Jeseque regarded the man whose life had become entwined with hers. They had little in common. She knew she was smarter than him. And she didn't believe in the Gods or the Velkren, whereas he accepted them without question. She had strong, firm views on most issues, whereas he was very malleable. Yet she wanted to be with him. She wondered if it was because he looked up to her and showed her the respect she'd never got at home, or anywhere else.

"Do you think much has changed?" he suddenly asked. "It's been thirty years."

Jeseque shrugged. "Little things, I suppose. But the big picture will still be the same. Most people will still be struggling through life."

"What about the Velkren leaving? You didn't know anything about that, did you?"

"No." Jeseque smiled. He truly wasn't very clever. He still believed she was Destlar's agent. To her, such a position seemed incompatible with her vociferous dislike and mistrust of the establishment. Earlier, she might have responded angrily, berating him for his blind stupidity. Now, she found it amusing. Delightful and charming like a child's innocence. But she also felt uncomfortable, her stomach tightening. She didn't like misleading him, lying to him. And yet she wasn't willing to risk the truth. Not yet.

"You're not afraid of him leaving us alone?"

"No," Jeseque answered between tight lips. It was difficult not to argue with such rubbish.

"Neither am I. He wouldn't leave if he didn't feel we were ready."

Jeseque clamped her teeth. She needed to change the subject. "Are you looking forward to seeing your mother?"

Ferist frowned. "I'm not sure. My brother says she's confused a lot of the time. She might not understand. And it will be difficult to see her so aged. But I suppose it will be nice to spend some time with her." He didn't sound convinced.

"And your brother will stand aside," Jeseque stated.

Ferist raised his eyebrows. "I doubt it, though I suppose the fact that he sent the plane for us is encouraging. It must be a shock to him. He thought I was dead. He's been the prince for decades."

"But he must give up the throne. It's yours." Was this Jeseque speaking? Not so long ago, she would have been complaining about the injustices of inherited wealth and titles. "Or maybe you can work together," she said.

"He might not go for that. Which is a pity, because there are many things I'd like to do, to make life better for the people of Zervnia. Ideas you've given me."

Jeseque smiled again. "I'll help you. You have the law on your side, as you're the older brother. And once you're in power, we can work together to make life better." Jeseque was excited. Here was a chance to do something real. Ferist would wield significant power; she would orchestrate. They would make a fine team.

Ferist got up from his seat and sat down beside her. He put his arm around her and gave her a quick kiss. "How was I so lucky to meet you?"

"Do you love me?" she asked, quite seriously.

"Of course."

"How do you know?"

He laughed. "I just know." Seeing this answer was not satisfactory, he pondered a moment. "I'm happiest when I'm with you, and I'm only happy if you're happy."

"But I wasn't, when you met me. I was miserable."

"And now?"

"I'm certainly more content." She smiled. Was that all there was to it? If two people were completely comfortable together, and if one's happiness reinforced the other, did that mean they were in love? With nothing to compare, she couldn't be sure if this was indeed the real thing. Perhaps love defied analysis. Maybe Ferist's initial response was right. Maybe one just knew. Being with him felt right. It felt good. And she loved that feeling. She loved. She was loved.

Oh in the name of Kerl, just say it. "I love you too."

***

The Church of Lurg was packed to capacity. The First Advisor entered the vestibule and stood to one side. A deep reverberation emanated from the golden gong held aloft at the back of the church, just inside the inner doors. Whispered conversations died. Accompanied by the regular sounding of the gong, a double line of priests made its way up the central aisle and branched around the basin. Sunlight shone through the glass in the roof to sparkle off the clear water and the gold tiles beneath. As the blue-robed figures spread across the back of the altar, the Prelate walked up the aisle, Princess Alyna following three paces behind, dressed in a simple white robe, a cowl hiding her features. Meanwhile, Luckran moved along the left wall to stand at the altar's edge.

The Prelate stepped onto the altar and turned to face the congregation. Alyna knelt before him. Some in the congregation grew impatient with the old prelate's talk of homage to the Gods and how they loved and cared for mankind and how they had sent an angel to protect and serve during the world's harsh winter. However, most were captivated.

"The Velkren has decreed," proclaimed the Prelate, "His time with us is at an end. But this should not be a time of sorrow, or of fear, but one of rejoicing. The Velkren has appointed His successor," he announced, with outstretched arms, "Princess Alyna. May the Gods protect Your Highness, as Your Highness protects us."

"May the Gods protect Princess Alyna," the congregation chorused.

"Let us bow our heads," the Prelate called, "for the Velkren, Emperor Destlar!" From the side appeared a black-robed figure, silently making its way to the centre. At the other end, Luckran smiled. "Very good, Arnelius," he silently said. "Build and posture are perfect."

"Why, thank you," came the reply. "Now here comes the good bit."

Arnelius halted in front of Alyna and threw back his hood to reveal the familiar pale face with the pointy nose and the supercilious expression. With hands clasped in front, he paused for a moment or two. The church was quiet. The thin lips uttered no words. Arnelius had wanted to make a speech, but Luckran had convinced him it would be more effective if he remained silent. He now saw the First Advisor was correct. He had the congregation's undivided attention. Words would only spoil the moment.

Arnelius raised his left hand, indicating the vacant throne. Alyna, having been earlier schooled by Luckran, stood up slowly, paused for a moment, then walked over and sat on the golden cushion upon the white marble. Arnelius turned to face the enthralled audience and bowed low. He then walked across the altar and out through a side door. "All bow heads for Empress Alyna!" the Prelate called loudly. "May the Gods protect Her Majesty."

"May the Gods protect Her Majesty."

And that was it. The ceremony was far from complete, but Luckran had no interest in the remainder. He slipped quietly away.

***

Rubyan settled into the large seat, adjusting the black robes about him. A young woman, dressed in the light blue airline uniform, welcomed him aboard. Depositing a glass of white wine by his elbow, she did well to hide her initial surprise at finding a magician amongst the first-class passengers.

Rubyan lifted the glass and took a sip. It was good. He thought of Luckran, the brandy, the armchairs and the fire in the Governors' Rooms. He already missed the place, missed his friend. But he would not return, despite Luckran's pleadings. The First Advisor was now a stranger to him. Luckran had tried to convince Rubyan that he hadn't suddenly disappeared into thin air, that he'd simply imagined it. He had been under stress and had suffered a blow to the head when the Velkren had thrown him from the MatScan chamber.

There were moments when Rubyan thought Luckran was right. Most of the time, however, he just wasn't sure. He was confused. He had been in the church to witness the coronation of the new Empress, the supposed daughter of the Emperor. Had the Velkren really returned to the Gods? If so, what was MatScan and the journey to the new planet all about? Over the phone, Luckran had claimed there had never been a new world. He had begged Rubyan to come to the Governors' Rooms so he could explain. But Rubyan no longer trusted the First Advisor. Obviously, the man had been lying to him for decades, so why would he stop now?

The plane began to taxi towards the runway. Rubyan buckled his seatbelt. The flight would last for about four hours and would take him as close to the Swutland mountains as possible. From there, he would charter a helicopter to take him to the Imperial villa. It was possible there was something there, in the basement. A precious item, one he didn't want anyone else getting their hands on. And while there, he would try to unravel the mystery. He wasn't confident of discovering what had truly happened. And he didn't have much time, now that the life-extending spell was no more. But he had to try.

Acknowledgements

I would like to thank the following people for helping me take this novel all the way from a vague idea to print: Bob Kelly and Carmen Dreyer for insightful editing of an early manuscript. Julien Remy for his constructive criticism of a later draft. Eunan Meyler and Abdul Sheir for their invaluable feedback on the final draft. Eddie McGlynn and Declan Byrne for providing technological assistance, back in the days when I couldn't even afford a computer. Leo Donlon for inspiring in me a love of books. My colleagues and friends, both in Ireland and New York, for their keen interest in my short stories, especially David Cisek, Chris Booth, Guy Young, Tom Lucas, JP Doran, Eamonn Doran, Tony Horswill, Gordon Dana and everyone at UNIS and at the IAW&A. My immediate and wider family, for their endless encouragement. Larry Kirwan for his gracious support. Nick Mullendore for his patience and for helping me to believe in myself. Colum McCann for his guidance and for having faith in me. Everyone at John Hunt Publishing for making me feel welcome and for ensuring the publishing process was stress free. And lastly, all the readers who took time to respond in any way to my published stories.

About the Author

James Rogers is a multi-genre writer whose short stories have appeared in online and print magazines, including *The First Line*, *The Galway Review* and *Inscape*. Originally from the west of Ireland, he now lives in New York with his wife and three children and teaches mathematics at the United Nations International School. This is his first novel.

Find more of the author's work at jameswrogers.com

COSMIC EGG
BOOKS

FANTASY, SCI-FI, HORROR & PARANORMAL

If you prefer to spend your nights with Vampires and
Werewolves rather than the mundane then we publish the
books for you. If your preference is for Dragons and Faeries
or Angels and Demons – we should be your first stop.
Perhaps your perfect partner has artificial skin or comes
from another planet – step right this way. If your passion is
Fantasy (including magical realism and spiritual fantasy),
Metaphysical Cosmology, Horror or Science Fiction (including
Steampunk), Cosmic Egg books will feed your hunger. Our
curiosity shop contains treasures you will enjoy unearthing.
If you have enjoyed this book, why not tell other readers by
posting a review on your preferred book site.

Recent bestsellers from Cosmic Egg Books are:

The Zombie Rule Book
A Zombie Apocalypse Survival Guide
Tony Newton
The book the living-dead don't want you to have!
Paperback: 978-1-78279-334-2 ebook: 978-1-78279-333-5

Cryptogram
Because the Past is Never Past
Michael Tobert
Welcome to the dystopian world of 2050, where three lovers
are haunted by echoes from eight-hundred years ago.
Paperback: 978-1-78279-681-7 ebook: 978-1-78279-680-0

Purefinder
Ben Gwalchmai
London, 1858. A child is dead; a man is blamed and dragged
through hell in this Dantean tale of loss, mystery and
fraternity.
Paperback: 978-1-78279-098-3 ebook: 978-1-78279-097-6

600ppm
A Novel of Climate Change
Clarke W. Owens
Nature is collapsing. The government doesn't want you to
know why. Welcome to 2051 and 600ppm.
Paperback: 978-1-78279-992-4 ebook: 978-1-78279-993-1

Creations
William Mitchell
Earth 2040 is on the brink of disaster. Can Max Lowrie stop the
self-replicating machines before it's too late?
Paperback: 978-1-78279-186-7 ebook: 978-1-78279-161-4

The Gawain Legacy
Jon Mackley
If you try to control every secret, secrets may end up
controlling you.
Paperback: 978-1-78279-485-1 ebook: 978-1-78279-484-4

Readers of ebooks can buy or view any of these bestsellers by
clicking on the live link in the title. Most titles are published
in paperback and as an ebook. Paperbacks are available in
traditional bookshops. Both print and ebook formats are
available online.
Find more titles and sign up to our readers' newsletter at
http://www.johnhuntpublishing.com/fiction
Follow us on Facebook at https://www.facebook.com/JHPFiction
and Twitter at https://twitter.com/JHPFiction